Exiles and Barbarians

Michelle Granas

ISBN: 978-0-9888592-2-7
LCCN: 2018905133

CHAPTER 1
Warsaw, 2014

If Yuri had been asked, on the day the statue fell, he would have said the universe proceeds by laws and accidents, some fortunate, some less so, but the shape of the human world can be shifted, a scintilla at least, by the long lever of our determination. Nevertheless, for some time past it had been the disorderly luck of living that forced itself most on his attention, whacking him over the head until he had to notice.

Thus he was not entirely unprepared when the half-ton angel began to tip from its plinth. As it keeled, spreading cement wings over the woman below, he sprang from his place, flinging his violin aside and catapulting across the street.

*

Seated daily across from the church he had had time to observe the crumbling cornice beneath the sculpture. He had even, at some risk to himself, pointed it out to the two policemen who passed regularly.

"Well, hmmm," they had said, halting their heavy tread of the Old Town street to squint up at the statue and down at his violin case on the cobbles. He had stopped playing, of course, when he saw them in the distance, but they knew what he had been doing. They chose the easier rather than the weightier question.

"Hmmm. Yes. Well. So, you will be here and you won't be playing your instrument, right? Because if we saw you doing that we would have to fine you 500 zlotys for disturbing the peace, right? So you won't be busy and you can warn people to stay away, right?" said one.

"You'll be the guardian of the angel," giggled the other, with more wit than Yuri would have given him credit for. And they moved on, unconcerned.

After that he had gone the length of leaving a note— written on a scrap of paper salvaged from a garbage bin— in the mailbox of the Archbishop's residence two streets over. No one had come to make repairs, and although he occasionally warned people if they passed too close, gesticulating to show they should walk on the other side of the street, for the most part he had other things to think about: Kant's *Perpetual Peace*, for instance, and food, and the pale young woman who passed so often; or the life similarities of Turgenev and Marx, and food, and the young woman; or the poet Lesya Ukrainka, and food; food and the young woman.

Still, sometimes he thought he should make the steps of some other doorway his habitual spot. These steps received the most sun, though, and here the tourists had to crowd close to his violin case as they passed. Other steps were taken, and moreover and most importantly the young woman walked this way. He suspected by now that she wasn't the one he was looking for, but she was nonetheless, as Dostoyevsky said, one of those persons who "begin to interest us all at once, before a word has been spoken."

He had seen her dozens of times already. He had seen her accompanying a man with a white cane, and carrying groceries for an elderly woman; he had seen her with a boy with Down's syndrome and watched her stop to talk to a woman with swollen legs. But he felt quite sure, from her air and clothing, that she wasn't a social worker.

He had never spoken to her. In earlier, better days, he would have found it easy to seize a pretext—any pretext, like the angel—to start a conversation. Now he was aware of his diminished status and that it behooved him to be reticent. If he were to leap up and ask her questions, she might say anything to get rid of a scruffy stranger. It would not be unreasonable. And probably she was not the one, but if he approached her clumsily he might never know. Three weeks ago he had had enough money to enter an internet café and after some searching he had found a nearby address, an email, and a photo, dated some years back. He had written to her, a botched missive, but she hadn't answered.

Yet whether she was the right woman or not she stirred his imagination. First, there was the line—whatever she was wearing the impression was always of a draped arrow. Second, she kept a supply of bills in her purse for the beggars the area attracted; as she walked down the street anyone who approached her with outstretched hand would receive a donation and a kind word. She had never tossed money in his violin case though, and he was glad of that. And not everyone appreciated her efforts. Once he had seen her emerge from a bakery to be accosted by a girl in a multi-colored skirt. She had instantly handed over her purchases and had had the bread thrown back at her. She hadn't noticeably reacted but had deftly caught the bag and continued on her way, cool and remote as before. But after all—and here was where a tinge of disapproval came in—one couldn't really pay homage to Fashion and St. Francis of Assisi at the same time.

She came down the street today at her usual time, and he had not been thinking about her, or the statue, but only about money, money, money, and alternately, food, food, food, almost on the intake of every breath. She interrupted these thoughts.

It had been a slow day.

He had just finished Pachelbel's *Canon* and his eyes followed the last group of walkers until they passed him without dropping a coin or even turning their heads, and then while resetting his instrument he looked in the other direction to see if anyone was coming and if it was worth playing—and that's when he saw her coming down the street.

She was not strictly beautiful if one were objective, but Yuri had ceased to be objective. She was rather tall, her hair was more ash than blond, there were defects that could be found, but somehow she radiated an intense refinement. She was wearing pale slacks and a raincoat—a raincoat that even Yuri realized had not been made in a distant sweatshop but somewhere close, by a designer with a ruler. Her hair was pulled into a loose braid and as always she was without makeup or ornaments. She walked in an aura of inner concentration, with the unselfconsciousness of a nun or mental patient, as if the outside world didn't matter to her. It was the combination of her aloofness with her charity that intrigued him particularly. Perhaps, he mused, remoteness was characteristic of saints and perhaps, as it was not an easily comprehensible quality, it was why they so often came to bad ends.

He wouldn't play while she was there. It would be like begging for a coin. She stopped to read one of the posters on the church's bulletin board, directly under the statue. Move away, he thought, move away—and raised his eyes to the statue and saw it starting to slide.

He had never moved so fast. He bounded across the street, grabbing the woman and letting the impetus of his leap carry them sideways until they collided with the wall, and—and nothing.

There was no crash. He looked up. The angel was still up there, still tilting. He hastily let go of the woman in his arms and stepped back. For many long seconds he looked into her startled eyes, contemplated the shame of his error, opened his mouth to apologize, and wondered how long it would take to walk to Krakow.

Then the statue fell, just missing him, and smashing to the ground with such force that the sidewalk shook and shards flew in all directions, riddling the wall around the woman. Something grazed his leg with a knife-like sensation, but he noticed the pain with only a fraction of his mind.

Then the world went on again. Somewhere down the street a troupe of tourists stared and pointed; somewhere a drunkard emerged from a doorway and stood gaping. The reconstructed 17th-century façades still lined the street; the chalkboard restaurant menus still competed; the windows were still full of amber; rooks still swirled in the early-summer sky, and the ice-cream vendor's sign still swung in the breeze.

She stood beside him, apparently unmoved by the near

catastrophe. Her voice, when she spoke, was low and held only the slightest hint of tremor. "Thank you. I don't believe you quite saved my life, but I imagine that was your intention."

He looked at her for a long moment. Then, the contact with her slight torso still reverberating along his arms and speeding his heartbeat, he straightened himself and replied, "Madam, there is no least need for any expression of gratitude as it has been an honor and a privilege to be of service to one whom I have long considered to be the pinnacle of elegance and womanly grace and even though I doubt the efficacy of your charity, it shows that you partake of that essence of kindness that is the most precious quality of humanity and has made me dream of being able to perform for you even so slight an office as to retrieve your dropped purse that you might turn and with one glance of your gray eyes uplift and exalt me, your humble servant, Yuri Yeremevich." Or that is what he thought, anyway. What he said, partly because he was a man living in the twenty-first century, and mostly because he had to speak Polish, which was far from being one of his five best languages, was, "No problem."

They stared at the pile of rubble at their feet.

"Rather a pity, all the same," she said.

"I do not think it was original," he said.

"Oh, true, to be killed by a fake angel would be in questionable taste." Her voice was lightly mocking.

"Did you want to be killed?" he asked, startled that she had construed his statement in that manner, and wondering if he misunderstood her.

But she didn't answer; her gaze was arrested by the approach of two policemen. Yuri recognized them.

"Well, sir, you were right," said one to him magnanimously, nudging a bit of the stone with his foot and giggling nervously. The other policeman took out his pad and a pencil, then looked at the church, considered, and rather sheepishly returned the pad to his pocket. "Not our affair," he whispered, shrugging, and the two moved on with rather more rapid strides than usual.

A family of tourists that had been watching from a distance now came striding over the cobblestones, pointing and exclaiming in British accents. "Look," cried a boy's voice, "a villain."

"Who?" thought Yuri in surprise, "Me?"

And then, of course, he realized the boy was pointing not to him but to his violin—which wasn't his violin actually but Andrei's—and he very much hoped it wasn't broken. It was lying neck down on the steps, as if it had drunk too much and collapsed there. Yuri crossed to it rapidly and picked it up. It appeared to be whole, thank God, although there was a scratch on the lower bout that he was pretty sure hadn't been there before.

Yuri stood on the steps with the violin. Well, that was that. It wasn't really the moment for asking the young woman the question he wanted to ask, so the idea was just to get back to work, because there was the problem of money, and the problem of food, and the Kremlin-sized problem of the future...but he wouldn't think about that, it was pointless. The British boy stood staring at the ground until his mother grabbed his arm and pulled him away, his neck craning back for repeated looks.

The young woman hesitated on the other side of the street, beyond the debris, and then crossed to him. "You're bleeding."

Yuri looked down then and saw that in fact a surprising trickle of blood was running down his shoe and down the steps. "It's all right," he shrugged, although he was, in fact, rather alarmed.

"Shall I call you a taxi? Do you want to go to a doctor or the hospital?"

"No, no, thank you, I do not want anything."

He knew he sounded surly, so he tried for a joke, in his slow Polish. "I am disappoint. In mythologia, the blood of the colossus is supposed to be gold."

She did not smile. "Yes," she answered, "I can see that might be disconcerting, but in your place I would worry more about quantity than quality. I will go to the pharmacy to get you a bandage."

"The pharmacy is closed. The owner is vacationating. I saw the sign on the door earlier."

"That's true."

"It is the back of my leg, no....no artilleries there," he said, struggling for the words. "It is all right. Please, do not disturb yourself."

She deliberated, biting her lip a little. Then, "Come," she said decisively.

"Where?" he asked, starting at her tone of command.

"You can't sit here bleeding all day. I live on the escarpment. Come with me to my apartment and I will find something for a bandage." She did not wait for an answer but turned and walked away.

He had a moment of hesitation. Perhaps this was the opportunity he had been waiting for, or perhaps it would be a mistake to have direct contact with a Polish person—even one who caused his heartbeat to accelerate, one to whom he might have something to say. She could report him as an illegal immigrant. On the other hand, although he knew his interest in her was only a fleeting crush produced by loneliness and isolation, he was also mighty curious. He hastily stuffed the bottom of his pants' leg into his sock to keep the blood from dripping, rose, and limped after her, the violin case in one hand and the violin and bow in the other.

CHAPTER 2

She was already halfway down the street. He hurried to catch up, slightly nauseated by the pain in his leg and the scents of food that assaulted him from various doorways. The sweet-sour aroma of *bigos* pouring out of a restaurant window among the din of plates in a kitchen, the oil-laden scent of potato latkes, the tang of dill, the aroma of butter, of garlic, tomato sauce, warmth...He was passing restaurant tables set up on the sidewalk now. He wouldn't look at the bread baskets, or at the lucky hands reaching for another slice. It was not yet the busy time of day, but someone was already playing *Besame Mucho* on an accordion for a handful of diners.

She was walking through the gate of a carriage drive and entering a building through a tall wooden door. She held it until he caught it. Inside, the hall was dark and the staircase only a little less so. The banister rail under his hand was bumpy with old layers of paint. They began to climb. The steps were shallow, possibly marble, but he couldn't tell in the murk. There was a smell of age about the walls. She shouldn't invite me to her apartment, he thought disapprovingly, I could be anyone—bad, dangerous.

She stopped before a door, touched the handle, and pushed.

Unlocked? he thought, his disapproval growing. Who left a door unlocked?

The room that opened before him, though, stopped a line of thought that was rising. Beyond the entrance hall was a large clear space with tall windows and through the windows a stunning view over rooftops to the Vistula River. The water was gray and shimmering under the clouds, with white specks of gulls wheeling above it.

"Ah," he took a quick breath: it was so unexpected. He gestured, "Your view is beautiful. Very beautiful."

She shrugged. "You can see the same view from the escarpment, in a hundred places. Please wait here." Leaving him to stand nonplussed, she crossed the room and began to rummage in a cupboard.

This was not good, he thought. Was she indifferent to beauty? How could she be? But after all what was it to him?

She said suddenly, over her shoulder, as if afraid she had been rude, "I only meant it is not mine. The view belongs to everyone."

"Ah," he said, relieved, "But you own the frame."

"If I could provide the same to everyone, I would," she said in a clipped and almost defensive tone.

"Ah," was all he could think to answer, as the inequality of the world hung between them. He looked about. The walls were lined with books on fitted shelves. There was old oak furniture of mismatched shapes, a folk textile from the pre-tourist era hanging on a wall, a number of paintings of varying quality, some pre-war photos in frames, and a large silver epergne on a table. It was not what he had expected. In contrast to the staircase, it was clean in the way interiors are clean only when there is cleaning help. It was also a little decayed, a little passé, a little gloomy, and aesthetically quite pleasing to him. It was very much like his family home. His former family home.

"It is your family home." He said to her back.

"It belonged to my grandparents."

"Do you live here alone?" He asked, looking around for signs of other occupants. A laptop and neat stack of papers lay on a table.

"Yes."

Tsk, he thought, you shouldn't tell me that, you really shouldn't. How did she know he wasn't a thief? This silver card case, lying beside the books, it was almost to hand and he could easily slip it in his pocket while she wasn't looking. He wondered how much it would bring. Not enough to solve his problems but enough for a few good meals…suddenly he shook his head, surprised at the sort of ideas that had begun to pass through his head recently.

"How can you tell me that? How do you know I'm not a murderer?" Or a rapist, he thought, but he didn't say that. The word was too embarrassing—but, he argued with himself, why should it be more so than murder? There was a clear perversion of priorities there. "Or I could be a thief."

He picked up the silver case and held it in his hand.

"Go ahead and steal something," she said, "my back is turned."

He put down the case hurriedly. "Are you always so …" he searched his mind for the word meaning cool, "so frigid?"

At that she turned and looked at him, with her eyebrows raised.

Ah no, that wasn't the word. "Cold, I mean—no, chilly, no, well, quiet."

"Calm, you mean?"

"Yes, calm, thank you."

"Yes, always."

Once again, he reconciled himself to the fact that as a foreigner he would perpetually be saying things that were absurd or misunderstood, reduce complex thoughts to Tarzan simplicity, and give offence where none was intended.

She didn't seem to be finding what she was looking for. He could feel that his shoe was beginning to grow damp with blood inside. He was aware of his less than pristine clothes and hoped he didn't smell; he had bathed that day, but only in the clay pit, of course. The homeless had few options. He shook his head to rid himself of these thoughts—this too, so be it—and let his eyes run over the books, noting here and there titles he knew. Something that had been in the back of his mind returned. Something evoked by "you can't sit bleeding here all day." Ah yes, it was a quote. "I can't stay dying here all night." *The Critic.* Sheridan. An English playwright he had written an article on once, early in his career. In his mind, he saw his colleague Grigori Petrovich picking up a volume from his desk, waving it about, and heard his voice: "All English writers are lightweights."

He moved forward and reached for a volume of Proust, setting the violin down on a marble table top. He had written a paper on Proust once too. Unfortunate French author, *salonnard, snobinard*—but still, he loved to read in French. "Of course," he heard Grigori Petrovich's voice, "they're all decadents, the French writers, and no one really knows that much about art." He opened the book and flipped to a page. The look of the print, the smell of old book. He raised it and inhaled. It was all so wonderfully far from the hard stone surfaces and pigeon dirt of the Warsaw gutters by which he crouched.

"Where are you from?" Her question took him by surprise.

He turned around, and shifted uneasily before lying. "I am staying in muddletown."

She looked at him with a puzzled expression, so he corrected himself, "Middletown. Downtown. I am living in downtown."

She politely did not say that that wasn't the question she had asked, but only held out to him a roll of gauze and pointed him toward a green-mosaic lavatory.

When he emerged, he handed back the remainder of the roll, picked up the violin, and hesitated. Now, he supposed, would be the time to ask her his question. He might not have another chance. But no, she probably wasn't the one and she might think his question odd. There had been no answer to his email.

"You have been very kind and I am very grateful," he heard himself saying.

"We have a mutual acquaintance," she replied, waving away his thanks. He looked his surprise, hastily wondering if she was going to mention his email after all, but instead she went on, "You know Pani Jadzia? She's elderly—always wears a green sweater and walks about with a sign asking for help to buy various medicines—she has a different one for every day of the week…"

He relaxed and nodded. There would be no need for difficult explanations in a foreign language.

"She says you give her whatever is in your violin case, whenever she asks you."

He shrugged, inwardly delighted that she had taken note of him. "It is never much."

"In fact, I hear about you wherever I go in the neighborhood. You were seen helping Julek."

"Julek?"

"You know—he's a man in the last stages of some alcohol disease. He's in a wheelchair; his legs are bandaged, he wears a catheter and a diaper; he can barely push himself, but he's always leaving the Social Aid building to go buy more drink. They told me you helped him get back one day."

"Ah, that man. I cannot decide whither he is a particularly pathetical case or whither I admire his determination not to change to the last."

"He's very pathetic."

"We choose our own handbaskets for getting to hell."

She did not answer that but said instead, as they stood together in the entrance hall, "I suppose you need stitches and should go to a doctor now. I could call you a taxi."

"Thank you, no." He smiled down at her, a long smile, and her eyes met his meltingly then flicked away, and a faint scowl appeared on her forehead. So, he thought with a sharp spike of enjoyment at the hint of human warmth, not solely a saint. But perhaps he was bothering her?

"If it's a matter of money—to see a doctor—I could help."

He was pleased—this was good; she was kind, even to him, beyond need. He vacillated—there, take the money and don't go to the doctor. He shuddered. "No, thank you."

He bowed slightly, said goodbye, and was out the door before she could say more.

CHAPTER 3

She closed the door and with her senses unusually and disturbingly a-shiver listened to the man's uneven footsteps retreat down the stairs. She had spent too many years reading reports. Her thoughts had a tendency to arrange themselves not in literary forms but in the bullet points of official memos:

- What an unusual man.
- You're not allowed to be interested in people anymore.
- Unless they need your help.

She moved away from the door and stopped to reshelve the book the man had taken out. Proust. How curious. She opened a page and read, "I would have liked not to think of the hours of anguish I would spend that evening, alone in my room, without the possibility of sleep." She snapped the once-familiar book shut and inserted it back into its space. Where had he come from? she wondered. Ukraine or Belarus anyway, from the accent. He was probably a professional musician, someone from a chamber group or orchestra, who was out of work in his own country. He was vaguely familiar; perhaps because he reminded her more of a professor, somehow: maybe one of her grandfather's friends as she remembered them from her childhood. There was something about his intelligent gaze or in his slightly old-man clothing when he was what—

probably not more than forty? Or maybe it was only because he had gone straight to the books? He had stood here, large, rumpled, dirty, slouching, and he had made her curious. And she must not be. She knew precisely the thought that would kill all curiosity; she also knew she had to keep the thought at bay. Work—she must return to work. Quickly she crossed to the table and turned on the laptop.

She was expecting an email that had not arrived. She searched again through the fifty emails waiting to be read in her inbox and then tried her spam box. There it was. She was about to open it when she was jolted by the title of an email below it. '*If you were in Cambridge...*' it said. With a sick feeling and a slowed hand, she clicked on it.

Seated at her desk of polished walnut, laptop in front of her, she was aware of the neatness of her wrists, the cuffs of her cotton-linen blouse, the slim fingers. Her reflection in the screen stared back at her—neat mandarin collar, long neck, a face with Slavic cheekbones, blond strands of hair, a mouth that seldom smiled. She was straight, and perfect, very perfect. Except for that one moment of the past that no one in Warsaw knew anything about. No one except her fiancé Filip, that is, and Filip had broken their engagement soon after.

Behind her, also mirrored in the screen, was her inherited home. Her parents had been too involved with the start up of their business to care for her when she was a child. Her grandparents had raised her here, with watchfulness and stringency: put your hat on, speak politely, study hard, read Miłosz and Tuwim, listen to the brave things we did in underground days. Aniela stopped the reel of memories. They had been dead these ten years now and if she still missed them terribly it was selfish to sit and yearn for their tenderness and support. They had been spared certain knowledge and her inner damage was her own.

At five-thirty she closed the lid of her computer. She was expected at Iza's party—at Iza's *cocktail* party, when no one in Poland drank cocktails—in twenty-five minutes. That gave her five minutes to dress, which was two and a half more than she needed—off with the slacks and shirt, over the head with the sheath dress, three strokes with a brush on each side of her head, on with the heels—and five minutes to walk to her car. She did not bother to glance in the mirror before leaving. This unconscious assurance or unconcern, coupled with a figure from which clothes hung as from a hanger, meant she was generally considered well attired wherever she appeared and in whatever garment. Most people thought her naturally elegant; quite a few, envious and offended by her reserve, were also inclined to suspect her, unjustly, of snootiness.

It was as she was about to turn the key in the ignition of her car that her cell phone began to beep. She extracted it from her purse.

"Nela!"

"Hey, Iza. I'm on my way."

She was answered by a staccato barrage of words. "Darling, you're an angel, and I don't know what I'd do without you, but I don't know what I'm going to do anyway, because it's all going wrong, and after I put so much effort into making it perfect; I've been working, working, working, and how that boss of mine has the conscience to ask anyone to work such hours I don't know, but I was up to two last night, and from seven this morning, and would you believe someone from the embassy called to ask about the catering? Because the ambassador doesn't eat ham or veal, I forget which, and I told them it was all under control, but the caterers said they were serving *carpaccio*, and how am I supposed to know what *carpaccio* is?"

"Did you ask them?"

"Yes, but I can't remember everything, can I?"

Aniela's thumbs whisked over her phone. "Italian *sushi*. Could be veal, ham, or, if you're lucky, fish. There's a company called Veggie-Might that will deliver suitable trays—I'm sending you the number."

"*Jesus and Mary.* And now there's a problem with the musicians, because it was supposed to be a trio, but one's sick or died or something—it doesn't matter, but he's not coming, and with just two it'll look stupid, and Pan Witold won't be happy, and I'll probably lose my j-j-job again…"

Aniela leaned her head against the window. She wondered vaguely what it would be like to allow oneself to go to pieces over the hors d'oeuvres, or some other minor difficulty of daily life, but she couldn't imagine it; she hadn't allowed herself to show anything outwardly for years. She simply, patiently, solved one problem after another, as they presented themselves.

"Iza, Iza, listen."

"Yes?"

"Can't you get someone to fill in?"

"I don't know where to find anyone. I've been googling and googling, but it doesn't say anywhere 'violin player for rent'."

"It's a violinist you need?"

"Yes."

"How much are you paying? I might know someone— if I can find him." She was already opening the car door.

*

By the time Yuri limped back to his usual spot it had been taken by a young man with a guitar, singing an American rock tune with three chords and an accent. He looked up as Yuri approached with his violin, and deliberately did not make eye contact. The inner velvet of his guitar case, open for tips, was an empty field. A beginner then, Yuri noted: he'd be gone soon. He sat down on the next set of steps, wishing he hadn't given up smoking. It cost too much, smoking.

At one end of the street a man in a green robe was levitating cross-legged. He had collected a good circle of gawkers, but Yuri knew the arrangement that held him aloft and his gaze slid over him now. Further on, restaurant tables spilled onto the sidewalk and an extended family sat in two lines: aunts, uncles, a matriarch; two girls in demure dresses and banal faces, the kind of girls, Yuri decided, who wouldn't bully a classmate but would titter when someone else did. But did he have a right to pass judgment, even in his imagination, when he was an outcast, or worse, a parasite? Who was he, cut loose from society and so alone? A gust of wind blew over the chalkboard holding the menu. Heads turned but no one moved; the waiters were inside. To the count of ten, Yuri pictured himself as an ant in a dysfunctional anthill, where each ant milled and scurried to its own ends. Slowly he rose, limped the length of the street, set the sign back in its place and retreated to his former spot.

The minutes passed, an hour, and he could see that the young man was growing discouraged—his singing was less confident and lower. Yuri shook himself, stood, and shuffled toward him. The young man looked up, dropped frightened eyes, and pretended nervously to tune his guitar. Yuri halted in front of him.

"Pardon me."

"What?" snapped the young man.

Yuri was aware that his size, and possibly also the long, barely healed scar on one side of his head, made him intimidating, so he tried to slouch, to make himself smaller.

"I want to suggest that people—are like monkeys—if they think other people put money in your guitar…thing," he gestured, "they put money in too."

"I'm done here anyway," said the young man, hastily collecting his things and departing.

Well, he'd tried, thought Yuri, sitting down in his usual spot and opening his case. He raised the violin to his shoulder, tuned it, and gritting his teeth slightly launched once more into Pachelbel's *Canon*.

It was as he was drawing the bow down on the last note that he looked up and saw her walking briskly toward him down the street. The crowds of people were thin at this hour; no one hid his view. She was wearing a dress of light fabric, which followed her contours, and low stilettos, which were surely difficult on cobblestones, but by force of practice or personality she didn't wobble. The bow and violin hung suspended in air as he watched her come. She was coming to him, it was certain. A number of conjectures flashed through his mind. She was coming to offer him more assistance, and he couldn't accept it. She wasn't really coming to him; he was imagining it; she would walk past.

He rose and descended from the step. She stopped in front of him.

"I came to ask if you were interested in a...a gig, I think it's called."

"A gig?"

"Yes. To play the violin. Tonight. I have a friend who is organizing a party. There was supposed to be a violin trio, but one of the players has fallen ill. Could you fill in?"

"I...am..." All the reasons why he couldn't do it rushed to his mind.

"She will pay several hundred zloty."

"...at your service."

"Come then. I'm going there now and I'll give you a ride."

"But...my clothes?"

She glanced at him and shrugged, "It can't be helped. Anyway, it's not a very formal affair."

"There will be many people?"

"Around a thousand."

He choked and coughed and she went on. "I have a friend who works for a policy institute. I am going for her sake, that's all."

"Then the people there will be from academia, journalists…government types?"

"Yes."

He gulped again. But after all, no one would approach the musicians and ask questions about their immigration status. He would be safe enough.

"What is your job, if I may be so…so incontinent as to ask?" He did not know why a quarter smile lifted a corner of her lip, but it pleased him.

"I am the Prosecutor General for Warsaw."

He nearly dropped his violin. But at once his fingers tightened again on the handle of the case and he strode manfully beside her as if the fact were nothing to him. Unformed ideas rose and sank in his mind as he found himself half looking for alleys down which to flee. He wondered if she had notified the police about him. Maybe she'd called them while he was in the lavatory at her place. Maybe she would drive him to the police station, stop in front of it, and turn him over to the officers who would emerge to arrest him.

She gave him a sidelong glance. "I'm joking."

His heart skipped a beat with joy.

"I'm the Deputy Minister for Labor."

Hardly better.

"Not really. That's my cousin..."

"You tell me falsations and it is the first time I see you smile. It pleases me, your smile."

She didn't answer and her mouth assumed its usual straight line. He accepted her rejection as just. What was it to her, of course, if he were pleased or not. He walked beside her heavily and was silent.

After a moment of consideration she added, truthfully. "I am director general of the Ministry for Disabilities."

"Ah...Good."

CHAPTER 4

They drove in silence. The car was too small for him. He sat with his knees pulled up awkwardly but still wedged hard against the dashboard, clutching the violin in his arms, watching the street. She drove too carefully, too slowly, gripping the wheel with both hands and looking in all directions. He wondered if she'd just learned.

They didn't have far to go. They left behind the massive brick walls of the Old Town and wound through streets lined with centuries-old apartment houses and last week's glass-and-steel office buildings, past restaurants, cafes, beer joints, and a stream of cars and bikes. They were crossing a bridge. He had a view of reflected lights below, of illuminated buildings beyond, and then they were among the decaying prewar tenements and spiffily renovated factories of east-bank Warsaw. They entered a large courtyard and she parked the car.

"I suppose," she said, breaking the long silence, "I should know your name, to introduce you."

"Yuri Yeremevich Romen." He would have liked to bow over her hand, formally and politely, but his arms were full of violin, so he had to make do with ducking his head.

"Aniela Solan," she responded.

But was she his particular Aniela? And was he even

looking for an Aniela? That was only a guess, after all.

She typed into her cell phone, and they got out of the car. A plump woman in a short cocktail dress was scurrying toward them, while a nondescript man in a bow tie and peevish expression brought up the rear. Introductions were made all around. The bow-tie man was the second violinist of the City Philharmonic. Yuri felt a trickle of sweat inside his shirt, but there was nowhere to flee now. The women departed.

"Come," said the bow tie, rather hurriedly. "I'll show you where we're seated and we can compare repertoires." He looked Yuri up and down disapprovingly as they fell into step together, "You're a bit underdressed…"

"I am underdressed but over-educated—I borrow from Oscar Wilde," said Yuri.

"Whoever Oscar is," muttered the man, half to himself, "I don't think much of his clothes."

Yuri slowed his step very slightly—he didn't want to do this, after all, he really didn't—and the man hastily added in a more conciliatory tone, "It's good you could come on such short notice—let people down once and your reputation for this sort of thing is shot forever."

Ahead of them, the ambassador of Ecuador's car, flags flying, pulled up and disgorged its passengers. Yuri and the violinist followed in their wake toward the building.

"I'm not…" Yuri began, "I don't…"

"I tried all my colleagues from the philharmonic, to get someone to fill in, but everyone was busy or unwilling."

"I am afraid I…" Yuri was interrupted again.

"It'll be light classical pieces mostly, easy stuff…"

They proceeded through doors and passages to emerge in a vast room filled with bevies of guests, scurrying waiters, shuffling feet, and the rising echo of conversations in too bare a space. Yuri looked at the mass of people and the flight impulse became almost overwhelming. What was he doing here? What had he been thinking? The money, yes, but...

He was being introduced to the other musician, a man whose bald head imitated architecturally the round end of his viola. Someone was passing with martini glasses on a tray. Yuri snagged one and downed it, aware of the violinist noting the move with pursed lips. They were sitting down, taking out their instruments. The alcohol splashed into his empty stomach and rose in his bloodstream. But he was a large man; one martini, even a strong one, would do little.

"Where have you been playing?" the cellist asked, but he didn't listen to Yuri's reply.

"The Old Town."

"So, first we'll play..."

Yuri could see Aniela walking through the crowd and to his mind she was the best looking woman in the room. She shook hands here and there, and eyes followed her as she passed, but her aura of remoteness prevented anyone from speaking to her for long, or so it seemed to him. Her eyes met his across the room and she did not smile but raised her chin in acknowledgement of his glance and he felt warmed. Only he was going to let her down badly. That was a sorry thought. Regret for the past surged through him. Now...He concentrated on tuning his violin.

Aniela's friend was making "play" motions to them with her hands.

Yuri waited for the axe to fall.

"…Pachelbel's *Canon*—you know it, of course?"

Saved! Yuri almost laughed, but instead he nodded seriously, raised his bow and launched into the opening bars.

But his reprieve did not last long.

"Dvorak's *Terzetto in C*—you know it, of course?"

Yuri shook his head.

"Well, Beethoven's *Serenade in D*," the cellist readied his bow.

Yuri cleared his throat. "I don't know it."

"Bach's *Sonata in E minor*? Any of C.P.E. Bach?"

He shook his head.

The violinist was getting irritated.

"It's because he's Ukrainian," put in the other musician helpfully. Yuri resented the implication, but he was in no position to object.

"Borodin's *Folk Song* then, in G minor."

"No."

"Why don't you tell us what you do know?"

"*Besame Mucho*."

"*Jesus Christ*. All you know by heart is Pachelbel's *Canon* and *Besame Mucho*?"

"Yes." In truth he also knew the Red Army song *Polyushko-pole*, but it was perhaps not tactful to mention it.

"*Jesus Christ*. Here, play from the notes then." He handed Yuri a sheaf of papers. Yuri had a kaleidoscope impression of the crowd in front of him, of women passing in colorful dresses, of men in suits, of waiters with drinks. He put the notes on the stand and blocking out the movements of the crowd before him, concentrated desperately on deciphering the music. The violinist was already counting one, two, three with his head. They played and within bars Yuri knew that something was wrong; he tried to play faster as they tried to play slower; he produced false notes; the music danced before his eyes. Please let no one be listening, he prayed. All those years ago, when he was being dragged unwilling to lessons, shirking his practice to run and play: "Someday you'll regret it," his mother had said. He did, he did.

"That was bad," muttered the violist when the end came.

"*Idiot!*" swore the bow tie. "You're *hopeless*, useless. Look, don't play, just pretend," he ordered.

Yuri, humbled, relieved, and wondering if they would pay him something, anything, after all, nodded obediently and concentrated on moving his arm up and down with the bow hovering minimally over the strings. Eventually, when he could no longer bear to look at the floor, he raised his eyes to the attendees. They were engaged in their own affairs; no one would notice he wasn't really playing.

The crowd passed back and forth. Men in suits but no ties, men in jackets, women in dresses that came to their ankles, their calves, their knees, their thighs, their upper thighs. Aniela's friend passed and re-passed before his eyes. She was forty pounds overweight and wearing a jersey tube around her middle and very little else; one hand held a martini, the other continually pulled down the hem of her dress behind to cover her posterior. He watched her absently, with a mingling of pity and disapproval—his tastes were refined, in spite of his appearance—and arousal, because regardless of refinement and so forth, there was still a lot of flesh before his eyes.

It was a prosperous crowd but not for the most part an ultra-rich one, not obviously a crowd where corruption and cocaine chinked the joints, just a euro-normal, influential, upwardly mobile one.

Time passed. Someone was giving a long speech, a famous movie director was making a toast about thinking and drinking, the ambassadors were displaying their teeth. The violinist and violist struggled on grimly, but no one was listening or could have heard the music had they wanted to. Waiters carried trays of canapés back and forth, back and forth. Chunks of skewered cheese and ham, of skewered cheese and ham, of skewered cheese and ham passed and re-passed before his eyes. A woman who looked like Aniela only younger appeared in the assembly, with a couple of young men in smart suits in close attendance. Perhaps he was seeing double. It had been a long time since he'd eaten. His leg ached, the music scraped on his ears, and his arm was tired of pantomime playing. The candles seemed to be multiplying. The young woman who looked like Aniela was approaching the microphone, was giving a confident speech about community and social care for the needy and the outreach of some charity and its corporate sponsors. "So I would like to ask everyone here to remember to reach out a helping hand wherever you can," she was concluding neatly, smiling and leaving the stage to applause. She crossed the floor and stopped beside him as the young suits rejoined her.

"Good speech," said one, and added something Yuri didn't catch but which was perhaps objectionable, as the other objected.

"Old man...!"

"Speaking of which," said the young woman, looking imperturbably into the distance, "that's my father behind you."

The young man started, looked hastily about, and moved away.

The other man also looked about, more cautiously, and then turned to the girl. "Your father isn't really here, is he?"

She shrugged, "I don't know. He said he might come."

"I'd like to speak to him..."

The girl almost but not quite rolled her eyes. "You can give him your *elevator speech*"—she said the words in English—"but it won't do any good. It's my mother who makes all the decisions."

They moved off. Others came and went. He got snatches of conversations. So-and-so's trip to the Seychelles, the Bahamas, and twice to Corfu; the prime minister, prime mover, and prime rates for loans; grants, tenders, subsidies, and seasons of asthma; real estate rises, lab test crises, tennis clubs, and tomography—the eternal hypochondria of Eastern Europe; problems with the customs office, tax office, every office; stupid laws, stupid bosses, stupid policies; *prosecco, mortadella*, migrants crossing the Mediterranean…

"One hundred and fifty thousand of them just this year; the Italians are fed up and I don't blame them."

"It may sound awful to say it, but my British colleagues believe it's kinder to let them drown than to rescue them. They say it just encourages more to make the crossing."

"What is Europe going to do with these waves of people? They have to be stopped. Libya, Syria—they're pouring out of there."

Barbarians!, Yuri thought, I'm one of those migrants; the only distinction is that I've come from a different direction. He leaned over in his chair and said loudly, in a pause in the music, "Perhaps if certain countries had to deal with the consequences they would be less interested in engineering regime change and violence." Or at least that is what he meant to say, but perhaps it didn't come out quite right, as the speakers only stared for a moment before moving away. Yuri muttered after them, "The Samaritan didn't ask 'what's your nationality?' before he took the traveler to an inn."

The musicians glared at him and the music began again. He looked up and saw that Aniela had been listening too, but she turned her back then.

After a time a man approached and spoke to her. Yuri didn't like that; he felt a surge of envy, of territoriality: Stay away from her! It was an absurd thought, he reminded himself as he went on with his mime. Time passed and he felt decidedly odd.

Aniela's friend with the tube dress stood in front of him, eating sandwiches and talking to a number of women. Her curled red hair, like lacquered snakes, swarmed over the back of her bare shoulders. The candles, impaled on long holders, made a barricade between the musicians and the guests. She'd better keep her hair out of the candles, Yuri thought, and glanced away. When he looked again, he saw that she had stepped back and what he had foreseen was coming to pass. The small flame caught and flared—unawares she went on talking and drinking. Yuri leapt from his chair and began to slap the woman's back.

Screams, cries. "Have you gone mad?"

"Crazy!"

"He must be smashed!"

"Madam, your heer—it was burning."

"My beer was burning?"

"No, yeer hair." Yuri found his tongue twisting. The lights were still dancing. The room was beginning to turn sideways.

"Oh, Iza, he's right—your hair is burned."

But Yuri was already beginning to fall; he was falling, falling.

"He's drunk."

"Call security!"

"They're never around when they're needed."

But in fact they were around. Someone—two someones—were grasping him with firm grips, were helping him in all indignity propel his unsteady legs toward the exit, were leaving him in a heap on the sidewalk, with the cool night air rushing in to bring him to his senses.

He sat with his head between his knees for a while, feeling ill. It was the memory of Andrei's violin that finally induced him to look up. He couldn't leave that behind. He would not be paid—he wouldn't think of asking for payment—and that meant he'd lost the evening's earnings from busking as well. So he wouldn't eat tonight. He wouldn't take the bus but would walk back across the bridge. Two hours, maybe three. If he walked slowly it would be all right. Tomorrow would be a new day. He'd get through it. Be a man, he said to himself. He raised his head, preparatory to rising, and saw that Aniela was standing a ways from him, the violin case hanging from one hand. She wasn't smiling.

"I am sorry," he said.

"For what?" she asked.

"I am not a very good musician."

"I don't care about that. But I saw what happened with Iza's hair. That's the second time today."

"That her hair catches fire?"

"No. The second time you were in the right place at the right time."

He shrugged and rose. "And I was starting to think my destiny was to be in the wrong place at the wrong time. Well, it doesn't matter. You have brought my violin— thank you. You are always very kind."

"You are not drunk, as they were saying. Are you ill?"

"No." He held out his hand for the violin.

She put the violin behind her back, and he stopped, puzzled and swaying a little.

"I think you are in need of help, and as a public functionary I would be derelict in my duty if I left you to your own devices." She wasn't smiling. She was saying these ridiculous words in all seriousness.

"Oh, this is not a popular idea—that the state is for helping people," he spoke slowly to form the thoughts into words.

"What, are you an anarchist?" the tone had that touch of mockery again.

He spread his arms, thinking, "Forgive me, centuries of pawn-ship have produced hedgehog reflexes," but what was the point? He was not going to discuss political theory with her when his head was spinning. Instead he said, "No, madam, no. You have nothing to fear. I am vair obedient citizen. Paragon of docileness—that's me."

Another woman was approaching, the one who was a double of Aniela but less soberly attired. Viewed up close he could see that she was also considerably younger, viewed conventionally—more beautiful, and, viewed from any angle, hard as nails. She was adding a leather jacket to her fluttering dress with a series of jerks. "My sister," Aniela murmured, but he had already guessed this must be the case.

"You aren't leaving already?" said the younger woman to Aniela.

"Yes. This gentleman needs a ride."

"Oh...well, can't he call a taxi?"

"'So I would like to ask everyone here to remember to reach out a helping hand,'" Yuri couldn't resist quoting.

Aniela's eyebrows lifted fractionally, while the other

woman shot him a look of dislike before pretending not to hear.

"Kasia, I'm leaving, are you coming with me?"

"Oh, I guess." The younger woman shrugged.

"Come, let's get in the car."

Yuri couldn't grab the violin from the woman and so had to follow. He would give her a false address, he decided, not too far from his destination. It would be better than walking. He was very grateful, because really he felt quite tottery on his legs—not at all like a hedgehog but more like a week-old kitten or an elderly giraffe.

CHAPTER 5

They squeezed into the car, with Aniela at the wheel and her sister in the back seat. Yuri leaned his head against the window and they were in motion. Lights seemed to be flashing or swirling before his eyes and he felt nauseated, hot and then cold and the clammy perspiration was even on the back of his neck. His knees were pulled up once more against the dashboard. He leaned his head forward on his knees.

"You really aren't well."

He could feel more than see that Aniela was taking glances at him as she drove.

"I will take you to a hospital."

"No, please, I beg of you!" He put the last of his energy into the plea. "It will be…bad for me. Very bad. With your excuses, I am just going to faint here a little."

And then, somehow, the world was going black.

"Oh, oh God, Nela, he's passed out." Kasia's voice from the back seat was more distaste than agitation. She had seen plenty of men passed out before. "In your car—that's disgusting. Couldn't he have waited till he got out on the sidewalk? Please God he won't puke."

Aniela was pulling the car over to the curb. What to do now? The two young women stared at the stranger slumped over the dashboard. In the small car he was very close.

"Sir, sir? Excuse me, sir?"

No answer.

Kasia grabbed the back of the man's jacket in her fist and shook the cloth. "Hey, sir, wake up! Wake up, you! You lout, you dunce, you jerk." Kasia's language descended to the level of the gutter.

No reaction.

"This," said Aniela, "is unfortunate."

"Drive him to a police station and let them take him to the sobering-up center," suggested Kasia, but she waited for Aniela to make the decisions. In spite of being considerably more experienced in many spheres of life, she was accustomed to take the lead from her older sister.

"I can't do that. He might have overstayed his visa or who knows what."

"Aren't you supposed to be upholding the law and all that?"

"My job is to help disabled people, not to turn migrants over to the police."

"This guy's a bad musician, but I don't think he's disabled."

Aniela regarded the inert form beside her. "He looks about as disabled as it's possible to be."

"So what are we going to do with him? Shall we push him out on the sidewalk?"

"Kasia!"

Aniela was almost distracted from the immediate situation. Sometimes her sister shocked her and she felt she didn't know her at all. Then she quickly turned her mind away from the idea. It was youth, or a hard outer shell produced by the life she was leading, but there was really a better Kasia underneath.

"Maybe he's sick. We have to take care of him."

"Take care of him? Us? We don't even know him."

Kasia's phone rang and she talked into it. "Some friends are going on to a party," she said, as she dropped the phone back in her purse. "I'm going to meet them at Plac Bankowy. You'll be all right, won't you?" She was already opening the door, already out on the pavement and scurrying away.

Aniela watched her go, disappointment in her sister momentarily overcoming all other emotions. Then she turned back to her problem. What was she going to do with him? Suppose he really needed medical help? Here was an awkward position for a high public official.

She stared at him in distress, reaching for her cell phone, and as she did so his body began to tilt in her direction. She bolstered him with her arm to prevent him from falling on her and shouted, "Sir, sir, wake up!"

The man moaned, and put out a hand, which met nothing stable, and then seemed to come to himself. He steadied himself against the dashboard and pushed himself back until he was more or less upright.

Aniela waited, thinking "stay conscious, stay conscious, stay conscious." The man took a moment to get his bearings then he turned and looked at her.

"I am sorry. I fent in your car."

"Yes, and it's not allowed," she said severely, "so now you have to tell me what's wrong with you and what I'm supposed to do with you."

"'Have to,'" he repeated musingly. "Madam, if I were in a less parlous physical condition I would be delighted to respond to your request by countering your imperative with my own interrogative, which would perhaps lead us by many pleasant byways to consider the ethics and semiotics of compulsion and indebtedness on the part of the recipient of a benefit; however, the state of the matter being what it is, I must, unfortunately, forego the pleasure." Or, at least, it was something along those lines that floated in puffs through his mind. What he eventually said was, "Thank you for your cencern. I am all right."

"Are you drunk?"

"I am not."

"Diabetic?"

"No."

"Epileptic?"

"No."

"Peptic, septic, narcoleptic?"

What he thought was "Leave me alone already"; what he said was "No."

There was a moment of silence.

"Where do you live?"

He paused too long. He could not tell her where he lived and he was not accustomed to lying; it had not been part of his former life. "You can drop me anywhere along your way. It doesn't matter. I can get out here."

"No, you can't."

"You are kidnapping me? You?"

"No, of course not." She shook her head impatiently.

"But surely you can see—I am a public official; you are a man in a dubious state of health. If I were to abandon you somewhere and then, heaven forbid, you were to die, where would it leave me?"

"To say nothing of me." In spite of everything, he smiled at the ridiculousness of the situation.

"My point exactly."

"Madam, I am almost chickmated. I live on the edge of the Włochy district, in that big new housing development."

"I doubt it."

"Why?"

"I don't know. I just do."

He didn't answer and they drove a way in silence.

"Do you share an apartment?"

"No."

"Then you don't live in a new housing development; you couldn't afford it—not on what you'd make busking. You're probably squatting in the former factory buildings beyond, in Ursus, the ones scheduled for demolition. Am I right?"

"So, you are very smart."

"Yes, that's why I'm head of a ministry at my young age."

"Did I congratulate you?"

"Not yet, but you may."

"Congratulations."

"Thank you."

"When were you elected to this ministry generalship?"

"It's not an elected position. I'm a functionary, not a

politician. I worked my way up the ranks then won a competition."

"I see." His interest in the conversation, which would normally have been lively, flagged under compulsion of his hunger. The hot and cold flashes were coming back. He leaned his head against the window.

They had come to a stop light. Ahead of them was the long stretch of Nowy Świat, but it was closed to ordinary cars. It was more pedestrian mall than street under the curving line of classical facades. All the shops were restaurants but not mostly Polish ones: their signs said kebab, or Starbucks, or Thai food, or Frida Kahlo eats here. The broad sidewalks were crowded with tables, and on a particularly warm weekend night the area pulsed with life. All the languages of Europe could be heard. He had walked down the street often, but one couldn't play there. The policemen came and chased one away at once.

Aniela looked at him for a long moment as he tried to focus on the crowds of young people passing in front of the car. Self-important young women in tight pants or short skirts, looking for attention; self-conscious young men in tight pants, looking for drink. One could get vodka, standing, at 5 zloty a shot. A few like that and one went out and collapsed on the sidewalk. He'd seen them, late on a Friday evening, being dragged into taxis by their friends, being dragged into ambulances, being left to lie. A stupid way to pass the evening, but *de gustibus non est* and all that. Hadn't he also been sitting in a heap on the pavement just recently? His thoughts swirled. He hadn't spent his money on booze though, and while he had enough to make sure of meals for Andrei for a day or two, that wasn't much, and if he didn't eat tomorrow as well, he'd be in bad shape. He knew he should be forming plans, but the lack of food confused him.

"What did you think of those canapés at the party? The ones with liverwurst and walnuts?"

"I did not have any."

"How about the prosciutto and avocado?"

"No."

"You were wise."

"I am, yes."

"When was the last time you ate?"

Too long again, he hesitated, trying to think back. "It doesn't matter."

"You can't remember?"

"Yes, yes, I can. It was…this afternoon. I had an enormous lunch. The table was laid with a white cloth…." What did Poles eat? "'It began with cold beet soup and gherkins.'"

"It seems to me, sir, that you are lying."

Silence.

"Is that a quote too?" she asked.

"Your own national poet, Mickiewicz."

She was pulling rather abruptly into a parking spot. "Prosciutto doesn't do anything for me, either. I'm a vegan. Thus, I am in desperate need of dinner. Will you do me the favor of joining me? I never like to eat alone at a restaurant. My treat, of course."

It was kind and tactful and something inside him cringed and something leapt with joy.

She was already out of the car.

He followed her up the street and through a door, into the dark room of a restaurant with white eco-leather chairs and wide exotic-wood floorboards. A white-aproned waiter appeared, deposited large bound menus in front of them, lit a candle, and departed. The waves of nausea receded for the moment and Yuri could look at the other diners. The women looked as if their clothes had been bought that afternoon from expensive boutiques, the men as if their shoes had never walked on dirt and their shirts had not yet lost the crispness of their packaging. He struggled to regain a sense of himself, to see their material well-being objectively in terms of commodification and oppression, of Hegel and the masses, but the odors of warm food, coffee, and perfume mingled together and clouded his mind with simultaneous longing and satisfaction.

And across from him was this beautiful woman, somewhat younger than himself, who was buying him dinner. He couldn't concentrate on the menu. He put it down, deciding to have whatever she had.

"Tolstoy was a vegetarian too," he said, to make conversation. "And I am also, of course, but that is less interesting, particularly as it has not made me into any kind of radicalist, as expected by Oscar Wilde."

"Why less interesting?" she took him up, "I am having dinner with you, not Tolstoy—fortunately, as I don't think he'd have been a pleasant companion."

This was said rather repressively, so he was silent, but in a moment his natural talkativeness asserted itself. "It is true Tolstoy had no sense of humor, not littlest bit. That is why I am glad you lie with me."

"*I beg your pardon?*"

"You lie with me—it is not the right word? Earlier. About your job. It shows you have this that Tolstoy lacked."

"Keep your voice down. Lie *to* you. To. To. To." Her look was fierce and not amused at all, and he fell silent, abashed, until with relief he saw a corner of her mouth curl up for a fraction of a second.

In a moment, she continued, without looking at him, as she studied the menu, "Your references are literary. Are you a teacher or a writer?"

"I busk in the Old Town. I am a violinist."

"No, apparently, you're not. Everyone saw you faking it—it was the best part of the evening. But if your profession is unmentionable, forgive me." She applied herself to the menu again.

What difference did it make? he wondered. She was buying him dinner out of compassion and if she was the right woman he'd never see her again, and if she was the wrong woman he'd also—he acknowledged it with a pang —never see her again. The least he could do was answer her questions. So he began to speak, slowly, aware that he was mangling the vowels and mixing Polish with Ukrainian suffixes and annoyed at some level by the impediment to his usual articulateness but dogged.

"I was a professor of literature and taught at a university in the east of Ukraine. It doesn't matter where, or what the name is. Suffice to say that it is a place of mixed population. There are Ukrainians who are Russian speakers, and Ukrainians who are Ukrainian speakers, and people who consider themselves Russians, whether they speak Russian or Ukrainian. This was never a great problem in my lifetime. However, after the Maidan events, matters changed, and after Russia invaded the Crimea, even more. You know what is happening in Donbass and Luhansk. Yes, well, this that I am going to tell you happened before the separatists and the government troops began fighting in earnest; maybe a handful of persons had been killed in skirmishes here and there but not many. We were all waiting to see what would happen. My ancestors are Russian and Ukrainian and even Polish. I do not care about nationality—it is a meaningless point to me. I was attached to the city where I was born and I have always looked forward to a day of greater democracy in my part of the world. Above all, I have—responsibilities—that come first. Peace is the most important thing."

He paused, watching her fingers curve around the base of a candle, as if seeking warmth. Her head was bent, listening.

"Go on," she said.

"At the university, though, the unrest was becoming harder to ignore. I do not know if you can imagine what it is to wait from day to day, not knowing whether the march of world events will mean that you must remake your life according to a quite new set of rules. What did they care, there in Moscow, or Washington, or Kiev, what would become of us? Well, never mind that. One was being asked to take sides. I stated my position when asked, but I am not an activist."

This was a bit disingenuous, he admitted to himself. Over the years he had made rather a habit of speaking up suddenly when it would have been more politic to pipe down.

He corrected himself: "I did not join protests or march in the street. However, in the face of various kidnappings and murders, I felt it would be wrong to remain silent and published my views on the importance of resolving conflicts by negotiations and concessions. There was nothing that hadn't been said a thousand times already on the internet, in the papers, in the street. I cannot lay claim to any special courage, as I did not expect what followed."

He paused and then went on, "You know, I have written very many articles on various topics—including various injustices—and I was certain that hardly anyone read a word of them, though some were rather clever, if I say so myself. Why this one should have found readers and produced so much anger on both sides…" he shrugged. "A certain group took my letter as a manifesto—a manifesto for peace—it went rather viral on the internet and they marched with it and were attacked, some said by pro-Ukrainians, and some by separatists. I was thought to be a ringleader.

The next day, I went to work. The building where I teach is a social-realist building, one of Stalin's progeny, with enormous columns. There are about one hundred steps to a gigantic doorway, and then inside, more columns and more steps, and a very high ceiling. One is meant to feel dwarfed, insignificant before the state. I am already aware of my insignificance in that sphere; I can not be diminished further, or so I thought, and thus I walked in as usual. At the top of the stairs I was met by the head of the department and also by my friend and colleague. The head of the department said to me, 'Yuri Yeremevich, you disappoint us.' And my friend said, 'We can not work together.' They blocked my path.

"'What does this mean?' I asked, because I was taken by surprise. It should have been obvious what it meant. They were for the new government in Kiev and claimed that I was for Russia; I was for settling the issue quietly, like reasonable beings.

"They were joined by a number of other professors, my colleagues, and some men I did not know.

"'You disappoint us and we can not work together,' they said. 'Go home.'

"There was that odor in the air—do you know it? When men decide to do something they know is wrong and they are frightened at themselves, perhaps. It leaves a trace in the air; perhaps this why sin is connected with sulfur. They formed a line against me. I did not think I could reason with them, so I turned, and walked down the steps, and went home.

"And the next evening I was at home and there was a noise in the street. I went out on the porch, and there was a group of men wearing face masks and shouting that I am pro-Ukraine."

Here he paused again, and the waiter brought their food.

"And then?"

"Ah, no, I have talked enough about myself. That is a

story for another time."

She smiled slightly, musing. "You are like Scheherazade, you tell one story and leave the next one hanging."

The food before him was shouting for his attention. He could not have told the rest of the story if he had wanted to. The warmth and odor of food, food, food rose beneath his chin. He felt that it was requiring all his willpower to keep his eyes on his dinner companion, to force his eyes to follow the waiter as he receded, to only then imitate the woman in reaching for his napkin while letting his eyes finally come to rest on his plate. He was not an animal; he would not fall on his meal. At last he allowed himself to pick up his knife and fork and eat one bite, and then he laid his utensils down again while he chewed. Then, like Ivan Denisovitch's fastidious fellow prisoner in the gulag, he felt that he had upheld civilization and his own dignity. He regarded his dinner companion.

"Now you must tell me something about you."

When she did not answer, he prompted, "About your minister, for instance. Have you always wanted to be his servant?"

She smiled faintly. "No, being a *civil* servant at the minis-*try* was never my aim. I studied law and social policy at the university, but later my interests changed and I wanted to work directly with people who have brain injuries."

"Nalurogy?"

"Neurology, yes, but in terms of rehabilitation. I wanted to study what can be done to help. My parents objected, however. It seemed to them a plan lacking in ambition...and I cannot hurt them, by disregarding their wishes, because...because..."

Her voice trailed away. After a long moment, she put down her knife and fork and squeezed her hands together, almost in a sign of prayer. Her head bent down and she spoke so low that he had to lean forward to hear. "I have been revolving in my mind, since we came in here, while we were ordering and eating, if I could tell you something—if I could seize this chance to tell one other person something I've never told anyone...Because I know I'll never see you again, and it won't matter to you, it will be just another story you've heard—like something from a newspaper."

Suddenly the waiter appeared to fill their glasses. She fell silent, waiting for him to depart, but her telephone rang, and she apologized and spoke quietly into it for a minute or two, giving advice to someone.

Yuri was too taken aback by his companion's words to pay attention. He reached for the wine glass the waiter had filled. Suppositions rose in his mind. Was he mistaken about her character? Did he want to know? She put her phone away and was silent, staring at the table.

"Please, go on, I am listening."

"No," she said finally, "Never mind. It doesn't matter." Her voice had lost its intensity. She spoke offhandedly, drily. Perhaps he had imagined it all, perhaps it was an illusion created by emptiness. He looked about the room: it all seemed solid enough and real, with its murmur of conversation and slight clatter of plates being removed.

"Eat," she said, "your food will get cold."

And then, when he had eaten most of his meal: "Now, the rest of the story, please."

He shrugged, suddenly embarrassed. "It is not so much of a story."

"Please?" Her voice had lost its usual clipped tone.

"Ah," he took a deep breath. It wouldn't do to be too happy or to think that the felicitous situation where he sat surrounded by cleanliness and warmth and was asked to speak by a woman with whom he very much desired to converse would prolong or repeat itself. It wouldn't do to think any of that. In the meantime, in spite of his perfect consciousness, his heart seemed to be growing larger.

"Ah, yes, well, as I said—did I say?—it was evening, dark, and my young son—"

"You have a son?"

"Yes."

Aniela, who had been leaning forward in her seat, leaned back. "And a wife?"

"No."

"Go on, please."

"Yes, so, my son was in bed already, when the group of men in masks came and stood in the street outside my house. The first I heard was the tramp of feet, and then I heard voices. Then they were shouting, 'Ukrainian fascist!' I didn't understand at first that they meant me. I looked out the window, expecting that it was a march going past, or something of that nature. No, they were stopped in front of my house, and that Ukrainian fascist, you see, that was me. They looked really very threatening with their faces covered and their torches—they were young men from the shapes I could see in the flicker of their lights and the street lamps. They were shouting slogans and obscenities and after a time they began to throw stones or maybe bricks at the wall of the house."

He had stood for a moment just inside his locked front door, shocked and angry, the adrenaline pumping through his veins and his heart pounding, pounding. He did not tell her that, though.

"I knew that if they continued, soon they would break the windows. My son was inside; I did not want them to come in. So I opened the door and stepped out. I thought, perhaps they will beat me up, perhaps they will kill me, but they will leave the house.

"I intended to speak to them, to reason with them. I did not get the chance. Something hit me on the side of the head." He raised a hand to the scar on the side of his face. "Then there was a great explosion and crash behind me. I do not know what it was—a grenade, a Molotov cocktail, something else—All I thought about was my son—my son was in there. I turned and tried to run back, up the stairs to my son's room. Bits of plaster and wall were lying or falling everywhere. Flames were shooting across the corridor. I saw my son open his door and slam it again. I yelled at him to jump—to jump from his window. I ran out the back, into the yard—from there his room gives onto a garage. He was already out the window and running across the roof of the garage, dangling over the edge. He was in his pajamas; he'd brought his violin, nothing else. I caught him, and we climbed over a fence and ran away."

He stopped. "Eat. Your food will get cold."

She raised her eyes to his. "I'm not so hungry any more. Did you go back? Was your house much damaged?"

"It burned to the ground, but that is no matter."

"No matter?"

Andrei woke in the nights screaming. His family had lived in that house for three generations.

"We're alive. We're okay."

CHAPTER 6

The shack had been a bit of luck. He had heard about it on the bus to Warsaw, from a woman who worked cleaning houses. She had sat beside him and he had smiled at her and attempted to make more room, though it meant squeezing himself against the window, and she had warmed to him in that way women often did—he wasn't sure why. The shack belonged to the great-uncle of her former employers, she said, a summerhouse on what was once a garden plot, a common thing in communist days, but no one came near it anymore. It was hidden in the thick overgrowth of a parcel of land a few streets from her employers' house. It wouldn't do for a woman, but for a man like himself, who could make do with rough conditions...

The district, on the edge of the city, had once been a pastoral village. For a hundred years, he supposed, it had consisted of tree-lined alleys, single-family homes, and small tenement buildings surrounded by orchards and vegetable gardens; now it was being landscaped, upgraded, divided, and overtaken by apartment complexes. It was still a quiet place to live, however, and there were a few empty lots.

He looked up and down the street to make sure no one was watching, put his foot on the bottom of the ironwork gate and vaulted over, then pushed his way in the dark through the tall grass, dodging clumps of ash maple and tangles of vine overhead. The shack was an obscure mass, with a light barely visible through chinks in the wood.

He pushed open the door, calling softly, "Andrei." His son, seated cross-legged on the bench that served as his bed, looked up from a magazine he was reading by a diadem light.

"I didn't expect you so soon." Andrei's pointed, eleven-year-old face shone with relief. The light caught the planes of his too sharp cheekbones and the angles of his thin shoulders as he twisted lithely round to face his father.

"I know. I had a gig, and then a lady invited me to dinner. I brought you my roll from the restaurant." Yuri pulled it out of his pocket. "I told the lady it was for my pet." He rumpled the boy's hair and handed him the roll. It wasn't the sort of restaurant where putting food in one's pocket would pass. The lady had noted the move impassively, but he had felt embarrassed. "I didn't do much busking."

He sat down on the platform they had cobbled together out of rotting boards and bricks to make another bedstead.

"Where'd you get the magazine?" he asked.

"A garbage container."

Yuri looked at the cover and recognized a trashy men's magazine, all guns and body parts.

"That's where it belonged. I suppose it'll help your Polish, but that's the only good you'll get from it."

"I'm studying biology," said Andrei, in a superior tone. "The habits of the locals are peculiar."

Yuri half snorted, half laughed.

"Okay, maybe it's pseudo-science," Andrei admitted, putting it aside. "Polish men aren't very smart if they read this."

"Most don't and you shouldn't either, although I'm not forbidding it...If you were looking in garbage containers, you were collecting cans. Did you get a good haul?"

"No, hardly any."

"Never mind. What else did you do during the day?"

The boy did not answer. After a long time he said instead, "I want to go back to Ukraine."

Yuri lay down on the bench and closed his eyes. "We can't go back," he replied in the tone of someone who has said the same thing many, many times before. "What would we do there, with no house and people shooting each other in the streets? Everyone who can leave is leaving."

"Yes," said Andrei tensely, rocking himself back and forth and then shrugging and biting into the bun Yuri had brought.

"Anyway," went on Yuri rallyingly, "a man shouldn't be afraid of a little adversity. The human spirit needs adventure or it grows stultified. It's good to do new things."

Andrei was silent. He'd heard it before.

"So what did you do all day?" Yuri asked again. "Did you go to the library?"

"No. The ladies there won't let me come in any more."

"Why not?" Yuri raised himself to stare at the boy.

"They asked if I'm registered in the district, and I said, I don't know, and they said I can't come in unless I'm registered and I should ask my parents to bring proof. I think that's what they said, anyway. I didn't understand a lot of words—only they were pointing at the door."

"Ah," said Yuri, and sank back. "Damn." After a moment of silence, he said, "Well, while you weren't at the library, I hope you repeated the lines of Shevchenko I gave you this morning."

"'You did not play me false, O Fate/You were a brother, closest friend/To this poor wretch...'"

"Good. What else did you do?" he asked for the third time.

"I studied slugs." The boy shrugged; he had recently developed an irritating habit of shrugging to punctuate every sentence.

"Stop shrugging. Slugs? Why slugs?"

"They're really interesting, actually." Prevented from shrugging, the boy jerked his head sideways. "I found a heap of them under some grass, so I made a habitat square and began by observing them, like in science camp last year. They have feelings, like people, did you know?" He sat up straighter, his eyes lighting with interest as he talked.

"Really? How can you tell?"

"Because they come together in a group, like people— I mean, there's the whole garden they could wander in— why would there be thirty all together under one patch of grass? I don't think it can be for protection, so it must be for company. Maybe they have conversations. Maybe they have political systems."

"Maybe. It wouldn't be hard to do better than people in that regard, would it? You keep watching and tell me if you find any wars among the slugs."

"I've named one Putin and one Obama; one's Poroshenko."

"All males—what about females? Do you have a Merkel slug or a Tymoshenko slug with a blond braid?"

Andrei looked at his father pityingly, embarrassed by his ignorance. His neck jerked. "They aren't male or female. They're herm…hermaphrodites."

Yuri was tired. He didn't want to contemplate a world where male and female was the same thing. He wanted to lie still and dream of a different ending to the evening than one where he had dinner with an interesting woman and then she dropped him off in a dark street and drove away. But he was a father first of all. He talked for a long time with his son about the subterranean natural history of a suburban lot.

The problem of the boy's schooling worried him in third place after the scarcity of food and the probability of being deported. Even without books, he could teach Andrei languages, literature, history—but math or science? Not so well. Andrei was missing half the school term already and autumn, with the new school year, would come soon enough and what then? He could hardly earn enough playing the violin to…The violin! Suddenly he realized he'd left it in the woman's car. He sank back onto the bench and put his arm over his eyes. Well, he knew where she lived. He would get it back. He would see her again. Had it been his subconscious that made him leave it?

CHAPTER 7

The rooms were large, empty, and silent, the ceilings obscured in a kind of gloom. Only the floors creaked slightly as Aniela stepped through the unused interiors. With the shutters half closed, the outer world of fields and trees was eclipsed, but through the open inside doors she could see the breakfast table at the end of the enfilade. There, in a shower of light like in a Renaissance painting, her parents sat motionless, murmuring with bent heads before a table scattered with porcelain. A casual observer, seeing them from a distance, might assume they were saying grace. Aniela stopped for a moment and tried to imagine them intoning, "Bless us, O Lord, and these your gifts…" She knew, however, that nothing could be further from their minds.

Her father, who had once studied the medieval history of the Low Countries, now found selling semi-products or subassemblies more engrossing. She had lost track of what those items were—brake calipers, heating units, spring locks, the list was long and he was always vague on the subject—but she was certain it was a long time since, for his own pleasure, he had read anything but his cellphone screen or his tablet. There, like a hunting beagle, he tracked his status and his assets through the spoor of communications. Her mother, on the other hand, had always had a mind for business and even as a schoolchild had auctioned her homework answers.

Now, as Aniela approached, her father lifted his head two centimeters and said in greeting, "Nela, darling, I didn't know you were coming out."

"Out" meant out of Warsaw, where Aniela lived most of the time, to this graceful and echoingly unpopulated house in the countryside.

"Good morning. I sent you a message yesterday that I was coming." Thinking "forgive me," she wondered how it would be if she could drop a kiss on his short gray hair and receive a hug in return, but it had been too long since they had displayed affection to each other. He was dry and she was unpracticed. They met frequently but fleetingly, like city buses on north and southbound routes.

Her father began to scroll through his messages to find hers: not because he doubted her word but out of a kind of habit of triangulation. She could see him searching and then abandoning the search as he was attracted by some other text. In the blink of an eye, she dropped out of his focus. The words that had been forming in her mind, "I have something to discuss with you," died on her tongue.

She felt in her pocket for the email she had printed. "*If*," it said, "*you are the woman who was in Cambridge ten years ago, I am wishing to speak to you.*" The very crinkle of the paper made her feel cold.

Her parents were so busy, though, so preoccupied with their affairs. If she spoke, it would startle and pain them. If she spoke it would change their view of her forever.

Aniela's mother, round and sharp-nosed, did not raise her head from her tablet, but only clucked to her husband, "paragraph four, point seven," and to her daughter, "strawberries, Nela. Candy." She indicated a large box springing cellophane and gold tissue paper.

There were always these boxes about; Aniela's parents received a lot of such gifts. The bottles of Monkey Shoulder went into a cupboard or sat unopened on a shelf; the Parker pens rolled off table tops and were never picked up; but Aniela's mother was always working her way through another layer of chocolates, always waving sticky fingers in the air as her eyes stayed riveted to her screen.

Now, without shifting her gaze, she tapped on the cover of a glossy magazine. "I see you're in *Gala*, Nela. But it's not a good image—you should wear makeup to look better in photos. I've mentioned it to you before. And Kasia's in *Viva*, but her mouth is hanging open." She flipped the magazine toward her daughter, "Never mind. It's the names that are important." She went on with her task.

Aniela sat down and helped herself to the first strawberries of the year and bread from a platter. She had ten years' practice in being calm, after all.

Pani Ola, their housekeeper, brought Aniela's coffee and set it down with barely a murmur. Other members of the household got a portion of complaints with their service, but Aniela inspired respect even in someone rude by nature and nurture both. If she knew, thought Aniela, what would she think of me?

Then Kasia came in, walking with the grace of a sleepy

young cat. She draped herself over a chair and dropped a book on the table.

"Strawberries, Kasia," said her mother.

"Morning," said her father, without lifting his eyes.

"Oh, God, I'm so tired," said Kasia to no one in particular, as she stretched and writhed. "I didn't get in till three in the morning."

No one listened or answered. In a household where achievement was the ruling principle, the minutiae of family members' schedules or emotions did not get much attention.

Aniela's father rose and began to pace back and forth with the phone to his ear, the floorboards creaking under his feet. Someone would come from Paris, to meet a lawyer, to discuss a contract with some Hans from Hamburg …Aniela wasn't listening. Her mind veered from her parents' activities like the north pole of a magnet from the north pole of another. She did not know that her father micromanaged and obsessed, multiplying problems and creating tangled webs, and that his wife followed in his traces, a reverse spider, undoing many of his maneuvers and steering him relentlessly in the direction she wanted him to go.

The phone rang again. Aniela's mother went placidly on with her typing, as her husband walked about the room, talking in cryptic bursts. She did not appear to be listening, but when he glanced round at her, her own return look and jerk of the head was perfectly choreographed. He relayed the negative to the caller, ended the call, and went on reading his messages in silence: a neat, good-looking man of sixty, without obvious vices, outwardly suave and inwardly eaten by nerves. Once, only, his eyes fell on his elder daughter and the thought perhaps crossed his mind that he should put aside his business to speak with her, if just for a minute. She was so silent, so distant, so unhappy. What would he say to her, though? Fine weather we're having? It was fine, wasn't it? He looked out the window for the first time that morning. Ask about her work at the ministry, or if she'd seen the news?—puerilities. His eyes were irresistibly drawn back to the screen before him.

Now, maybe now, would be the time to speak after all? Aniela's heartbeat began to pick up speed. To speak or not to speak?

- I was criminally irresponsible.
- What I did cannot be undone.
- It is coming back to haunt me.
- What next?
- God knows.

The dining room was small and looked onto a small lake. Aniela stared out the window, feeling disjointed from her surroundings. The house, which some called by an imaginative leap a "palace," had been bought on impulse a few years earlier. Her parents' plans for its eventual restoration had grown increasingly grandiose with the passing months. Someday, they said, there would be chandeliers, gilt, damask, marble. The house would be a showplace and there would be domestic staff in uniform, not Pani Ola. That someday was enough. In the meantime, their lives centered on the city. They came here to get away, they said, but they hardly noticed their surroundings and had no interest in making the house a home. Thus they were eating breakfast sitting in white plastic garden chairs, around a plywood slab on sawhorses.

Aniela looked about at the other members of her small family. They shared certain characteristics, she knew. They were all articulate, determined, and hard-driven by inner spurs. Nevertheless, it sometimes flickered across her consciousness that her life aims and those of her family were deeply divergent. It wasn't an idea she ever cared to explore. In her imagination her parents were worthy of esteem and admiration, pinnacles of self-made propriety. Kasia—Kasia was a work in progress. And if her parents and Kasia did not form a very supportive or attentive group, they were all she had now. The thought of any event weakening their thin bonds produced something on the order of an existential angst in her mind.

The door to the kitchen swung open and the housekeeper came in again. She lived two fields over and considered she was doing a favor in working for them, or anyone. She clapped a cup of coffee onto the table.

"Hey, careful, you've splashed my book!"

There wasn't a drop anywhere, but Kasia knew how to vanquish Pani Ola, who waddled back to the kitchen, banging the door a little behind her.

Aniela always tried to ignore these exchanges, which were not to her taste.

•Judge not that ye be not judged.

She watched her sister take a strawberry between two fingers and flip open her book: *The Master and Margarita.*

"Why that book?" Aniela asked, surprised out of her own thoughts.

"It's the prime minister's favorite."

"You aren't seeing him?" She asked, startled again. But with Kasia anything was possible.

"Not yet, but I may."

"He's married—he wouldn't."

"Most are—more will than you think."

"He's thirty years older than you."

"Doesn't bother most guys."

Aniela gave her sister a reproving look, and when Kasia looked back, the faintest spark of amusement passed between them.

"Yes, you look disapproving," Kasia said softly, as she neatly decapitated a strawberry, "but my misbehavior is the only thing that makes you smile."

"But since you know it's misbehavior…" Aniela objected.

"Yes, but are you in a position today to object?" Kasia purred, "What about that lowlife you picked up last night?

"I don't remember any lowlife."

"Ah, and I distinctly remember that when I left you, there was a man slumped over your dashboard," Kasia teased.

"Oh, that one. He needed a ride."

"So, do you usually pick up drunks?"

"Don't be silly."

"Who was he?"

"Yuri something. I don't remember his name exactly."

"There, you see. And I thought you'd taken a vow

against men. Nela *contra mundi*—oh, except for men who are old, sick, paraplegic, schizophrenic...those are all right."

"Kasia!" Aniela protested, but her protests were half-hearted. She knew her sister enjoyed being provoking. Aniela glanced at their parents. Seated at the same table, they gave no sign of hearing. But her sister had reminded her of yesterday. Yesterday—what an odd evening it had been—odd enough that it had almost distracted her from the email. Yesterday's lowlife rose before her mind. A homeless man with a reputation for kindness. A man who could be witty even in a language he spoke imperfectly. Yuri the professor; Yuri the philosopher. History is repeating itself with odd distortions, he said. Nationality is the new serfdom, and the internet turns the world into a village, where no one escapes identity or the local gossip. I am a runaway serf, he said.

They had talked for a couple of hours, on a variety of subjects, but after their first exchanges not on personal ones. Since Filip, she had not met a person to whom she positively wanted to speak. In an aberrational moment she had almost told Yuri everything and that was very strange. She picked at her breakfast in silence.

She weighed telling her story to Kasia, but it was only a hypothetical imagining.

Kasia, finding her sister unresponsive, pretended to read, but made little headway through Bulgakov's novel. When Aniela raised her eyes she found Kasia's gaze fixed on her own reflection in the French window.

No, not Kasia.

She turned her eyes to the pond instead. A brown duck

splashed from the bank into the water and paddled pur-
posefully across the pond on some important quest of its
own, the wavelets ribboning out behind it. There, in the
middle of the lake, the water was pale green and almost
inviting in the sun.

She too could swim out there, to the middle, sink below the cool waters, and never have to think again. But
no, she remembered, she couldn't drown herself in the
pond. It wasn't deep enough.

She shook her head to rid herself of these morbid ideas and picked up the thick report she had brought to
breakfast: *Compliance Statistics in Regard to Access Facilities for
the Handicapped in Lower Silesia*. She could not be put to
shame by the industriousness of a duck. She opened the
report and began to read.

After fifteen minutes of starting the same paragraph
over, she closed the report and decided that after all ducks
doubtless had more soothing memories. Her parents' heads
were still bent. Kasia had disappeared.

She rose, uncertain suddenly why she had come. "I'm
going for a walk," she said, "and then I'm going back to
Warsaw."

Her mother raised her head. "Did you get enough to
eat, darling?" she queried, as she gave Aniela's clothes an
up-and-down glance. The question was rhetorical. Her
daughters' sartorial and nutritional needs had lasted a little
longer in her consciousness than other parts of their lives,
but basically all maternal concerns had been replaced by
the equally primal instinct for power.

Now, as she watched Aniela walk away, she said to her

husband briskly, "Have you talked to her?"

"I've tried," said Aniela's father, without turning his head from the screen, "She doesn't seem to listen, you know. Maybe she doesn't intend…."

"Her intentions have nothing to do with it," snapped his wife. "We all have to make efforts and sacrifices. She's growing too comfortable where she is. The disabilities job was all right as a stepping stone, but she's walking in place now. Where's the use in it?"

"Director-general, you know, dear, it's something, after all."

"A civil servant. My daughter. At thirty-two, for God's sake. It's time she moved up."

"Yes, dear. Although—when we were thirty-two we lived in a one-room apartment with no running water and had debts, you remember."

"Remember? Remember? How could I forget? Don't remind me. It's burned on my consciousness. I want better for my daughters."

"Sometimes I think my biggest regret about those days is that we had to leave Nela with my parents."

"What, you don't remember the conditions? The mold on the walls? It was no place for a child and we were up to our ears in work. I have no time for sentimentality."

"No, no, of course not."

"Talk to her," she said, and even though Aniela had scarcely left the room, her father reached for his cell phone.

"Nela," he said to his daughter, who paused before a

window, phone to her ear, fifty feet from him. "Your mother thinks it's time for you to think about the future—about what you want in the future."

"What I want?" said Aniela, evasively. She knew what the call was about. "Let's see. To make the world a fairer, kinder place, I guess."

"Well, of course, of course, we all do, darling." Her father's voice was smooth but held a hint of uncertainty, as if speaking to his daughter was unfamiliar. It might also be that she frightened him slightly, but this did not occur to her. "And the experience you've gained at the ministry will be useful—that is, what I want to say is that we think, your mother and I, that you have everything needed for a really great career in politics."

A long silence. Aniela had never openly resisted her parents' desires. At last she said, "My opinion of the political class is not high."

"Maybe it needs more women," he tried.

Aniela's memory tossed up a televised debate where two female politicians jabbered at each other simultaneously like angry parrots while the interviewer sat by helplessly and the cameras rolled on minutes of unintelligible noise. She couldn't see herself competing in that milieu; there were more serious impediments, though.

"I haven't observed that gender makes a difference. Once in power all seem to succumb to the same forces."

"Well, you could be different anyway."

Aniela paused for a second to think of what she might attempt as a politician. Admirable as they were, her parents wouldn't like the remedies.

"But you wouldn't vote for me then, would you?"

"Aniela, *darling*, please."

Aniela passed back through the enfilade of rooms and went out into the courtyard, waving at the two security guards seated glumly behind the wheel of a small car. They had nothing to do and little to look at here. The furtive visits of Pani Ola's daughter to the nearby parish house had ceased to amuse them. Their combat equipment had never been put to use.

Aniela circled the vehicle. In what had once been the front sweep of the house there was now an enormous pile of rubble and boulders. Where the boulders came from, no one knew. Possibly there had been a fountain that had been destroyed, or perhaps the former communist authorities, figuratively thumbing their noses at the past, had used the spot as a dump. Someday—next week, or next year—all this would be returned to its former glory. So far her parents had only surrounded the whole with a high chain-link fence and motion detectors.

She looked up at the house. The pillared porch was held up by pine scaffolding, and the courtyard failed to be a sea of mud only because it was hardly used. Her small Mercedes was parked to one side, in the grass. She did not go to it, but instead passed out of the gate and into a district preserve that bordered the local priest's neat grounds. She skirted the church and followed a path between hedges until she came to the woods and the lake.

Perhaps in a past century she would have become a nun. Closed away in a convent she would have risen rapidly to be Mother Superior. Novices would have trembled in her presence but they would also have felt enveloped in her tender care. No one's prayers would have been more impassioned. In the contemporary world, however, she had to make her own framework of good works and repentance. So far, her attempts had been unsatisfactory. Her every fiber was taut with a love that sprang forth in abundance, searching for an object, only to be tamped down, far down, by her family's concentrated monetary interests, by her own official position, and by a sense of her contribution to the world's disorder. She could not be the person she was meant to be.

She walked through the scent of conifers and new leaves, and hardly noticed. The path led under the trees, through carpets of Kenilworth ivy, and brought her to the pond, where the banks were steep and lined with reeds and stakes. She should have been in love with spring and her own youth, in love with love and with—someone. Instead every image brought her back to the past.

A man with a fishing rod sat by a bridge and the branches of a willow shed catkins into the water. In Cambridge, where she had worked briefly as an au pair, her employer had had a set of china with such a scene. She remembered laying the table with those blue plates. She closed her eyes and was instantly transported to another bank.

When she opened them she spun around and walked with rapid steps toward the car. She used nature simply as a backdrop for restless physical activity: for years it had ceased to ease and comfort her. Now only a total immersion in some difficult activity would help. The sole means of compensating for the past was to do good—passionately, frantically—in the present.

She reached her car and had her hand on the door when her eye was caught by something in the back seat. A violin case! That man had left his violin in the car. And what was she going to do about it?

She felt a sudden intense relief. Here was something she could do for someone. Here, at least, was a practical problem, and she was good with practical problems. She had a reputation for no-nonsense efficiency. Some of her colleagues, she knew, even called her "the ice machine" behind her back. She maneuvered her car out of the courtyard and began to think again, with an interest she repeatedly tried to stifle, about Yuri.

CHAPTER 8

Yuri opened his eyes to darkness in the moment after dawn, when the first birds began quietly to stir and chirp. He gave himself only a moment to gather his wits, to remember he was not in the room where his grandfather was born, to remember a blond woman buying him dinner after a trying musical interlude, to remember a statue splintering—these images flashed across his mind and were gone.

"Andrei, wake!" He rolled out of bed and shook his son, who pulled the cover over his head.

Across the road a city park had been extended to turn a series of clay pits into an elongated body of water where ducks, coots, and sometimes swans lived, and small fish shared the depths with beer cans.

Barefoot, they pushed their way through the dewy grass, climbed over the gate, and ran down to the reeds at the water's edge. There they stripped off their remaining clothing and cautiously—for the water was very cold and the sludge at the bottom held broken bottles—waded into the glinting water, gasping as they went. At waist height, Yuri lowered himself into the water and began to swim. A dozen strokes took him into the middle of the lake, where he tossed his hair and the water—and no doubt a lot of pollutants that didn't bear thinking about—out of his eyes and looked back. Andrei was just visible in the dawn light, standing at the edge of the water, his thin boy's body bent over the water, his fingers hovering over the surface of the lake. He looked very small and alone, and Yuri's throat tightened with protectiveness. He would keep him safe. But Andrei's concerns were different from his father's: a splash and his excited voice, half whispering, came clearly across the water. "I caught a frog! A little one! Tiny!... There, I let it go!"

Soon he joined Yuri in the center of the lake, and they trod water together. Andrei looked back toward a pedestrian bridge over a channel on the lake and suddenly exclaimed, "I want to jump from there." Even in the semi-dark, Yuri could see his eyes lighting at the idea.

"No, the splash will be too big; it will make too much noise."

"I meant *I* should jump, not *you*," teased Andrei.

Yuri put out a hand and pushed his son under water.

When the boy came up, spluttering and laughing, Yuri felt lightened—so, it was still possible for his son to find joy in life. The rest didn't matter so much. Afterwards, as they had no towels, they ran dripping back across the road to the shack. There they went to sleep again, until the day had come and a magpie knocking its bill on the roof and cawing woke them once more.

He was returning from the local shop with breakfast for Andrei, strolling along past bridle-wreath hedges and crabapple trees, the virtuoso racket of a family of nightingales mixing with his thoughts about Aniela, Aniela, the newspaper headlines, Bakunin, Akunin, and the hole in his shoe, when he saw a van pull up by the gate to "his" lot. A head stuck out and called in Ukrainian, "Do you want a job?" He had been asking for work at construction sites. They had found him by the grapevine and were short a worker. It was an opportunity he couldn't miss. With a pang, because he had been counting on seeing Aniela, at least for a few moments, he squeezed himself into the crowded van, and as he sat swaying shoulder to shoulder with men whose overalls were covered in paint and plaster even before the day began, he realized he would have to leave the violin to another day.

*

Aniela, arriving in Warsaw with the violin, realized that all she could do was wait until Yuri appeared to claim it.

•You are unreasonably pleased at the idea.

•Stop it.

Her phone rang. She saw that it was her friend Iza, groaned inwardly, and stifled that feeling too.

"Iza, hey."

"Nela, Nela, listen, I have to know who that guy was— the one who helped me when my hair caught fire. Where did you find him? Who is he? Tell me everything!"

Now why did the idea of Iza pursuing Yuri strike her as so offensive? It was nothing to her, after all.

•Nothing to you.

"I found him in the Old Town. He says his name is Yuri."

"You found him? What, like, he was just wandering around?"

"No, sitting. He was just sitting around."

"He's very handsome, don't you think?"

"No."

Be honest, she told herself. "He has a certain something," she conceded.

"He's a great violinist, isn't he?"

"If he practiced for ten years he'd be decent."

"I wonder what he's like when he's not drunk?"

"Iza, there are lots of more suitable men out there for you."

"Why? What's wrong with him?"

"I don't know. Maybe nothing. Anyway, I don't think he was drunk."

"No?" Iza sounded disappointed, "Oh, well, what's the matter with him then?"

"He's an independent thinker and it's rare to be independent and popular."

Stop it, she scolded herself, but Iza wasn't listening. Iza had been her friend from schooldays, and because she was silly and needy, Aniela couldn't avoid the relationship, even though it was all give and no take.

"Nela? Nela? Nela?"

Aniela realized she wasn't listening.

"I'm sorry, Iza. What were you saying?"

"Maybe you want him for yourself? That would be something new."

"I…no."

*

She had agreed to meet her parents for lunch, but, as

she strode down Foksal Street, oblivious to the heads that turned and the television cameras waiting for someone to emerge from the opposition party headquarters, she wasn't looking forward to it.

She entered the restaurant, passed pillars and short-skirted waitresses, and saw her parents seated at the far end of the room. Her mother was dressed in the manner favored by the German chancellor; her father had left off a tie—because a tie was excessive for lunching with his daughter—but he had the buttoned-up look of a man who frequently wore one. As Aniela walked to their table, she was struck again by the idea that wherever she encountered them, however often, they always seemed slightly like strangers. Their heads were down over their phones. The table had changed and the backdrop was different—now vaguely art deco, with touches of city street through the window—but otherwise the scene with her parents mirrored the one in the countryside a few days before. They ignored her until the food came. Then they put aside their phones and got down to the business of the meeting, which was their campaign to push her into politics.

These were their dreams, not hers, Aniela might have said—their aspirations for power and publicity. She couldn't quite bring herself to add disappointment of her parents to her other burden of guilt though.

•How little they know me.

"Why don't you suggest it to Kasia?" she said evasively. "You might be able to interest Kasia."

"Kasia's not suitable," said her mother, "You know it well."

"She's knows as much about the political scene as I do. I'm sure she knows a lot more people anyway."

"Kasia sleeps around," said her mother, never one to mince words. Aniela's father winced.

"Havel, Clinton, Hollande..." murmured Aniela.

"But *not* with *other politicians*."

"Kasia's too young, anyway," put in Aniela's father, to end this line of conversation. "Much too young."

"But in a few years time, she'll be ready, and I won't be in her way."

Aniela's mother shook her head firmly.

"You're both in the public eye, but you're the one with moral authority—"

If she only knew, thought Aniela.

"—Kasia's unpredictable."

"And I do what I'm told, you mean?" said Aniela, outwardly calm, and inwardly beginning to curdle. Aniela Solan, head of a ministry and her parents' puppet.

"Kasia's too hard to pin down. You're reliable. The thing I admire about you, Nela, is that you're so phlegmatic. Always cool and rational. Always."

Aniela felt an unaccustomed warmth at her mother's praise, regardless of its unappealing nature.

"You would have our fullest aid and support, of course," said her father.

Just say yes, thought Aniela, and her parents would be made happy and life would change, between one bite of coconut quiche and the next.

"But suppose the policies I promoted weren't ones you approved of, what then? Suppose, for instance, that our views on welfare, or immigration, or national security differed radically, what then?"

"What do you mean?" said Aniela's mother, her attention on her salad, where she was sifting the feta from the cabbage.

"I'm sure," said Aniela's father, "that whatever surface differences there might be, we basically think alike—families do, you know. When you get in office you'll take advice from experts, I'm sure, and be sensitive to the needs of the people who support you—."

"You mean the voters?" asked Aniela, suspecting that was not what her father meant.

"Those too, of course, but primarily, the people in positions to help you out—that's the way the world works. You know it."

"But I don't like it."

"But darling, you don't have to *like* it. You have to accept the world the way it is and work within it."

"I want the world to change. I don't want to accept it the way it is."

"But that's what we're talking about—you should go into politics, because then you'd be in a position to get things done."

It occurred to her fleetingly that now would be a good opportunity to ask her parents what they wanted to see accomplished, but she was silent.

"We've always helped you out," her father was saying, "and we expect you feel some gratitude, don't you?"

"Yes, of course."

"So think about it. We know you'd never let us down."

A passing couple then interrupted their meal. Aniela's parents rose with an abruptness that signaled the stature of the arrivals, kissed hands and cheeks with their acquaintances, tossed out polite phrases that collided in midair with the phrases of the other couple, and sat down again, glancing covertly about to see who had noticed, their smiles lingering for a few seconds.

"I would hate to let you down," agreed Aniela, and her parents, wisely deciding to stop while they were ahead, turned their attention to their pasta and beefsteaks.

*

The construction workers who had picked up Yuri were renovating a house in Ursus, they told him, the next district over. By the time they arrived at the site, he could tell that his educated speech and different mannerisms had already given rise to suspicion among the crew members, who were work-worn men with years of drink, labor, and rural households behind them. He climbed down from the van and looked with ignorant eyes at a two-story house whose innards, in the form of whitish plaster, bricks, and Styrofoam, appeared to have burst through its empty windows to coat the garden. He had never constructed so much as a house of cards, but he was ready to work and determined to prove himself a useful member of his new community.

"Can you put up that chipboard?" asked the foreman, handing him a drill.

"Er, sure," said Yuri, shooting the drill bit into a bucket of mortar.

When he had fallen over a stack of gyprock, and de-formed the sander head on a nail, and proven that he did not know a spatula from a trowel, they set him to hauling buckets of rubble to the garbage container.

He was naturally a strong man but unused to physical labor. Twenty years of university life had prepared him ill for fourteen hours of hard work. By the end of the day, in the choking atmosphere of wood and plaster dust, his breathing was labored and his heart beating erratically. His hands were skinned raw. The cut on his leg pained him.

"Have a drink," said the foreman on the last break of the day, holding out a bottle that had already passed around the crew and bubbled with spit. Yuri sipped.

"Have another."

"No thanks," said Yuri.

"You don't drink?" asked the foreman, exchanging glances with the other men as they sat in the garden, ciga-rettes clasped in leprous-looking hands. Incompetence was forgivable; temperance wasn't. At Yuri's shake of the head, it was decided to get rid of him at the first oppor-tunity.

In the evening, Yuri dragged himself into the shack and dropped, in his plaster-covered clothes, onto his makeshift bed. He would never move again, he supposed, his mus-cles were so sore and he was so achingly and all-over tired. He lay on his back with his eyes closed. One of his arms dropped from the bed to the floor and he couldn't gather the energy to pull it back.

Andrei came in from the slug center and sat down on

the other bed.

"Are you dead?"

"Yes."

"So did you have a good day?"

"Fantastic," Yuri gurgled.

"That's good: because a man shouldn't be afraid of a little adversity, the human spirit needs adventure or it grows stultified. It's good to do new things."

Yuri closed his eyes, and after a moment Andrei rose and went back outside.

But after a time he returned and sat staring at his father until Yuri opened his eyes.

"That drunk has been hanging around again. That one I told you about."

"What does he look like?"

"Like a drunk." Andrei shrugged. "Species *homo drunkus.*'

"Don't shrug. Young, old, tall, short?"

Andrei jerked his neck and considered.

"Medium."

"An undistinguishing adjective."

"He could come in and steal our stuff while we're gone."

Yuri tried to concentrate on the prowling drunk, but he couldn't get up the energy to feel threatened.

"What do we have to steal? I keep our money in my pants' pocket, anyway."

He closed his eyes again but as soon as they were shut Aniela rose before him, sad and accusatory, like his better self, because he'd left her, or someone, believing what wasn't true and he had to set all that right. He had to make sure she wasn't the one and then somehow continue his search. He'd do it as soon as he got paid. He'd have done with her. He'd collect the violin and cease these painful dreams of romance. He was asleep.

For a week he hauled himself out of bed each morning and stumbled through the long hours of back-breaking, socket-pulling, muscle-aching work, coughing in the dust, his hair and clothes and shoes gradually growing coated. The end of the long week came at last. The workmen headed for their van, to return to their quarters. Yuri caught up with the foreman and reminded him that he was expecting to be paid.

The foreman swung round, smiling slightly, and the crew by the van looked round, grinning too. Obviously the joke had been discussed before. "Come tomorrow. I'll pay you after you work tomorrow."

"Pay me today."

"Are you making demands?"

"I'm asking for my money."

"You're such a rotten worker you should pay me for training you. I'm not paying you anything. You're fired. Go to the devil."

Rage boiled in Yuri, rage so that he saw black and an impulse to physical violence almost overcame him. He had a tremendous desire to run amok, to crack heads together and bash the windows of the van with a shovel. But he got control of himself and stood without moving. He didn't hold with violence. He was also outnumbered, ten to one.

The foreman got in the van; the workers got in too. Grinning out the window at him, they backed out of the drive and roared away, leaving him standing. Yuri watched them go and swore softly to himself.

CHAPTER 9

She had waited all week for him and he had not come. The violin case sat on her sofa and mocked her. By Sunday, she had nearly given up hope. Perhaps she was wrong about him; perhaps he wasn't a reliable or rational person. Her interest flagged, with a curious depth of disappointment. Nevertheless, she left a note on the door for him— '*suis à la rivière, de retour sous peu*'—when she went out. Perhaps fresh air would clear her mind.

She left the confines of the Old Town and hurried down the escarpment. At the bottom the fountains sent up silver splashes beyond a shifting wall of children, parents, tourists, and young people. Five or six Yorkshire terriers, the dog of the moment, skittered at the end of thin leashes and looked longingly toward the hotdog stands. A soft-drinks container the size of a small store squatted under the trees and the garbage cans were already overflowing with bottles and paper plates. She left it all and hurried on to the embankment, where she had a strip of woods on one side and the river beside her.

She walked with long strides, feeling the stress begin to drain from her in the contact with nature and the physical exertion. The breeze lifted her hair. There had been a brief downpour in the morning, but now the sky was clearing, leaving the day new and clean. The river was dark blue, almost purple, and clouds heaped in blinding whiteness above the strips of sand and gray-green vegetation on the distant bank.

She passed a pub, banked against recent floods, where some cask had broken and seeped out in a bubbly rush toward the river. Stepping carefully over the puddle, she walked on past dilapidated dinghies, and restaurant boats, and barges whose prows were guarded by mongrel dogs, until she came to a chain-link fence that blocked her way and read a sign informing her that she was looking at the EU's 70-million-dollar waterfront project, whipped by the wind.

She turned back and saw him, coming in the distance. She knew it was he, even at a quarter kilometer. For one thing, he was large and there was something bear-like in his physique and too-long hair. For another, she was curiously aware of her heartbeat. She had a momentary impulse to cross up the grass bank to the street and thus avoid him. But that was ridiculous; all he wanted was his violin. She set out to meet him with determined strides and her chin at its usual haughty level.

He had a transient impression that she looked like a cornered deer, trapped between the fence and the water. He stopped at once, wondering if she wished to avoid him. But then she came towards him, and with relief he walked on.

They met shortly. She had her cell phone out, but she dropped it in her pocket as she came up to him. He turned to walk beside her back in the direction of the parking lot.

"You left your violin in my car."

"I did. I came to your door and saw your sign."

"How is your leg?"

"Fine, fine, thank you." How pleasing it was to have someone inquire of his health; Yuri's spirits rose.

"And breakfast? Have you had breakfast today?"

Yuri's spirits rose further. How pleasing it was to have someone inquire of his appetite. The sunlight glinted on the water and on her hair as he looked down at her.

"I have not, but it does not matter." Because I have seen you, he thought; it is enough for now. In half an hour perhaps I will be hungry, or very hungry, but now to be walking beside you is enough.

"You don't make enough busking to eat?"

"Sometimes."

"You would have more if you didn't give your takings to beggars. Why do you do that?"

He thought for a moment: Because he knew now what it was to be hungry. But he couldn't say that. He thought: because even if I have doubts as to the various values to be attached to performing trivial acts of kindness as opposed to pursuing a reasoned course to promote the greater good at the policy level, my situation leaves me only one sort of action. Out loud, he said, "Partly for them—because it is denying their humanness to say no when asked for help. Partly for myself. Because feeding the sool, sool…soul is important like feeding the body. Because it makes me feel like a man to be able to say 'your need is greater than mine'."

"I like your answer," said Aniela quietly, "Few people I know would answer that way, I think. But to be practical...Is it impossible to find a regular job? If you had more you could give more."

"I have been working all week as a construction worker, but I was fired."

"Oh. What did you do?"

"Er. I was working with the rabble."

"The rabble?" she repeated, slightly offended. Was he some kind of snob after all? "Oh, you mean rubble. But I mean, why did you get fired?"

"It might be because I dropped a brick out a window."

"Is that so bad?"

"The foreman was underneath." Yuri shrugged. "An accident. But, he was wearing a hard hat. And hard hat, no hard hat, he has a blockhead anyway. Or it might be because I tripped over a can of paint. Eh, it was open." He waved a hand. "But probably it is because I don't drink vodka."

She almost smiled. "You're exaggerating, I think."

"Ah, you smile almost—it's good. About the vodka, no—about the rest, a little."

They were strolling slower and slower, hardly progressing, sometimes stopping in their unconscious desire to prolong the encounter.

"Why are you here? I mean, why, when your house burned down, didn't you just go to some other part of Ukraine—to Kiev or Lviv, for instance?"

"If the authorities thought I was pro-Russian when I lived in the east, they will not stop thinking so because I move to the west of the country. I was afraid. I have no living relatives. If anything happens to me—if they put me in jail as a subversive element or if I disappeared, as has happened to many, my son will end in an orphanage. They are not good places to be."

"Yes, I see."

"Perhaps I am unwise to tell you this. But I think you are trustworthy."

"Yes." Then she remembered and added to be quite correct, "No. But you have nothing to fear from me."

He puzzled over this answer but said nothing and they walked in silence for a ways, thinking their own thoughts. They began to speak simultaneously.

"I have something to tell you…" both said.

Yuri smiled. "Women lead the way."

"My friend Iza—the organizer with the hair"—she was going to say 'extensions' but stopped in time—"that got burned wants to thank you in person. I sent her a message that you were here. I think it likely she will show up."

As a matter of fact she was positive that Iza was at that moment rushing for her car and was soon to be breaking a succession of traffic laws in her hurry to emerge from the parking lot at the end of the embankment before Yuri left.

"Ah. That is not necessary."

This, Aniela thought, was where she had to put in a good word for her friend. She searched her mind for Iza's good qualities, but they seemed elusive.

- …
- …

"She's a very, um, energetic person," she said at last.

"Enthusiastic." When she wasn't sobbing melodramatically.

"Dramatic."

Yuri felt uneasy. He did not quite grasp the situation, but it occurred to him that perhaps there *was* a situation.

"I see. And this enthusiastic-dramatic person is coming now, to meet me, here?"

"Yes. Or perhaps you're in a hurry?"

Did she sound as if she was hoping he was in a hurry, as if she wanted to get rid of him?

The breeze lifted a strand of her hair. Her eyes were large and gray, kind and wary like the eyes of a Byzantine saint.

"Madam," he thought, "Your slightest inclination is my command and I will go or stay, stand on my head or walk on my hands, as you please."

She was looking at him, waiting for his reply.

"I follow your wishes like a pull toy follows its string."

She frowned and dropped her eyes. It was just his odd foreign mannerism—it didn't mean a thing. And she wasn't allowed to be interested in anyone.

He was waiting patiently for her to speak, head inclined, half smiling. She could make neutral conversation with him as they strolled, or she could tell him everything there was to know about her, in one story. Then he would:

•Never say anything like that to her again.

Iza could come and perhaps he and she…who knows. It was nothing to her. Even as she thought the words, she knew how untrue they were. Why this man? she wondered. She had no answer beyond the rare certainty that he too was trustworthy and that his ideas on every subject would interest her. Once again the inaccessibility of a normal relationship surged to mind. Soon, she supposed, everyone would know about her past and perhaps she would rather tell Yuri herself than have him read about it in the media. Better to get it over with. Uncharacteristically, on the moment's impulse, she plunged into speech.

"Does being a literature professor mean you like stories? Or only ones in books?"

"All ones. You will tell me one? I am all ears. As earful as Eeyore."

"It's not a funny story," she shook her head to admonish his light tone. "Less funny even than your story of leaving Ukraine. You're certain you don't mind listening?"

"Certain." He adapted his expression to her seriousness.

They walked a few more steps before she began. "I received an email recently. The sender wants to know if I was in Cambridge ten years ago. I was...and something happened during that time that no one in Poland knows about. I'm afraid the person who sent the email may want...I don't know—blackmail, perhaps?"

"No," said Yuri, startled. "I am—I assure you this is not so."

But she wasn't listening, she was thinking:
•I went on a picnic, by a river.
•There was a child.
•I was supposed to be watching him.
But no, if she was going to tell it, she couldn't reduce

it to bullet points. She looked far into the distance and after a moment ceased to be uncomfortably aware of the physicality of the man beside her, and was wholly in the past.

"I am going to tell you all the details, even the unimportant ones because that's the way I've relived it in my mind over and over all these years, imagining that if only I could have changed this moment, or that, then maybe that day—the day that ruined so many lives—would have ended differently. But nothing exculpates me.

"It was in England. I had been taking a summer course at Cambridge, but I wasn't a regular student there; I studied in Warsaw and this was just for a month. After it ended I worked for another month as an au pair in place of an acquaintance who had to return to Poland for some family problem and didn't want to lose her job. I didn't need the money, as my parents gave me all I needed—it was just to help her out. My employer and her husband were professors. My grandparents had been academics so I thought I would feel at home, but the situation wasn't as pleasant as I'd hoped. They had a five-year-old daughter who was rather smarmy, the house was dirty by our standards, and my employer—her name was Sarah—was a bit impolite. She laughed at my accent. She didn't like her husband speaking to me. But these things were too slight for me to say reasonably, I've had enough, I'm leaving. I had engaged to work for a month and intended—unfortunately—to keep my word. I experienced briefly what it is to belong to the underclass and that has been useful, at least...Anyway, that doesn't matter.

"It happened on almost the last day. Sarah had orga-
nized a picnic, which we were supposed to eat along the
banks of the river. She had invited a number of other
couples, two or three unattached men, and a married professor who came without his wife. There was also a woman
with her small child—they were Ukrainian, like you. I suppose the child had a father, but he wasn't there that day,
and I never met him. I don't know why Sarah had decided on a picnic, or why she had gathered this group of
people. Perhaps she was paying off social dues or perhaps
it was in aid of certain—shifts—in her social sphere.

"We travelled to the river in cars and then had a ways
to walk. The Ukrainian woman and one of the men stayed
together. The other men formed a group, the women another, and there was distance between them. They weren't
very attractive people—balding older men in sweaters and
glasses, weedy younger ones, the women looking like the
men—yet obviously they all thought very highly of themselves. I was an outsider.

"I am not fond of picnics—I was not, even then. I don't
like flies and ants and bad food tipping on plates. Here,
picnics are about sausages and fires and charred potatoes.
In England, they involve a hamper and sandwiches and
wine, and they're still awful. The glasses clinked in the basket as we walked. Sarah's husband led the way. I came last
with Emma, Sarah's daughter."

"The guests walked ahead of us in single file, lifting
their feet in the grass, following the food in the hamper.
The line strung out and I suppose the men in front of me
imagined no one could hear them. One asked the other to

remind him why they were doing this thing, and the other said it was because of Nigel…um…Do you speak English?"

"Yes," said Yuri, wondering if he really wanted to know exactly how it had been, all those years ago, and finding with only a bit of surprise that it had ceased to matter to him. Nothing she could say could hurt him and his curiosity was only to know how she would tell the story. What happened—he knew that already. He had had a research fellowship at Cambridge that year. "Yes, I know English well," he repeated.

"So I'll quote their words in English then," she continued. "'It's Nigel,' said the one, and he gestured with his chin to one of the men ahead of us. 'He's interested in the Ukrainian.'

"'What, the young thing behind us?' said the other.

"'Shh, no, the one ahead, the pretty one,' said the first.

Tsk, thought Yuri, and then, be just, Oksana was beautiful.

"Then one of them made up a verse. It went like this: 'For the stealing of husbands, a Slav/ Is far better equipped and more suave/ And in addition to that/ Not nearly so fat/ As your average Brit in…' But he never finished because the other one told him he was an idiot and that I'd hear him. So he turned around then and spoke to me: the 'not pretty one,' you understand. I was so stupid—I minded that. 'Where are you from?' he asked.

"'Warsaw.' I said, 'It's in Poland.'

"'Yes,' he said, in a very drawling voice, 'I know where Wahsaw is, thank you.'

"'Our house looks onto the Neisse River.' I said, 'Do you know where the Neisse runs?'

"He hesitated. 'Through Wahsaw obviously.'

"'No,' I said, 'I'm joking. It's nowhere near; it forms the border with Germany. I would have thought a Cambridge professor would know that.'

"I don't know why I had to put him in his place that way. Maybe if I'd been kinder, less full of myself, what happened wouldn't have happened…" She stared unseeing down the concrete walkway by the Vistula.

"Please, continue," Yuri prompted after a long pause.

"So at some point the group stopped walking, but no one knew where to sit or what to grab hold of. There was some bickering and not much stiff upper lip because someone—Sarah thought it was her husband or maybe I—should have brought something to put under the blankets. I helped pass around the food and glasses. Perhaps the wine helped. There was a murmur of talk. At one point, I found myself beside the Ukrainian woman at the hamper. She spoke pleasantly and had an unusual face—possibly part Tatar."

Yeah, thought Yuri, Oksana had a face in which dark Tatar combined with fair northerner to devastating effect.

"She looked at me and then at the English people and her eyelashes batted. 'Most of them shouldn't be eating this food,' she said to me very softly. 'Most of them shouldn't be eating this week at all. Pile their platters.' She made me feel like we shared a joke—"

Yup, thought Yuri, she had that kind of charm.

"And while she was saying this to me, she was smiling

at the nearest don, and then I saw her eyes travel on and meet the eyes of the man who came without his wife. But at that point she had to drop the plate she was holding and chase after her toddler who was heading for the river. When she brought him back, he was struggling and crying.

"'Maybe it's an instinct pushing them toward the water,' I said to her when she put him down.

"'All children are lemmings,' she said. 'Right to the water and in they go.' Her hand made a diving motion.

"Emma, Sarah's daughter, turned to her mother and asked if she was a 'wemming' too.

"Sarah didn't answer her but ordered me to take the two children to the side and keep them amused as 'we' were getting in the way and disturbing the meal.

"I didn't mind being banished with the small fry, but Sarah's tone annoyed me. Interesting as England was, I was glad I was going back to Poland. I picked up the Ukrainian's little boy and he was surprised enough to stop crying. I carried him fifty feet or so away from the group, a little too far, Emma trailing in the rear.

"He was maybe a year old—I'm not sure. He walked as if he'd just learned, every step precarious, tilting forward too far then taking quick steps to catch his balance, or not sometimes: sometimes he fell on his hands or sat down abruptly. He didn't seem to care.

"I set him down, spread out the blanket, and invited the children onto it. He followed Emma. I found a Kleenex and wiped his face. He was kind of cute; he had a pointed chin and hair that stood up in tufts, like an elf. He looked back at his mother a time or two, but she was talking to her friend, and he was willing to be distracted. He babbled meaningless syllables at me with an expectant look in his eyes and I started to like him. I started to think he was quite a smart kid for his age. I fed them the chocolate biscuits one after the other until the boy's hands were so sticky that Emma complained in disgust that he was getting the blanket dirty. I carried him down to the river then and helped him swish his hands back and forth in the water. He was very pleased, and afterwards not happy about stopping, but I couldn't leave Emma alone, so I coaxed him back to the blanket.

"Then we collected the dandelions that grew around the blanket and played with them, until Sarah called out that we mustn't pick the wildflowers—her tone said 'stupid Polish girl, how could she not know that one mustn't pick wildflowers?'

"I sat and felt aggrieved, and then my better self struggled up, and before long I was ashamed. How could it be that I, who wanted to love all my fellow men, should feel such hostility over minor slights and rudenesses?

"I watched the group, telling myself that I had to try to see them objectively, not as unappealing people who thought they were superior but only as human beings. I told myself that no doubt they had complexes and disappointments of their own so large that if one could judge them truly, look into their hearts really, all one would feel would be compassion and pity. Probably, like so many people, none of them were loved enough by anyone: not by their spouses, or the partners of their affairs, or even by their children. I told myself these things and it didn't help. I felt angry and wounded. How hard it is to remember it."

Again she stopped and took a deep breath.

"I saw them tipping their wine glasses, watched the food slide on their plates. Occasional bits of their conversation came to me on the breeze.

"'Did you hear that slight splash? A trout, I suppose. We should have brought a fishing pole,' said one.

"'The child-minding Pole is more useful,' said another, adding words that I strained to hear.

"And then someone else said, 'So long as it wasn't the lemming again,' and the Ukrainian woman rose and said, 'Where's Andrei? I don't see him.'

Here Aniela's voice faltered and then went on.

Yuri too felt a strange tightness in his chest.

"I looked around and there was Emma beside me, playing with the dandelions still, but no toddler.

"I don't remember the next moments so well, only the feeling of horror. The rest is disconnected images in my mind. The Ukrainian woman with her mouth open, moving towards me, the entire group beginning to rise behind her. And then I was sliding down the river bank…"

Aniela took a steadying breath.

"And there in the water was a small body, floating, face down.

"He didn't move when I lifted him. There was a long moment when I stood in the water, holding his limp body, and was paralyzed. Then someone grabbed him from me and began resuscitation efforts. I wish it had been me, but it wasn't. The limerick don was effective, and sometime later, the ambulance people came trotting over the grass, and they took the body away, limp but alive.

"And then, you know, they were gone, and most of the guests went too, and I was left with Sarah. Maybe she spoke to me, but I don't remember. I remember watching her pack the hamper and seeing it all very clearly with one part of my mind, while the other was almost catatonic with shame and horror. My fault, my fault, my fault—that was all I could think.

"And I had to follow her back to the car, and as we were getting in she said, 'Oh, God, how could you do it? You were supposed to be watching him. I hope you're happy.' I wanted to run then back to the river and drown myself, and I've wanted it ever since, but I didn't.

"Afterwards, we went to the hospital and I met the boy's mother in the hallway. As soon as she saw me she began to scream that I was to get out of her sight—that the harm I'd done could never be undone, that the child would be…" Aniela whispered the word, "severely brain-damaged…and they would all have to live with that now. That little child, who hours before had been babbling to me about the water and the blanket and the flowers—all that eager baby desire for knowledge—all that was gone.

"His mother was shrieking with grief and I couldn't speak to her. What was there to say, anyway? Later, I tried to call her, to ask if there was anything I could do—Sarah tried too for me, but she refused to speak to us. The third time she said that if I called again she would lodge a complaint against me. I don't blame her. What could I do? I think I had some idea of paying damages—maybe I even said it. How could she not be angry? I suppose she thought it would be a travesty to accept money—as if that could make up for what happened to her child.

"And then I went back to Poland and never told any one—but one person—about what happened, but I've lived with the guilt of it every day for ten years. I ruined that child's life."

Yuri listened until she had quite finished. She was staring into the distance at nothing. He felt his chest expand in pity, and pleasure too, that he would be able to bring her this relief. In his mind he tried quickly to arrange what he wanted to say. He mustn't mix the words at this important juncture. He had to be clear, even in a foreign language.

Madam, he would say, I am deeply distressed that you have suffered all these years from an incident that had no serious outcome. I must say, however, that I think you are wrong to have allowed yourself to be so burdened with guilt. We all of us, without exception, have lapses of attention or judgment that could result in someone's serious injury or death. We are absent-minded while driving, clumsy on a staircase in a crowd, talking to someone as a small child crawls toward an open window; we place a flowerpot precariously on a balcony, forgetting the pedestrians below; we are abrupt to someone suffering suicidal thoughts. The list could go on forever, and mostly these things do not happen. Neither the child nor the flowerpot falls; the car drives itself; the person commits suicide, but we never know about it…This is part of living. Every single active human being has committed errors of this sort. The difference between lifelong regret and a forgotten moment is only luck. Thus to blame someone for incidents of this sort when the consequences occur is the worst sort of hypocrisy. It is only the motive that matters. You didn't mean to, and it could have happened to anyone. You must forget about it and go on living—particularly as I can tell you, since it's my son we are talking about here, that there is nothing at all the matter with his brain.

She sat tensely, staring at the water, not looking at him, waiting to hear what, if anything, he would say. She couldn't decide yet whether it was a relief to have spoken or whether she was already regretting she had said anything. Still he didn't speak. What had she been thinking? She rose abruptly and took a few steps toward the river.

•Why had she said anything?
•What a stupid thing to have done.
•She had no right to inflict her past and someone else's tragedy on him.
•What a stupid, stupid thing to have done.

"I'm sorry," she said, her back turned to him. "I don't know why I told you all that." And she really didn't—that she had acted on a need to share and communicate already seemed aberrational, even in the hindsight of thirty seconds. She felt herself freezing back into the calm, efficient civil-servant persona that had been progressively overwhelming her nature during the course of the past decade.

Yuri's consoling speech was ready and his mouth was

opening.

But her telephone was ringing. She picked it up and he could hear both sides of the conversation.

"Iza, hey."

"Nela! Nela! You have to help me. I've run into a lamppost."

"Are you injured?"

"No, but it's leaning. The lamppost is leaning. I think it's going to fall on me."

"Are you in the car?"

"Yes—Nela! Nela! It's leaning further!"

"Iza, get out of the car! Iza, do you hear me?"

"The door won't open."

"Try the other."

"No, Nelaaa!"

"Get as low in the car as you can. Call emergency; then call me back."

"Nela!"

"Just do it, Iza." She hung up but stood staring at her phone. It rang again.

Obviously, thought Yuri, this wasn't the moment for whatever reassuring comments he might have made.

"Oh, okay, it's all right," Iza's voice rang from the phone, "I got out and it looks like it's not going to fall after all, but you have to come, Nela. Because my c-c-car is smashed and what am I g-g-going to do?"

Aniela agreed wearily to come to her, and turned to Yuri. "I have to go help my friend." Her voice was curt and she was already turning and striding off.

He started after her.

"Wait, please! I have to tell you—it was I who sent that email."

"You?" She stopped then and stared at him, realizing she'd been an idiot. How could she have told all that to a stranger and now...In a voice like an Arctic plain, she asked: "What is it you want then?"

"I want..."

Nothing, he was going to add. Maybe he would go hungry; far worse, maybe Andrei would go hungry. He did not intend to ask for help.

Aniela looked at him in surprise and revolted distaste. Here was a man, a stranger, who had inspired such trust and such a sense of connection that she had recounted to him the pivotal point of her existence, and it turned out he was a sleazy extortionist. She wondered how he'd known about it all, but it didn't matter much. Maybe the Ukrainian woman had been his neighbor or university colleague. There were a thousand possibilities. What would he want? Money, of course. Assistance with his immigration status? She cut him off in mid-sentence.

"If it's money, I won't give you any." What did he intend to do? Take the story to the newspapers? She had been waiting for this for ten years. She went on, "And if it's to do with your immigration status, I can't help you." She spoke with cold precision.

"I want nothing." Yuri finished his sentence, stung by her rebuff and all atremble. "Nothing...ah, except my violin."

"Yes," she said, beginning to walk away with long steps. "You can have it."

It sounded like "take your damn violin and get lost."

She turned and was walking backwards away from him. "You know where my apartment is and you know the door is unlocked. Your violin is on the sofa." Steal something if you dare, she thought and even as she thought it she knew deep down he wouldn't and that his silence was not because he was a blackmailer but because he despised her. She spun around and the sun caught her hair as it swung against her rigid shoulders.

Feeling mutually injured and having missed understanding and shared joy by mere seconds, they separated.

CHAPTER 10

Yuri trudged across the Old Town to Aniela's building and up the stairs. The apartment door was open and he went in, but today he hardly glanced at the beautiful view. He was too wrapped up in Aniela's anger. She had told him her story and at once, afterwards, she had been angry. He wasn't sure what he'd done and he hadn't even had the opportunity to answer her. There was no doubt that her eyes had been full of pain.

The violin was on the sofa. He had only to cross the room, grasp it, turn, leave. He started forward and his eye fell on Aniela's desk with its neat pile of paper and pens.

He felt like an intruder, but he went to the desk, seated himself, and pulled a sheet of paper towards him. He had something that had to be said.

Madam, he wrote, almost word for word as he had wanted to speak before, *I am deeply distressed that you have suffered all these years from this incident. I must say, however, that I think you are wrong to have allowed yourself to be so burdened with guilt. We all of us, without exception, have lapses that might result in someone's serious injury or death…You didn't mean to, and it could have happened to anyone. You must forget about it and go on living—.*

He was startled to hear the apartment door open and rose abruptly, without reaching the last lines. He recognized Aniela's sister at once, but she jumped at the sight of him and exclaimed—*Jeezus!*—before recognizing him too.

"Good-day," he said, picking up the violin and intending to leave immediately. Now he really felt like an intruder. "Good to see you again. Good-bye."

"What are you doing here?" Kasia demanded.

"I am stealing a violin."

"That's your violin."

"That is my point precise-mently."

"Where's Nela?"

"With her friend who has the red hair in carls, who has run her car into a lampstreet and needs help."

"That might even be true," conceded Kasia, settling herself in a languorous pose on the sofa, drawing on a cigarette, and eyeing him thoughtfully as he bowed himself toward the door.

"Are you seeing her?" asked Kasia, looking at him speculatively.

"Whom?"

"Iza."

"No!"

Yuri was almost gone. Years at a university had taught him to retreat rapidly from young women who looked at him speculatively.

"Nela then?"

"No."

"Why not? Don't you like her?"

He stopped with his hand on the door. "Yes, very, very much, but I do not think the feeling is mutualistic."

"You have to show up in a wheelchair; then she'll be nice to you."

If I find myself in a wheelchair, I'll hotwheel it over here, he thought. "I will remember that," he said, and was gone.

*

It was raining by the time Aniela arrived back at her apartment that evening. Kasia was still there, a cigarette gripped between her teeth, typing rapidly on a laptop.

"I'm staying the night with you. Mama and Tata are holed up with a man with a Cypriot passport," she announced cryptically without looking up. "The atmosphere's too much for me. Even a pendulum would go off-kilter after taking as many pills as Tata has." Kasia's hand sketched a jerky zig-zag in the air. "Mama's fuming. I've got work to finish."

Kasia wrote a lifestyle blog that—to Aniela's continual but unspoken puzzlement—had half a million followers. It was filled with dessert recipes, diet advice, articles featuring Kasia photographed in elegant clothing against interesting backdrops, and banalities of all sorts parading as social responsibility. Advertisers flocked to it and Kasia had a surprising income.

Now she stopped typing. "I've had an idea—I'll get dark glasses and a Labrador and have myself filmed being turned out of supermarkets. A citizen's report on how shops discriminate against the blind. What do you think? I'll wear the coat from Simple and get Wiko leatherworks to match my bag and the dog's harness."

"No one would turn you away when you're followed by a cameraman," said Aniela wearily. Poland had won the FDR Disability Award for inclusion but there was still a lot of work to be done on public attitudes. Discrimination was serious business; Kasia's self-promotional use offended her. Everything grieved her. She felt a headache coming on and it was difficult to think, particularly when she didn't want to think. She wanted to curl up in a ball somewhere and be oblivious to the world.

"What's wrong with you?" asked Kasia, looking up, but she lost interest before Aniela answered. "You never like my ideas, anyway." She went back to her laptop, but in a moment she said again, "Mama and Tata would have fits if they knew you leave your door unlocked. That guy with the violin was here when I came in. He left you a letter. It's there on your desk. I didn't read it—I hope you're impressed—well, actually, I can't read his handwriting— it's crazy bad," Kasia's eyes creased in a grin.

Aniela was already lifting the letter, with a hand that shook a little. She took it to the window to read in the pallid light. Impatiently her eyes scanned the words. Whatever his purpose in contacting her, he wasn't a blackmailer, that was clear. It was kind—it was very kind of him. She appreciated that he had written these words, but his letter didn't tell her the one thing she most wanted to know: namely, how badly was the child damaged? Was he able to function normally at all? Whatever "normal" meant. He didn't mention the boy once.

Outside, dark clouds lowered while a cold small rain fell on roof tiles and new leaves and a slash of grayness that was the river. It was far brighter outside than in her thoughts.

*

It was raining hard by the time Yuri arrived at the shack that evening, footsore, weary, and sick at heart. He pulled on the door and the rotting fiber of the frame separated from the hinges. He propped it up and went inside to find the water dripping through the roof in several places. Andrei greeted him with a mumble and didn't look up.

"What's the matter?"

"Nothing," Andrei shrugged.

"Don't shrug."

"*You* shrug. You shrug all the time."

Yuri raised his eyebrows. Andrei wasn't usually rude. The boy turned his head away and the movement revealed a dark bruise on his cheekbone.

"You're supposed to be better than I am. That's why we have children—to enjoy the sight of our better selves without having to change. What happened to your face?"

"Nothing…Some kids didn't want me at the park. They threw stones."

"Ah." Yuri lay down. That was worse even than his rejection by Aniela. "What did you do then?"

Andrei, whose conscience wasn't clean, didn't answer.

"Well, I'm glad to know you walked away."

No answer.

Yuri continued, "Because you know how I feel about fighting. Fighting is *stupid*. If people hadn't been fighting, we wouldn't be here now."

"I didn't fight. I waited until they went into the Amicus store and then I smeared dog poo on their bicycle seats."

"You didn't!" Yuri sat up in consternation. "Did you wash your hands afterward?"

"I used a stick."

Yuri lay down again, chagrined.

"I should make you apologize." He neither expected nor received an answer.

From his lying position, he studied his son's heart-shaped face as the diadem lit it under its messy fringe of locks. The boy's hair was too long, and perhaps that made him a target. He could try to cut it with their one knife, bought for a zloty at an open-air market, but it still wouldn't have the buzz-cut look that was usual for Slavic youngsters.

Andrei was cradling a plastic carton in his lap. Now he reached in and extracted a large snail. He held it in his hand and it uncurled, extending its neck and waving its eye stalks. He watched it slide across his palm.

"Putin?" asked Yuri.

"No, this one's a snail," said Andrei with a touch of impatience. "Oleg. Just plain Oleg. He's my friend."

Yuri sat up and looked closer. He wasn't sure if the drop of water slipping across Andrei's face was a tear or a drop from the leaking roof. He made some inarticulate sound of sympathy, but Andrei turned away.

Before long the water oozing from the ceiling became a steady drip over Yuri's bed. He moved off the platform and propped himself against a wall, there to doze until the night was over, the rain had stopped, and he rose stiffly to bathe.

Andrei wouldn't rise with him, but mumbled and gripped his blanket without opening his eyes, until eventually Yuri let him lie and made his way alone to the lake.

CHAPTER 11

The water was cold in the dawn—bracing, Yuri said to himself, bracing, brrrrracing. On the next warm day he would bring his pants to wash and hopefully by the time he had to leave for town and his b-b-b-busking, they would be dry. He had only the one pair. After the construction work, all he could do was to shake them to get the dust off and beat them with a stick, which always seemed like a sort of self-flagellation. Holding back his general sense of loss, he swam back and forth with fast strokes until he warmed up; then he turned over to float on his back in the dark center of the lake.

So it was back to playing Pachelbel. That was infinitely easier than carrying rubble, etc., but the pay wasn't as good —if he had been paid for carrying rubble, etc., that is. He lay in the midst of the water, so still for a time that a family of ducks floated past almost within reach. They stop-ped him from something like the heartbreak of loneliness, but even so, he had to take deep breaths. God, God, what were they going to do? Seven billion people in the world and to none of them was his and Andrei's plight a matter of concern. And that was the devastating truth of poverty, of migrancy: they were nothing; they were refuse; he was an empty beer bottle bobbing among the pond scum. If he were to drown now, Andrei would go to a

refugee center and then be repatriated to a Ukrainian orphanage—out of sight, out of mind. Orphanages were
horrible places where abuses of all sorts flourished. A boy
might be better off in the street.

Of course, he had to keep things in proportion. He
was in an infinitely better position than most homeless
persons. He was educated and that meant he could always, like Don Quixote, connect his situation to that of
some literary figure. Someone he knew from a story had
always suffered similarly or far worse. He could call to
mind Hugo's wretched man, overboard in the depths of
the ocean, watching the ship disappear. He could scroll
down the list of Soviet atrocities from history and the oral
record of acquaintances. He could congratulate himself
that he was educated and living in the Western world and
that he didn't truly believe his current situation would last
forever. He was educated and that meant he could call to
mind the horrid Nazi experiment where educated persons
took longer to drown because, perhaps, they couldn't
really believe what was happening to them.

What to do, what to do? Nothing in his past had prepared him for living from day to day, from hand to mouth.
The next day, the next month, the next stage had always
been planned down almost to the hour. From childhood,
in a family of intellectuals and artists favored by the Soviet
system, his future had been mapped out for him—good
grades in elementary school, successful exams in secondary, university degrees one after the other, a professorial
position, steps up the academic ladder, marriage (the di-
vorce was unfortunate, but not without precedent), a child

or two (who would get good grades, pass the exams, etc.), some modest achievement added to the sum of civilization—to which younger colleagues would point as they breathed a sigh of relief and bid him farewell with insincere speeches upon retirement—then there would be friends and drinking vodka for old-times' sake; books and his old wife at the kitchen table; a sudden interest in gardening; walks leaning on a cane, with a grandchild, and a small dog. That was how his parents had seen his life no doubt and he had too.

None of it. The future was unimaginable. He could only plan to the end of the day. He must get dressed. He must walk into town with the violin and play. He must frequent the bus and train stations to seek out other Ukrainians, in case someone had heard of a job, somewhere, that he could do. This would not be today—working without pay for the construction site had set him back—but perhaps in two or three days, if all went well. If matters had gone differently with Aniela perhaps she might have become a friend. Perhaps he might have asked to use her computer to look for jobs, just for a minute...Perhaps, perhaps.

He wondered if she had read his letter and if it had made her feel better. But of course it would, how could it not?

He was growing cold in the water. He flipped over and looked back toward the shore, where he had left his clothes in a heap on the concrete step. Shock coursed through him —a figure was bent over the heap, and as he looked the figure grabbed, straightened, and began to run across the grass, clutching the garments, pants' legs and shirt sleeves flapping behind. Yuri bellowed at the figure—which only sped its flight—and began to swim with all his strength, splashing wildly in his hurry. Soon his feet were touching ground and he was staggering, cursing, through the water, then pelting madly across the grass after the thief with all the speed fear and adrenaline could give him. He ran unmindful of his nakedness or the terrain beneath his feet. All he possessed in the world was in his pants' pocket.

The thief looked back once and perhaps recognizing Yuri's fury increased his speed again. He ran with the uncertain gait of the alcoholic, but he had a good head start and a grasp of the local geography. He scaled a five-foot fence, dropped with a crash into a yard, and had disappeared over the other side of the lot before he roused the sleeping guard dog. By the time Yuri arrived and put his hands on the top of the fence, the dog was yodeling confusedly, hackles raised. Yuri backed away. He looked up and down the street, but the thief was gone and there seemed no way to pursue him further. The dog continued to bark and a light sprang on in the house. Remembering his unclothed state, Yuri backed rapidly into a hedge and away from the light until he was certain he couldn't be seen from the house. Then he ran.

When he got back to the shack, Andrei was waiting for him. Yuri picked up a blanket and wrapped it around his waist.

"What's the matter?" Andrei asked his father in a trembling voice, "I heard you shout and went to find you but you were gone."

"That drunk you mentioned?" said Yuri, still struggling to catch his breath. "You were right. He got my pants and the money."

He sought out a dry place on his bed and sat down heavily. There was a long silence.

"A man shouldn't be afraid of a little adversity?"

Andrei's voice held no provocation, only anxiety, and the question hung oscillating in the still air of the pre-dawn hour.

Yuri made an effort to take stock of the situation. They had no money, no papers, no food, and now he had no clothes. They were calamitously out of luck, but he had to put on a good show for his son.

He roused himself, clapped and rubbed his hands together. "Now things are getting interesting!" He cheered.

"Ye-es, but what are we going to do?" The end of the sentence was lost in coughing. "You're naked and I'm hungry. I need a handkerchief too."

Yuri rose and felt his son's forehead. It was warm, too warm.

Now things were getting serious.

That Andrei should be the victim of a clash of imperial agendas that cared nothing for the demolished lives of small people seemed to him hideous, monstrous.

"Let me think," he said, and stared into the total quivering blankness of his mind.

"First, a little fashion design." He folded his blanket in two and cut a hole in the middle, then pulled it over his head. He could wish, when he looked down at the effect, that he were a smaller man and the ends came further down his legs, but hopefully he would look like someone wearing shorts and a poncho. It was unfortunate, of course, that the blanket was covered in a grotesque flower design, but that couldn't be helped and perhaps if he walked fast it would look like camouflage.

He marched down a damp chestnut alley and through a tunnel where the cars came past close, up the hill toward a vast intersection and a McDonald's. Everywhere thickening hedges and greening lawns softened the outlines of new construction, old fences, and ubiquitous concrete. He strode along Połczynska and Wolska streets, past the old Catholic church and the old Orthodox church as the sun began to shine, past the Mormons' new compound, past cemeteries and parks and tram tracks, past the Wild West of high-rise business buildings, where later the employees would hang about the entrances in clouds of forbidden cigarette smoke.

It was still early, too early, but later there would be more people. He wanted as little public exposure as possible. The cool morning air felt odd on his legs in a city setting. He was not a man who ever wore shorts. He felt distinctly and overwhelmingly vulnerable and ridiculous in his vestiary shortcomings.

He tramped along Jana Pawła II and Solidarity streets, where most of the boutiques were still closed but the sidewalks were beginning to crawl with people and lines were forming inside small grocery stores. He walked through a scent of bread and longed for breakfast. Walk on, he told himself, breathe deep; enjoy the scent of the linden flowers. Try as he would, the idea held a tinge of bitterness.

He stopped beside a mock orange bush fronting an apartment building and it dropped an occasional pure white petal onto his shoulder as he stood with bent head.

He had failed. The standard demanded by modern society was self-sufficiency, and whether he ascribed to the ideology or not, that was the yardstick the world imposed. In spite of being half a head taller and a hand broader than most men, he was now a very small person—an impecunious little runt. But no. He was prepared for his place in a community that rejected its unlucky members but not that his child should suffer too. He was prepared to accept the inequality of adults but not the inequality of children. That—no. And yet he was expected to take care of himself, and his own child, and yesterday even Aniela had recoiled at the idea he might want something from her. She hadn't known, though, before he wrote the letter, that the boy she nearly let drown was his son. Now, however, perhaps she would remember what she'd said about wanting to help…Not that he thought she should feel obliged in any way—

He turned around then and almost started back.

But humans need each other and have a right to expect help from one another, he argued. And yet, he reminded himself, when he had been living comfortably in his house in Ukraine he hadn't felt quite the same urgency to share with other people either. He had noted all the ways society agrees to let the unlucky die—by poverty, or disease, or violence, preferably out of sight somewhere—

but he hadn't thought he would ever belong to that group. Not, of course, that he was in great danger of dying—probably, so long as he kept his head down—but he had always confidently expected to be able to take care of himself and his child—and look at him now.

He walked on until he reached the Old Town, where the sun was beginning to strike the bricks. He passed the maudlin statue to the boy soldier, with its outsize gun and mushroom helmet, simultaneously sentimentalizing and exalting murder—God Almighty!—He'd keep his son from ever having anything to do with such idiocy. That, at least, he could do. He had been right to flee his home.

There, down that street, was the step where last week he had been busking. Here he had followed Aniela. They had turned here. He strode along, head up, the blanket swinging against his thighs like a kilt. This was the door. It was ajar, but there was an intercom and it would be more polite to announce himself, he decided. He pressed a button.

Nothing happened. Here were two municipal guards passing as he waited. They were looking hard at his costume. He caught the eye of one and smiled at him. The man looked away instantly and the pair continued.

Now a low, calm voice was saying "hello?" over the crackly intercom.

At least, he reminded himself, he was not like ship-wrecked Odysseus, having to hide his nakedness behind a branch as he begged for help. And if that heroic ancient king could beg, why couldn't he, Yuri Yeremevich, unheroic professor of literature?

"Excuse me, madam, it is I, Yuri Romen, he of the violin, I...if I may, I would like..."

The buzzer rang before he finished, and he pushed open the door, panting. What if she told him to go away, what if she looked at his strange costume and slammed the door on him? What, precisely, would he do then?

He dallied momentarily in the cool, dank stairwell and admitted to himself that he hadn't a clue. He climbed the stairs.

"Come in," she said, opening the door to him. He went in. She was wearing some sort of gray jersey garments that might have been pajamas and her hair hung loose. She looked as if she had risen recently and this rather unsettled him. She waited, without smiling and with her brows faintly raised, for him to speak. He did not see that she was struggling with a mixture of apprehension and unaccountable, bounding pleasure at the sight of him.

He began by stammering.

"If...because...when..." He stopped then and tried again in a rush. "Forgive me for appearing in this unfortunately costume, but I have been the victim of a thief or maybe a joker, who knows, but that is not a matter, that is not why I have come to you. It is because of my son..."

"Your son!?" She was staring at him.

"Yes, you said you would not help me, and truly, I appreciate your sentimentation. I have no claim on you and indeed, as I said in my letter, I do not consider that my son does either. However, it is my most sincere belief and fervent wish that you have a good heart because the boy has fallen ill. I have no one else to turn to."

Aniela crossed to the sofa and sat down, clutching her hands together. It was becoming clear.

"He's your son? The boy I almost drowned is your son?"

Hadn't he written that? Yuri wondered. He must have been unclear in some fashion. It was so difficult when one had to communicate in a foreign language.

"Yes. My son. His name is Andrei. He is asleep now, in a shack, but it is damp from the rain and he has a fever. We have only two blankets and a thief has my clothes. We have no money for food."

"Ah-ha." She drew in a long breath. "Yes. Of course I will help you. I must help you." She looked away from the enormous relief that shone in his eyes. This was all wrong.

Later, later she could think about what it all meant. Now she must concentrate on the practical aspects.

"Aren't you afraid to leave your son alone? What if he wakes? I will buy you clothing, but I think we should go to him first."

"He is all right, I think. I do not like to leave him, but it is a quiet residential area and he will sleep till I return. I do not think he is very ill—a cold, perhaps."

Surely it was unwise to leave a disabled child alone, she thought, but it was pointless to speculate at this point. The boy's father must know best. "What is your size?"

"I will repay you someday—as soon as I can—I hope soon," he murmured, but she ignored him, and only asked again for his size.

He was waiting for Aniela to return, sitting on a sofa, staring at his own bare knees and at the edge of the blanket that did not cover them, thinking that this was what it was like to be a woman, when a noise jerked his head up. Kasia, dressed in something that might have been gym clothes or pajamas, was standing in a doorframe.

"You again?" she asked in surprise, looking about. "Where's Aniela?"

"She is gone to buy me new clothes, I think." He added in explanation: "I was rabed."

"Holy Mother," said Kasia, after a pause, "How weird …Ah. Robbed, not raped." She eyed him curiously. "You keep reappearing. Who are you really?"

"I am like Oscar Wilde of the East."

"I hate it when people make references I don't understand."

"He was a play wrighter. He wrote plays about forgiveness. But no one forgivenessed him when he needed it and he died in poverty in exile."

"Now I remember. He was gay, wasn't he? Is it your sexuality that needs forgiving?" Her tone was mocking.

Yuri pulled the blanket down over his knees. "No, there we differ."

"And you're not a playwright, are you?"

He shook his head.

"You're also not a violinist, so…?"

"I am the non-wanted refuse produced by clashing interests of the powerful classes in two civilizational spheres."

Kasia observed him with half-closed eyes. The effort to see a larger picture was arduous and she abandoned it.

"So you're an immigrant who can't manage for himself, is that right?"

"Whose home are you living in?" he countered.

She grinned at him then as she reached for a cigarette. "You sound like Aniela. You'll make a good pair. You're the man who needs everything and she's the woman who wants nothing."

"We are not a pair! Look at me—I'm not in position to pair with anyone. She is nothing to me!"—he was protesting rather too vehemently when the door opened and Aniela appeared.

"Just as well," breathed Kasia softly, through a cloud of smoke, as Aniela unpacked a number of shopping bags with a rustle of paper. "Our parents would never roll out the welcome mat for you."

"And you and your sister always do what your parents want?" Yuri asked, startled.

Kasia shrugged and nodded.

Ten minutes later, Yuri emerged from Aniela's bathroom feeling light and invigorated, like a freshly shorn sheep or just-molted bird, and suddenly convinced that new fabric on skin was one of the world's great sensations. The clean cotton was both familiar and beyond his imagining, so much had a few months of homelessness reduced his sense of what was normal.

He held the hideous blanket in his arms, but Aniela took it from him and gingerly set it aside. He thanked her warmly for the clothes, with a pleasure not even embarrassment could diminish.

Aniela's sentiments were very different. "She is nothing to me," she had heard him say and the words came as no surprise but sank into the deep well of her sadness. He had every reason to loathe her. If he didn't it was to his honor, but in no way lessened her guilt. Now she would shortly be brought face to face with the consequences of her irresponsibility.

CHAPTER 12

He followed her to the car and soon they were driving past the boutiques, the trams, the cemeteries and parks, the Orthodox church, and the McDonald's—how quickly it all passed now—and he hardly noticed it as his whole awareness was on the woman beside him, who was in turn giving her over-intense concentration to the weaving traffic.

"Why did you send that email anonymously?" Her voice, coming suddenly in the silence, startled him.

"I am sorry. I did not mean to. I was typing it on the computer of a print shop—because I cannot find a real internet café here, you know?—and the management came then and say they forgot to ask for my ID. So I got nerves and clack "send" before they throw me out. I made an account with no name to be safer. Afterwards, I had to beg strangers with smartphones to let me check my mail. Once someone agreed."

"How did you find me and why now? Why not any time in the past ten years?"

He was glad of the chance to explain, but she was answering her own question. "I suppose it's because you're more in need of help now."

"No, no, truly—before this morning I had no intention of asking for anything. I wrote that email only because I wish to speak with you, to set matters straight." He paused to gather his thoughts, remembering the doctors who had jumped to conclusions and his wife who was always dramatic.

"It was like this: My wife Oksana, my ex-wife, came to visit us rarely—only two times, in fact. Andrei has seen her only twice since he was a year old. She did not return with us from Cambridge. As I think you were noticing, she met someone else there. We divorced."

Oksana had told him, in a moment of awful frankness, that it was the split-second sensation of relief when Andrei's limp body was lifted from the river—of freedom accompanying the horror—that decided her. She was fond of her son but she wanted everything life in England could give her and family life in Ukraine couldn't. She had a chance to start over and she took it. Not everyone was born with an equal capacity for motherhood.

But Aniela was waiting. He paused to let resentment for his son die from his voice and his mind.

"The last time she came it was shortly after the disturbances began. She came to settle some affairs after the death of her mother. Andrei had the influenza then, and she only…"

There, he couldn't keep to his story in an objective manner. He must do better. Perhaps she was right, perhaps it had been better for all of them that she made the break definite.

"She waved at him from the door of his room and then we—she and I—had tea together in the kitchen. There was nothing to say and it was uncomfortable. How long does it take to drink a cup of tea? Much too long it seemed. For something to pass the moment, I showed her his last school report."

That must be a special-education school, thought Aniela.

"She sort of laughed, and when I asked her what was funny, she said she was remembering what she'd said to that au pair, the time Andrei almost drowned. 'What did you say?' I asked, because I didn't know she'd ever spoken to that girl—to you. And she told me what she'd said to the girl—to you—about Andrei."

The woman beside him kept her eyes glued to the road.

"'Why did you do that?' I asked. She said it was what the doctors said, and when you came in she told you. Later, after the tests, she wouldn't talk to you because she wanted you to suffer for what she went through—that's what she said. I don't think she knew how cruel it was. Or maybe she did. I never understood her. She said all this casually—chitty-chatty, you know—it was of no importance to her. She refuses to help Andrei if anything happens to me—she doesn't want to be burdened with him in England. She is not such a stable person. Marriage number three is going kaput.

"After she left I was upset by what she told me. I hoped the girl—you—hadn't believed her. I hoped that if you believed her, you were a heartless girl and hadn't cared. But I didn't know. And it seemed to me I had an obligation to tell you I wasn't angry and that accidents just happen—they can happen to anyone.

"I had time to write to an acquaintance in England and ask him to inquire the name of that au pair. No one was certain after all these years, but it was thought her name was something like Anita Solo or Salon and she was from Warsaw. I searched on the internet and found some people with similar names but not of right ages. So I wrote my contact again. He wrote back saying that perhaps the name was Alina or Anila not Anita, but by then events in Ukraine had come over us, and I—I didn't forget about it entirely, but those events…required a reorganization of my priorities. We had to survive and run first. Trying to find that girl was of very far secondary importance. Later, in Warsaw, I used the computer at the print shop, and that is how I found you. Also I found photos and your address in the Old Town and I knew I had seen you in the street."

Afterwards he had watched for her, followed her, and changed his usual place to see her pass more often, but he would not tell her that, of course.

He directed her around the lake and they pulled up in front of the overgrown lot. There were people about now: women pushing prams, children on bicycles, an old man walking a dog. Yuri waited until their heads were turned and sprang over the gate in two movements. Aniela remained on the other side. She was hugging her arms across her chest and once her teeth chattered nervously. It was the first time he had seen her look perturbed and he was uncertain why.

"I can't go in there. It's trespassing."

"Yes, I know."

"I'll wait here."

He found Andrei squatting listlessly beside the slugs. "One's disappeared," he coughed. "And I let my snail go too."

"Come," said Yuri, feeling his son's forehead. "There's a lady here I'd like you to meet."

In a moment he reappeared at the gate with Andrei, helped him over it, and stood before Aniela. Andrei's fever had increased and he didn't look healthy. All his usual sparkle was gone and his eyelids drooped.

"My son, Andrei."

Aniela extended her hand. "How do you do."

Andrei began to put out a limp hand, only to pull it back and rub it hard on his pants. "Slug slime," he muttered incomprehensibly.

Aniela could feel the tears starting to her eyes, but she made an effort. "Is this where you live?" she asked slowly and clearly.

Andrei started to shrug and then, remembering, jerked his neck to the side and did not answer.

Aniela felt the tears begin to roll down her face. She couldn't help it; she knew it was shameful, but she was overwhelmed by what she had done to this child.

Andrei and Yuri stared at her. Yuri was dumbfounded.

"It's not *that* bad a place," whispered Andrei to Yuri.

Aniela pulled herself together. Her behavior was tactless and her feelings, after all, were irrelevant to the situation. There were practical measures to be taken: first, these people needed to be provided with a decent place to stay. They needed to be fed and clothed, and then—being a functionary her mind was already glancing over legal ramifications. That was too complicated for the moment, though; she'd leave it for later.

"Gather your things together," she said. "I will take you to a better place to stay."

Yuri and Andrei looked at each other. Yuri climbed over the fence again and in a moment came back carrying the violin, a blanket, a knife, two spoons, and Andrei's one change of clothes in a clutch in his arms.

The car crossed town and Yuri lost all sense of direction. They were driving on a highway whose kilometers of sound barriers shut out all perspective and suggested, in their excess, malfeasance in some government office. Then finally these were left behind and they were traveling past empty fields and pine forests; he didn't like to ask where.

"Do they not expect you at the ministry?" he asked at last.

"Yes. I've called in that I will be late. This is more important."

It was extremely flattering, of course, to have one's humble self so suddenly elevated to more importance than ministerial matters, and yet it was also deeply embarrassing.

"I do not want to make problems for you at your job."

"I intend to speak to a lawyer this afternoon," she replied coldly, to keep her emotions from showing. "But I may have to give it up."

This was the point at which any self-respecting man asked for the car to be stopped and got out. He turned around to look at Andrei and found that the boy had fallen asleep in the back seat. *Damn*, he thought. But he did not ask Aniela to stop the car.

"I have to be in Warsaw in the evening, too," she said, suddenly stammering slightly, as if shy. "It's...I always babysit on Monday nights for a woman who...who needs a babysitter. I...maybe it seems like your needs should come first..."

"No," said Yuri, "of course not."

"But I can't let her down. So you'll be on your own tonight."

He didn't like to ask where.

"I'll be back tomorrow, though. And if I'm going to help you, I need to know about your legal situation. Do you have a visa?"

"We do not have even passports. When the house burned down, all our papers were in it—all our identity documents. I could not get my savings from my bank, even. Many offices had closed. I borrowed a small sum of money from friends—but it was difficult, you know, at that time—everyone was worried about what would happen and no one could give much. I was afraid of the authorities and of the separatists and did not want to wait around. We went to the border on a bus and...we crossed there."

"Not legally then."

"Not exactly."

Thus he reduced to two words the most stressful ten hours of his life. He had paid a trucker to take them across, hidden, at night. It had been very uncomfortable and very dangerous. He hadn't fit in the space provided and he had been separated from Andrei. He had worried about the oxygen supply; the wait on the border had been long and freezing cold; and he had expected discovery every moment. When the trucker finally stopped and dumped them out in the morning, by a field of rotting cabbage in Poland, he had been unable to walk and Andrei had stood beside him, shaking, on the edge of the road.

"Perhaps you can claim political asylum."

"I am afraid...If the new Ukrainian government considers that I am pro-Russian, perhaps this information will be available to the Polish authorities as well. They will not want me here."

"Yes," said Aniela thoughtfully.

They drove for a ways in silence. "Why did you come to Warsaw?" Aniela asked at last.

"We stopped first in a small town to the east of here. It was very prospering. The people are thriving on EU funds and fortunes built on Mercedes and things they stole from Germany twenty years ago. There is much free time and much alcohol. A day or two after we arrived a man went drinking with his friends—one of them owned a forklift. When the man woke in the morning, he found the friends had tied him with—how do you call it? duct tape?—to the upper part of a light-pole, meters off the ground. It was thought a very good joke. Me, with my one violin tune, how can I compete with such entertainment? So we came on, to Warsaw."

They had been driving along a narrow country road for a time. "We are not going to such a place?" Yuri asked tentatively.

"No," said Aniela, slowing the car. They were passing through an automatic gate and into a yard filled with boulders, beyond which loomed the imposing façade of a large villa or mansion in a state of disrepair. Yuri stared in surprise. An interesting house, yes, but was she going to suggest they squat there? He looked about at the fields, the forests, the parish house, and a distant, indistinct row of small houses that had no doubt grown out of the peasant dwellings of the manor. Where would he work and what would he do in this deserted place? He was just opening his mouth to protest, when she said, "This is my parents' house. There are few beds, but lots of room."

Yuri's eyes flicked to her and then shifted uneasily to a man in black uniform, who was watching them as he leaned against a car with a logo on the door.

"It's all right," said Aniela, "that's just one of my parents' security guards. There's another about too and cameras and stuff all over, but don't let any of that bother you—it's just my parents—they have an obsession about security. I don't know why."

CHAPTER 13

Aniela, having settled Yuri and his son in one of the bedrooms and having provided everything in the way of tea and towels that sprang to the mind of inexperienced hospitality, was wandering around the lake in restless circles. The boy had curled up at once on a bed, eyelids closing over dim eyes. She shook her head to rid herself of the image, but it stayed. She walked on, unreceptive to a day that sparkled now with sunlit grass, quickening leaves, and the darting of birds and winged insects over the pond. She stopped on the bridge and leaned on the railing. The surface of the water held shades of brown and jade and shimmering chartreuse, but she saw only a blur. Shortly, shortly, she would go to tell her parents about the boy.

She closed her eyes and felt the warm rough wood of the bridge beneath her hand. This was all the support she could get.

She thought briefly of her long-ago fiancé, who had so decisively left her in exchange for her honesty. She whispered his name experimentally to the air—"Filip"—but he was in no way the embodiment of her indistinct yearning. He had not loved her enough and all that was dead and gone with the person she used to be. If she remembered him, it was only because he was such an enduring prognostic of what she could expect from others.

She looked up and saw Yuri emerging from the house onto the terrace. He saw her in the distance and raised a hand, asking in sign language how to reach her. She signed back and before long watched him come out of the trees and follow the bank toward her.

"How is your son?" she asked, when he came up to her.

"Asleep again," he answered, shrugging, "In normal circumstances—a dry room, warm food—one would not worry about such a little illness, but as we are living, such small diseases grow fast, I think."

"Yes," she said. "Particularly in special cases—for children such as your son, I mean—I imagine he will need special care if you stay here—special education, too."

She was embarrassed by her words: Why did she keep saying "special" as if to drive the point home? All her years helping people should have made her more tactful, she thought, biting her lip at her strange mental overthrow. But Yuri was pretending not to notice.

"Yes." Yuri thought of Andrei's struggles with Polish. He was learning quickly, but was far from fluent. "It is my biggest wish that he is attending school, but it is true he could not go into school normally. Yes, he would need special education."

Aniela wondered inwardly at the man's calm acceptance of the fact, standing before the woman who was responsible. She forced herself to look up at him, her gaze travelling up his shirt front until it came to his face. He smiled at her, a peculiarly sweet half smile, and she looked away at once, down into the water.

"Madam, how can I express my gratitude for all that you have done for us?"

She felt her body growing rigid and did not answer, not being entirely certain if he was being sarcastic or sincere.

"We will not stay long to inconvenience you, I hope. A day or two—Andrei's illnesses are frequent but not usually long or serious…"

Sincere then.

"…When Odysseus asks for hospitality on his journey, he falls on the ground and grasps his hostess's knees in his arms. Madam, I would like to encircle your knees."

She glanced at him uncertainly and moved a foot away along the bridge.

He took a step back too, still watching her.

But then, as if the thought of Odysseus at Alcinous' banquet had brought to mind the idea of food, he turned to face the water himself, and asked in a different tone, "Are your parents vegans too?"

"No. Dedicated carnivores. My father's whole diet is meat and lemon vodka, and my mother's is meat and chocolate, and my sister's is meat and nicotine. But when I'm here Pani Ola—that's our housekeeper—makes some dishes without meat, although it goes against her upbringing and she doesn't like it."

"I must try to mallify Pani Ola."

"Mollify."

"Thank you. I feel that if you were to speak with me often I would soon be speaking Polish almost peerfectly."

"Yes, well, but I must go to speak to my parents."

"Of course, forgive me, I do not mean to keep you."

"I mean," she explained, seeking comfort from this man even as she was surprised at herself, despised herself, for it. "I must go to tell them about…what I did, and your son, and…all that."

"Why? You have no need to tell anyone anything, it seems to me."

"But soon everyone will know. It cannot be kept hidden."

He did not understand that, so he was silent, and the sunlight warmed their shoulders as they stood together on the bridge and Aniela was aware of her trampling heartbeat and of the man beside her, watching her, and of a suspicion, growing by amazing bounds, that she could end ten years of solitude if she let herself forget—.

But this was all wrong. She turned abruptly and walked away.

Her parents were hunched as usual over their screens when she entered the dining room. She had texted earlier that she was bringing guests and her parents had texted back their unconcern with the fact. With the exception of Iza, who came often, they were not in the habit of having guests; still she knew they would not feel obliged to act as hosts and would not thus be disturbed. Now she must explain the situation to them.

She sat down at the plywood table and waited until her parents lifted their heads from their work.

Then she took a deep breath and condensed the story, without reliving it in detail as she had with Yuri. She was concise because her voice, though cool, was slightly trembling. These were her parents, after all—and if some connections had never properly solidified between them and if they were strangers to her in many essential ways, they were still the people whose opinion mattered most to her in the world.

They listened in silence and when she was finished she waited, staring at the table, to hear what they would say. The silence continued. She dug her fingernails into her palms and looked up. Her parents were regarding her with mild surprise. She saw their eyes, noses, and cheeks —features that hazily mirrored her own, her flesh and blood—and she waited for a sign of empathy, for the relationship to bridge the gap of separate entities and for her parents really to understand. She looked into their eyes at complete incomprehension.

She had ended the story with the boy's mother shouting at her in the hospital. She made no mention of her intentions with regard to the boy now. She was concentrated on the past—regretting, regretting, regretting.

"Well," said her father, grimacing and running his hand over his hair. "Well." He remembered now that he had wondered briefly, after his joyous, extroverted, wise-cracking daughter came back from Cambridge subdued and extinguished-looking, whether she had had an unhappy affair, or even—been assaulted. This story couldn't be all there was to it.

"Well," said her mother testily, "Why wasn't the child's mother looking after him? What kind of woman lets her child out of sight on a riverbank? She must have been abnormal—a bad mother. The English are known for being bad parents. Even the prime minister left his small daughter behind in a restaurant. It was in the news last year."

"No, you don't understand—they weren't English. The mother, the little boy, they were Ukrainian…"

"Oh, Ukrainian…" put in Aniela's father, waving his hand.

"But listen to me, please, these Ukrainians…they're…"

There was a buzzing sound. Her father glanced at his cell phone. "It's Krucyk" he said to his wife.

Aniela's mother was instantly alert and diverted. "Answer it," she said.

No, thought Aniela, no, don't answer it. I've just told you about an event that has lacerated my conscience for years…

Aniela's father was already talking about some schedule and some contract. He was striding about the room with the phone clapped to his ear, occasionally banging his palm lightly against the wall. "Listen, Irek, listen! Here's what we'll do…"

Please, thought Aniela, please put down the phone and speak to me. Here, all these years I've dreaded telling you this thing because I thought it would pain you exceedingly and now…

Slam! She jumped as her father slapped the wall again, his jaw clenching. Aniela's mother was following the conversation with complete attention.

Desperately, Aniela said to her, "It will affect my chances for a political career."

Aniela's mother's head snapped round. "Of course not. Look at who gets elected. Does anyone know about it?"

"No, but…"

"Anything in the media?"

"No."

"The others were responsible, not you. It was bad luck you were there that day but no one could make a thing out of it. Forget it. I'm glad you've made up your mind about politics—"

"No," Aniela tried to say.

"—but we'll talk about that later. Right now I want to listen to what your father's saying."

Was it worse even than she had imagined that her parents didn't seem to care? The world was out of kilter, and she struggled to set it straight in her mind. She felt the ice returning, creeping slowly up her arms.

Ten minutes later, her father was hanging up. He and Aniela's mother were speaking between themselves. Aniela waited until they stopped and were turning back to their papers and laptops before she spoke, very calmly. "I brought my acquaintances here because it seemed to me a better place for them than my apartment. Is it all right if they stay for a few days while I find somewhere else for them?"

"Of course, of course," murmured her father, eyes on his screen. "No problem at all." Then after a pause and the clicking of the keyboard, he added, "Who?"

"Those guests of Nela's," Aniela's mother prompted him. "Right, Nela? They won't bother us. Tell Pani Ola to make more food. She can leave it on the stove for them."

No, thought Aniela, her parents would not be disturbed. She looked at her mother, whose round contours were somewhat disguised by a suit, her blond hair cut in a professional helmet. Her father was dressed with equal crispness. In a while perhaps they would jump in a car, or in two cars, and speed into town to meet with their business partners or their customers or someone they wanted to lobby about something. They would have dinner with someone influential—champagne and veal, which they would hardly taste, at the Amber Club or the Ambassador's Garden. Then they would speed back and once again, around the plywood table, begin the endless round of answering and making calls, the endless calculations of profit and status.

They were, she suddenly realized, as addicted as drug takers.

She had reached the next room when her telephone rang. It was Kasia.

"Nela, what do you think if I ..."

"No, Kasia. Whatever it is, no."

"You never like my ideas. Okay. So never mind that. I'm in your apartment. Can I borrow your Baczyńska dress?"

"Yes." Kasia was so focused on her own affairs she hardly took heed of anything else, thought Aniela. Still, she couldn't help asking. "Kasia?"

"Wha-at?"

"What do you think it would take to get Mama and Tata's attention?"

"Mother of God. Why would you want to do that?"

"I just wonder if they ever think of anything besides their business. Sometimes I feel like they're complete strangers to me."

"No, in our family, we're even more foreign to each other than strangers. That's a bit weird, if you consider it, but why bother?"

"I'm beginning to."

"As to attention, you might not have noticed, but anyone who interferes with their plans is—ho, ho!—in trouble. It's not a good kind of attention, but…"

"What do you mean?" asked Aniela, startled.

"Well, I was speaking for myself, mainly. For the rest —it's just what I've heard. Mama always gets what she wants, you know? A 'tough broad' people say—I admire that."

"I can think of preferable labels! No, I don't believe that, Kasia."

"Don't start talking in that tone, Nela, like you just stepped out of the grave and don't like the look of the world now."

"Okay. Tell me what you heard."

"I don't remember the details. It doesn't matter, anyway."

"No, tell me."

"I'll tell you something else. You remember I had a boyfriend my last year in secondary? Artur?"

"No."

"Jesus Christ. You know what, Nela? You're sleepwalking through family life too."

Aniela shivered a little as she registered the truth of these words.

Kasia was continuing, "But the point is, I was really in love with Artur, only his parents lived in a social-housing apartment and had a tiny electronics shop, so Mama and Tata decided he wasn't good enough. And when I wouldn't end it, they put pressure on his parents—told them they'd use their contacts to make sure they had trouble with tax inspectors and lose the apartment and that sort of thing."

"They didn't! I don't believe it! That's a serious thing to say, Kasia."

"Okay. I won't say anything more."

"That's—that's awful…What happened?"

"He dropped me. And that proves they were right, see? Because if he'd been worth anything he'd have stood up to them. Anyway, later he had to drop out of university and now he's nothing. He just helps his parents with the shop. I see him sometimes from a distance, but I wouldn't even speak with him anymore, he's such a zero." There was the slightest catch in Kasia's voice.

"He was in a hard position, Kasia," said Aniela, shocked. "I'm sorry. I didn't know."

It crossed her mind that she had just been given a clue to Kasia's worldview, but before she could follow it to a conclusion, she looked back at her parents, saw them again framed in the Renaissance light two rooms away, and sought hastily for excuses. "I suppose Mama and Tata thought they were acting in your best interests."

"Doubtless. And theirs too," agreed Kasia, and hung up.

Aniela's phone rang again almost at once and it was her assistant with a question; then it rang and it was one of the persons she helped on a regular basis—just lonely and wanting to talk; then it rang again and it was Iza.

"Iza, hey."

"Aniela—so, what about that violinist guy? Did you get his address for me yet?"

"Iza," she almost snapped, "the violinist guy is an immigrant. He's homeless."

"I could give him a home."

"He has a son. Eleven years old."

"Nnnnn, that could be a problem."

"With a disability."

"Ohhhh. I just have no luck. I'm not so good with kids. You remember that guy I went out with for a while? The divorced one with two little girls? They looked just alike, I mean, really, like twins, or sisters, anyway, and I couldn't remember which was which so I called them both 'duckie' and one day he says to me—that guy, that is—he says 'you can't even remember their names, can you?' And he was right, but I don't know why it made him mad. He had some sort of unhealthy attachment to his children, I guess. He thought they were brilliant, can you believe it? Do you think this guy—the violinist one, not the other— thinks his kid is brilliant?"

"Ah...I," Aniela almost stuttered as the words "neurological damage" flashed in her mind. Then she recovered. "All parents think their children are great, Iza."

"I wonder why? The way they're always wanting attention, always underfoot, always there? That would drive me crazy." A pause, then brightly, "Still, nothing's perfect in this world." A pause. "I want to see him again. The violinist, that is, not that other one."

Now why, Aniela wondered, did she feel curiously relieved that she could say the violinist would be staying with her parents overnight, with the knowledge that Iza's car wasn't running?

She turned off her phone, feeling a need to concentrate. She felt the anti-climax of some martyr who is steeled for the stake but is instead freed with a dismissive "you're not worth it." Clearly she had over-imagined her own importance and in her self-absorption had been as heedless of what was happening to her family members as they were in regard to her. Perhaps the past had drawn such a dark veil over her mind that her whole outlook was deformed. She was considering these things with humility and depression when she saw a shadow cross the threshold and then Yuri stepped quietly into the room. Her heart skittered unexpectedly at the sight of him, but she turned away and went to stand at a window, staring out at the lake as his footsteps approached. He stopped some six feet away.

"I am disturbing you?"

"No."

"You look very unhappy and I am hoping that it is not because we are making troubles for you. Doubtless, though, I am ridiculous in my thinking and it is some much larger question that is disturbing you."

Aniela fixed her eyes on some distant point, too unsettled to turn and look at him. He was a stranger and one of the persons she had irreparably injured. Even if he did speak sympathetically it was absurd to feel encouraged by his presence, and even by his respectful silence.

"I told my parents, just now, about letting your son fall in the river. I don't think they even understood it was your son."

"I wish you would forget it."

"I wish they had been able to remember it long enough to say something kind to me. We were interrupted by a phone call. All my conversations with my parents are interrupted by phone calls."

"But you see—it is not an important thing."

How could he say that, she wondered? "It is to me and would be to most people. Only my parents aren't interested." She paused but then went on, explaining hurriedly:

"I had a boyfriend in Warsaw when I went to Cambridge. He was a graduate student in political science and I loved him. He seemed to love me too—I was sure of it. When I came back, I told him what had happened. I don't know what I expected. Perhaps I was hoping he'd say something similar to what you wrote me, but it wasn't like that. He didn't know how to react, and at first, for a time, he pretended it didn't matter. But it did, and eventually he told me he couldn't feel the same about me, knowing what I'd done to the child. That knowledge would always be between us, he said. 'Suppose we had a baby of our own,' he said, 'how could I trust you to look after it properly?' He was right, of course. So we broke up. He's a member of the European parliament now, and has a son and daughter. I determined never to have another relationship or a child of my own. That was to be my atonement."

Yuri's answer was a stunned silence.

What could he say, except that her ex was an idiot? In any case, there are moments when words are less valuable than gestures. The gesture that sprang imperatively to Yuri's mind was to wrap his arms around her, pull her towards him, and attempt to assuage the pain of living in the consoling contact of their warm bodies. And perhaps he even made a slight move towards her, and perhaps she felt the same impulse toward him, but she remembered her guilt and doubted her worthiness, and he remembered his failures and doubted her response. His gesture was a question, and she answered it by stepping back abruptly, far back. Yuri, his heart pounding, did not say anything and she turned and breathing too quickly walked away from him, through the echoing room and out the door to her car.

After Aniela left, Yuri continued his slow, wondering tour of the house. An occasional room looked as if its sofas and chairs had arrived yesterday from a high-end furniture store; others were empty entirely or contained only the oldest and most rudimentary items. He came to a large, antiquated kitchen of high counters and faded tiles. A heavy older woman was there in clogs and a print apron, cigarette dangling from her lip as she stirred something in a large pot. The scent was enthralling.

"Good-day, madam," he said.

"So you're the one making more work for me?" she growled, looking up from the pot, cigarette bobbing.

"I could help out," suggested Yuri humbly, but he was answered with a hoot of derision.

"A man helping in the kitchen! That's the day! Thirty years I've been married and never once has my husband offered to help in the kitchen. Out, go on, out of my kitchen!" But as he was leaving she added, in a tone that suggested she was mollified and he was going to get a large portion, "I'll call you when it's ready."

CHAPTER 14

Andrei, much restored by several warm meals and twenty hours of sleep, emerged from the house onto the terrace and sat down in the morning sun, observing with interest the fields before him, the lake, and, with a sudden sharp focusing, a small feline face that peered back at him through the stone railings. He slid slowly from the fallen pediment on which he had been seated. "Kitty, kitty" he called softly, holding out a hand. The cat hesitated, took a step forward, then whirled and ran tail up in the other direction, toward a man who had emerged from the house.

The man looked startled to find himself face to face with an unknown child as well as the cat, but he made an effort to be nonchalant.

"Here," he said, holding out a can of cat food, "you can feed it, if you like. Only don't let my wife see you—she doesn't like cats." Or kids, he added in thought.

Andrei took the cat food from Aniela's father, and was soon kneeling beside the kitten as it ate.

"What his name?"

"It doesn't have a name. It's just a homeless cat. I shouldn't have begun feeding it, but I didn't have the heart to let it meow, so now I'm stuck with it. Does it need a name?"

"My father say that Adam walk about naming, naming

the whole world, and then the world was his."

Aniela's father pondered this for a moment, trying to decipher the mix of Ukrainian-Polish, and could think of no answer. He was unaccustomed to children and it was hard to say whether it was a sudden impulse of kindness or the qualities of this particular child that kept him from returning indoors at once.

"We're homeless too," added Andrei, "but I have a name."

"Pardon me," said Aniela's father, almost amused, "I should have introduced myself. Marek Solan, and you are …?"

"Andrei…mm, Romen."

They shook hands. "What happened to your face?" Aniela's father asked, as the boy stroked the small cat.

"Some boys threw rocks at me."

"Goodness. What did you do?"

Andrei shrugged. "I walk away."

Aniela's mother appeared. "Marek, I need you," she gestured toward the house, meaning back to work, and to Andrei, she said, "You should have thrown a *bigger* rock back, *harder*."

"No, no, you did well—it's much better just to go away," said Aniela's father, alarmed.

"How can you tell the boy that? Do you want him to think it's all right to let someone push him around? He should stand up for himself."

"Yes, dear," said Aniela's father, meekly.

"I think fighting stupid," said Andrei, "If people not fighting I would no be here, I would be in my home."

"Let's be grateful more people don't think like you then," said Aniela's mother tartly, before turning away. "Where would Poland be without its uprisings? Each one was crushed completely—so many brave boys died—but did that prevent the next one? Certainly not. Fighting is a patriotic duty."

*

Seated at her ministry desk, Aniela signed her name under "respectfully yours," just after "effective immediately" at the end of her resignation letter, and sent it off with a feeling in her stomach as if she'd eaten a slab of sidewalk cement. If she had not loved anyone in the past ten years, not enjoyed anything, she had held to her job at the ministry as the one sustaining force through the years. She had appreciated the very necessity of rising every morning at a specific time in order to arrive at the office.

She looked out the window where the sun was warming the stucco of the baroque façade opposite. The high windows were close across the narrow street and below there was a constant bustle of small cars squeezing into parking spaces.

There were things she wouldn't mind leaving, of course. She would not miss the infighting and the backstabbing, the eternally shifting politics and loyalties of the ministry's employees. But she would miss her office, the presence of her respectful underlings, the stacks of binders, the personal events that penetrated even to a ministry—Paweł's engagement, Ewa's baby—and most of all the occasional feeling of being at the center of affairs, of working on something that could matter to many people.

She would also, she admitted to herself, very much miss the respect. One way or another, her culpability in regard to Yuri's child would become known, she was certain. The social media mob was ruthless in such instances and she could expect to be hounded in forums and twitter accounts. Hopefully, if she was no longer at the ministry, the fallout would not harm its work.

She put on her light raincoat and prepared to leave the office. She had spoken earlier to the minister and other colleagues, but now she stopped to shake hands and murmur a few words about "personal matters" to the lower-ranking employees. The reaction was one of confounded surprise but not particularly of dismay, she noted with an additional pang. What had she expected? She had fulfilled her duties with an abundance of diligence but she had not made a friend in all these years. Soon, with her associates' eyes on her back, she walked through a series of doors to the sidewalk and was unemployed.

Later she could grieve for what she had lost, she told herself. Now, she had a clear sense of where her obligation lay: she must do everything she could for the child.

Two hours later she left the lawyer's office with a quantity of notes in her hand and uncertainties buzzing in her mind.

The lawyer had not been entirely sympathetic. He had said airily that, after all, he himself rather thought it better for the country to keep foreigners out, though Ukrainians were admittedly less undesirable than some kinds of refugees. Aniela had said quietly that if "desirablility" were to be made the requirement for residency, it would be curious to know how many natives would have to leave the country, but the lawyer had neither the mind nor the time to dissect his own opinions. He had shuffled his papers; even used as he was to courtroom debate—those endless sentences rolling off his tongue, the anger, the wounded egos—his client's over-earnest gaze and unsmiling face rather unsettled him. "Fanatic," he thought. Aniela did not press the point.

He might think he's safe, the lawyer had said of Yuri, but in reality he won't last long. Perhaps he's been lucky so far but any day he could come across a policeman who'll decide to check his status and then he'll be deported very quickly. Or he can file for asylum, which will lengthen matters, but less than a fraction of a percent of such applications are granted, and in the meantime, given his lack of documents and the regulations on minors, separation from his child and incarceration seem certain. So if you want to take preventive measures—here the lawyer had permitted himself a dry smile and a glance—you have to move quickly—er, take action—because once he's arrested as an illegal alien, it will be difficult to…effectuate. He had been joking, of course. He hadn't for a second thought she would act along the lines he had sketched, or at most, he had assumed she would search for a proxy.

How far would she be willing to go to save Yuri and his son? Because it was beginning to look as if the only solution—the only one that would involve her, that is—

would have extremely close and personal ramifications.

*

Yuri, searching for Andrei, wandered down a corridor and found himself suddenly in the dining room, facing Aniela's parents, with whom he had exchanged only the briefest of greetings on the previous day. They stared at him in such obvious mild alarm that Yuri stepped back with the intention of excusing his intrusion. Aniela's father, though, remembering his manners, rose slowly and invited him to join them: They were just having a break for coffee, or maybe he'd prefer tea? If the invitation was rather too obviously a case of "have to say a few words to the fellow sometime, might as well get it over with," Yuri was equally constrained by etiquette not to notice. He seated himself beside the table and was soon looking with pleasure and greed at a cup of tea into which he was dropping spoonful after spoonful of sugar. He saw that Aniela's mother was counting the spoonfuls as they fell and he smiled at her. How kind she was to provide him with tea, he said. She blinked.

He looked out the window and remarked on the fineness of the day and the beauty of the scenery.

Aniela's parents had not taken note of the scenery or the weather for many days. They turned their heads and looked vaguely out the window and then back at him. They were unused to small talk.

"You're here in Poland for work?" Aniela's father said at last. "Something to do with the ministry?"

"No. With the ministry, no. I am not here on business."

156

"On holiday then?' Aniela's mother recovered from Yuri's smile and took over the interrogation briskly.

"No."

"You've come to Poland to look for work." said Aniela's mother. It was a statement, not a question. Her eyes travelled over his new clothing, down to his old shoes, and he could see himself suddenly sinking down, down, in her estimation as he went from being Aniela's presumed colleague to another of Aniela's charity cases.

"Yes, but in the meantime, I am busking. I play the violin in the Old Town." As Aniela's parents stared, he added a bit defensively, "The tourists like me."

"They like those awful daubs and the mass-production carvings and the fake folk art too," returned Aniela's mother.

This was unanswerable and Yuri was silent, contemplating the justness of his grouping.

"What else can you do besides play the violin?" asked Aniela's mother severely.

"Er...I know six or seven languages."

"So does Marek here," Aniela's mother was dismissive. "What else?"

"I have thorough knowing of world literature and philosophy and write Russian and Ukrainian vair beautifully." He could not answer them in the cultivated language that, had he been speaking his native tongue, would instantly have informed them of his high education and social background. He felt unintelligent and not himself.

Aniela's mother looked at him disbelievingly. "Nugatory. What practical abilities?"

Yuri hastily searched his mind for practical abilities, and decided not to mention that as a student he had once spent a summer fetching and carrying for a trainer of brown bears.

"Organization, computers, technology, science, security, machinery?"

He shook his head sadly. His tea had ceased to taste as good.

"Come, I expect you want us to help you." Some part of Aniela's mother's mind was standing by, ready to riffle through a mental rolodex of connections. "What are you good at? Construction work? Plumbing, at least?"

I am, he thought, a good father, a good husband—at least I tried to be—a good friend, a good citizen…none of it mattered.

"And your documents, are they all in order? Do you have a work permit?"

"No, no permit. We left in a hurry."

"That was unwise of you."

Aniela's father interrupted his wife to add, in a kinder tone, as if speaking to a person of deficient intelligence, as he spoke to almost everyone: "But, you know, the red tape may be a hurdle, but it can't be disregarded, you know. Ukraine is a different story, but Poland is a law-abiding country, part of the EU. Matters can get difficult if you don't have all those papers and stamps."

Yuri answered slowly. "But what is it to me, their red tape, their papers, their documents, their stamps, their laws regulating matters that should never have been regulated? I am alone, only myself and my ethics; the world, when it takes leave of morality, cannot bind me...I will not stay and be shot like a dog—or shelled—Am I to have my child made into pulp, like a chick in a meat chipper, because we do not have the right papers?"

Aniela's mother stared, shuddered lightly, and looked away. Aniela's father said sharply, with distaste, "You exaggerate." Then after a pause, he added carefully, "It is difficult, you know, to see how anyone can help you if you don't have documents."

Aniela's mother said, "Without documents, you don't exist."

"*Cogito, ergo sum.*"

"Maybe, but it won't cut any ice with Immigration. What do you expect will happen?"

But one could only take so much questioning. It was time to turn the tables. "And what is it that *you* do, if I may ask?"

There was a brief pause. "We produce sensors. For CBUs."

Yuri set his glass down in consternation.

*

Aniela was just getting into her car when her phone rang. It was her father, leaping directly into his topic. "Nela, I've been trying to get hold of you but you don't answer your phone. Who is this man you left here?"

"He's the father of the child I injured in England. That's what I was telling you about..."

"Somehow you weren't clear, darling. So, listen, did you know him personally, or was it just a chance meeting?"

"Then—in England? I didn't meet him at all; I met his wife, briefly."

"Where is his wife now?"

"They're divorced, he says."

"So how did he get in touch with you here in Poland? This is all very strange. Because, listen, Aniela, we wonder about this man—he was talking a bit wildly to us about Ukraine and asking odd questions—I think your mother should have been more careful—"

Here her mother's voice could be heard in the background protesting and then there was silence for a moment before her father's voice came back. "Anyway, never mind that, what we've started worrying is—if he isn't, you know…"

"He's not a Russian agent, if that's what you think." Some other time she might have been slightly amused. This time she answered sharply, not amused at all, "He's homeless. A refugee."

"So he says."

"No, really. We met when one of the statues fell off the roof of St. Sebastian's. He was slightly injured and I invited him back to my apartment. He couldn't have arranged that."

"You'd be surprised."

"Even a secret service wouldn't think up anything that far-fetched."

"Exploding cigars, radioactive tea…No, really, darling, the secret services prefer to do things the hard way."

"But why bother, when we were going to meet anyway? He'd already sent me an email."

"Ah ha. You see?" Aniela's father, had he been observant, might have noticed the stress thinning his daughter's voice.

Aniela continued, "He couldn't have made his infant son fall in a river in England so we could meet under a collapse of masonry in Warsaw years later. And what possible information could you or I have that would be of interest to anyone anyway? I've been working in the ministry of disabilities. I know nothing of any use to a spy."

"Not *you*. Us. You're forgetting our business."

"I don't understand. Why do you think your business would interest a spy? I know it's growing, but it's not a large corporation with secrets or anything—"

"This isn't a conversation for the phone," said Aniela's father and ended the call abruptly, leaving Aniela staring uneasily at her phone. Her parents were not only obsessive, they were growing paranoid, she thought.

And if they thought Yuri was a spy, they really weren't going to like the plan that was forming in her mind. She wasn't sure she liked it either:

•You have to make up for what you did.

•What Yuri and his son need most is to stay in Poland.

•There's only one way to do it, and it's not a paper marriage.

•Better think this through carefully.

It would be impossible to carry through such a plan while remaining emotionally detached and her detachment was all that had kept her together all these years.

CHAPTER 15

On the road, Aniela reminded herself to concentrate on her driving. She worried constantly that in dwelling on one tragedy, she might cause another. The more preoccupied she was, the more carefully she drove. This made her rather a dangerous—or at least rather an irritating—driver. Trucks barreled past and a number of cars flashed their lights and rushed up on her bumper. She drove as far on the right shoulder as she could until she turned off the highway onto a small country road. There she stopped beside a field of flowering rapeseed.

She needed a moment to think. She tried to imagine a long future in which she would have an unbreakable tie to Yuri, a man who stirred her in unaccustomed ways but who might be totally different than she imagined him to be, a future in which she was a mother and was involved with a disabled child—who was not her child, and who would grow into a disabled man, still needing care. She quailed and yet—and yet—after ten years of internal repentance, she accepted the demands of justice. It would be a bold move, but wasn't it precisely such leaps of faith into the unknown, for a higher purpose, that added value to pedestrian existence? She couldn't do much for all the needy of the world but she could help two people if she were simply brave and determined enough to do it.

She got out of the car and paced back and forth rapidly, then stopped and looked down at the earth. Without quite knowing what she was doing, she slid to her knees among the chamomile and poppies of the verge, feeling the earth and air around her pulsing with life—with an infinity of plants, birds, and insects all intent on multiplying. She alone had resisted the forces of nature. No longer. She too could be elemental.

•Yuri.

•Yuri.

•Yuri.

The sound of an approaching tractor in the distance disturbed her communion with fecund nature. She rose, brushed the dirt off her designer skirt, and got back in her car.

Strung up with resolve, she drove on until she stopped again in the courtyard of the house, where her exaltation took a nose dive. The hardest part, of course, would be putting the matter to Yuri. No, if he accepted, the hardest part would be...

•Don't think about it.

She pulled forward and parked, but hesitated before getting out. One could be clinical and rational, she reasoned: here was the problem; here was the solution. Emotion need not enter into it. It was absurd that who-could-cross-what-borders should depend on such intimate foundations, but many things in the world were absurd. Making the world a better place for Yuri and his son was completely justifiable. Yes. She forced herself to get out of the car and walk indoors.

*

Yuri paced back and forth, back and forth, from the window to the door, across the room Aniela had given them. Outside, a dark cloud momentarily blocked the sun. He stopped at the window to look at it, hearing again his question to Aniela's parents. "And what do you do?" And the answer, "we sell sensors for CBUs." Cluster bomb units.

Intolerable; it was intolerable; his position here was intolerable and he must leave.

Andrei was sleeping deeply, under a mound of comforters. Yuri stopped and looked down at him. After seeming much better in the morning, he'd had a relapse. Heat radiated from the boy; his breathing rasped and there were lavender circles under his lashes. What to do? Impossible to stay here; and yet, would he be endangering his son if he were to wake him, force him to dress and start walking? He had no very accurate idea of how far they were from Warsaw, but he thought it must be at least thirty or forty kilometers. Perhaps they could hitchhike, but if no one picked them up, what then? And once they reached the shack again? He would still be out of money; they would still be out of food; the shack would still be damp and cold.

None of that could matter. He hadn't lost everything over his stand in Ukraine only to equivocate with his conscience in Poland because he didn't want to be uncomfortable. If it were himself only, he'd be gone in a minute. But there was Andrei. He stopped pacing and stood by the bed. "Andrei," he said softly, "Andrei, wake!"

But Andrei didn't stir.

Louder. "Andrei!"

Andrei's lashes flickered, but his eyes didn't open and he pulled the blankets tighter.

Yuri gave up. Tomorrow then; they would leave tomorrow. He had been wrong about Aniela. He'd been wrong about a woman before and this one—he'd nearly been in love with her, and now, to find that she belonged to such a family, well, it was a good thing he'd found out before things went too far. He'd been obsessed with remembering how she avoided his arms the day before, but now he knew it was fortunate. He'd be off as soon as he humanly could and never see her again. The idea was so searing and left such a lunar landscape of the future that he knew there was no "nearly in love" about it.

As he leaned against the window frame, grappling with these piercing thoughts, he saw Aniela's small car pull up in front of the house. He turned from the window and set out with quick strides to meet her.

They met by the front door.

"I must speak to you," both said at once.

Yuri stepped back, and Aniela led him through the enfilade to an empty room and stopped under a listing chandelier in a cracked ceiling. She turned to face him then and opened her mouth to speak.

Yuri glanced up at the chandelier and put out his hand to move her gently to the side.

The touch shook them both, so they forgot for a second what they wanted to say. Aniela gained control of herself first. She took a deep breath, and calmly, rationally, outlined the problem. Yuri perhaps didn't see the bullet points, but they were there.

"I've spoken to a lawyer. Your situation is not good. If you are picked up by the authorities, without documents and without a visa, you will be sent at once to an immigration center and then deported. I believe you are aware of this fact."

Yuri nodded. "Yes, yes, but that is unimportant at the moment. I must speak to you about something else. I…" He ran his hand over his hair and tried to see her objectively, but she was too close, and she was talking.

"You could ask for asylum, but you would have to prove that you have been the object of persecution and this would be difficult for you to do. Under the UN norms, the mere fact of living in a war zone does not qualify a person for political asylum. The burning down of your house before the start of open hostilities might be an arguing point, if you could prove it."

"How could I? But never mind that…"

"Yes. Asking for political asylum would seem unlikely to succeed. Particularly as you would be asking asylum from both sides. To continue: there is an article in the Act on Foreigners that aims to prevent the separation of families." Here, her voice lost some of its calm rationality and began to pick up speed. "Your son, however, would be deported with you and there would thus be no separation, so what you need is a family member who is Polish…"

"I do not have a family member who is Polish, and…"

Aniela sped on. "I know. I have considered this problem and I have...I..."

"Yes?"

Aniela gulped. "I have decided to provide you with one."

Yuri looked at her with his head on one side, "How will you do that?" he asked, arrested and bemused.

"We could get married." She stopped abruptly, turned away, and went to stand by a window. She could feel him staring at her. "If you had papers, but you don't—"

"I—no."

She didn't know if he was affirming his lack of papers or refusing her already, before he'd heard her plan. "Wait!" she pleaded, looking very hard out the window. "Let me finish!"

But finishing wasn't easy. What she was going to suggest was so incredibly awkward. She took a deep breath of air. She had to remember that without drastic measures Yuri and his son would be deported. She might be able to delay it, but in the end there would be nothing she could do to prevent it. She owed them.

"The only way for you to have a Polish relative, at this point, is to have another child, with a Polish woman. I am offering myself."

There, she'd said it.

He stood dumbfounded for a moment and then began to stammer.

"You would—will—want—to do this for me?"

"No. Of course not for you!" She shook her head, mortified almost to the point of combustion at his embarrassment, his obtuseness, and a sudden sick doubt at her own motivation. "Not for you! For your son. I owe it to him."

"Because of an insig—insag—nificant accident years ago?" asked Yuri in disbelief.

"How can you say it is insignificant?" Aniela protested vehemently. "What I did left your child with permanent brain damage and you say it's 'insignificant'? What on earth—in your opinion—is significant, I wonder?"

"Wait!" said Yuri, "Wit. Wat. Wait! There is something here I am not understanding. I have told you that he is not and never was damaged, have I not? Was I not clear?"

"Not?"

They stared at each other for long seconds.

"Not...not damaged?" stuttered Aniela.

Yuri plunged on, embarrassment causing his speech to have only a remote connection with his ideas, which were in turmoil. "For the rest, it is extremely kind of you, madam, and I am infinitively grateful that you would think of me, even if it was only on account of your overacting conscience, but truly, I must tell you that there is no need at all for you to marry me or—or, or to have childrens with me—or indeed, for us to have any further contact, and, anyways, I can not stay here in the house of an armamaker. I assure you absolutely: I will leave as soon as Andrei is well enough to uprise."

Aniela gaped at him.

"This," she said very coldly, "has been most unfortunate."

Then, her face scarlet, she turned and left the room.

She had expected surprise, but never had she expected such a snub. Her footsteps rang through the empty rooms as she walked away with all the dignity she could muster.

Yuri returned to the room he shared with Andrei and leaned against the doorframe, his mind a white buzz of noise. Incredible, it was incredible what had just happened. That she should have offered herself to him! And that he had refused her! But of course he was right to have turned her down, wasn't he? He had refused at once, without thinking, because he had been keyed to a renunciation, but perhaps he had been too hasty? What if— what if—but no, he couldn't overlook the family business, not even for Aniela—and surely she was tainted too. She couldn't be what he thought she was and belong in such company. His intractable crush had blinded him because even now he was making excuses for her. His imagination was throwing up alternative futures where they were together. She had looked very shocked when he turned her down—he had been deeply unkind. Perhaps if he went to her now and apologized? Perhaps there would still be room for some kind of friendship, if not the relationship she'd offered? He was making too much of her parents' activities. Children weren't to blame for their parents. Maybe she had tried to stop them and couldn't. He paced back and forth, terribly tempted. No, he had to leave.

In her room Aniela sat at her window, motionless, as

the light sank into the woods and the shadows gathered. She knew she should be overjoyed that the child she had thought was injured—through all these years—was all right, but somehow humiliation—deep, annihilating humiliation—was her foremost emotion. Momentary waves of angry resentment at Yuri crashed over her. She thought back over all their conversations. Was there something she'd heard but not taken in? Perhaps when he was telling her about his ex-wife? She couldn't remember his words exactly enough.

The child was all right—that was good. Very good. Her action hadn't changed; she was just as culpable then as now, but it seemed an entirely different event—already dropping from top spot on the list of things to feel bad about. Now she had a far more immediate source of self-torture. She had offered herself to Yuri and been rejected. But after all—she tried to reason with herself—she had made the offer solely on an impersonal basis: there was no cause for humiliation if she hadn't asked because she *wanted* to have a child with Yuri. Or had she?

She tried to imagine what her subordinates at the ministry, who watched her covertly and said "yes, madam director" and scurried to do her bidding, would think if they were ever to hear of her private errors. She dropped her head in her hands. She could swim out into the lake and—but no, it still wasn't deep enough.

A distant commotion somewhere in the house made her raise her head to listen, then look out the window. A small gray car, which she did not recognize, was parked in front of the house. She heard a high pealing laugh and another voice exclaiming. Iza and Kasia. That was all she needed! How had they got here? A replacement car from the insurance company, probably—she hadn't thought of that. She listened, but after the first burst of noise, the house hid the newcomers. No sounds came to her. Where was Yuri now?

"I can not stay in the house of an armamaker," he had said, but what had he meant by that? And why should she care what he said or whether he stayed or left? He wasn't her concern. She wasn't responsible for the child. She wouldn't be pilloried in the media. She needn't care what became of them. She was free of all of it. Those subordinates at the ministry, those colleagues, those myriad acquaintances in the Warsaw *monde*—none of them would ever know a thing about it.

Her job! She had resigned her job. And now it was for nothing! Perhaps there was time to retrieve her resignation? With an inner cry of anguish, like fingernails raking a chalkboard down, down, she rose abruptly to search for her cell phone, but as she did so she heard a clacking of heels down the hallway and then Iza burst into her room, followed by Kasia.

"Nela!" shrieked Iza, "What have you done? It was just in the news—why did you resign? Why? What's happening?"

"Mama and Tata are going berserk!" put in Kasia.

Too late then.

"You might knock before you enter," she answered distantly, wrapping the ends of her cashmere sweater about her and climbing internally back to some cold, calm citadel.

"Oh, I never do," said Iza truthfully. "You know me. But come on, tell us what happened!"

"I have decided it was time for a change."

"Mother of God," said Kasia, "has this been a long time coming? You never said a word."

"About ten years. Now, if you don't mind, I would very much like to be alone for a while."

Iza looked hurt, and shrugging, left the room. Aniela called Kasia back as she too turned to go.

"What does 'armamaker' mean?" Kasia always knew the arcane terms of contemporary life.

Kasia raised her arms and let them fall. "No idea. Why?" And then, looking more closely at her sister she added, "Are you all right? You look peculiar."

"It has been a superlatively peculiar day, but never mind that. Yuri said he couldn't stay here because our parents are 'armamakers'—what does that mean?"

"Oh," said Kasia, after a moment's thought, "maybe he means 'arms manufacturers'."

Aniela received the words in silence. This was undoubtedly one of the many misunderstandings that had occurred. "Why would he think that, do you suppose?" she asked, irritation at Yuri returning.

"Well, I'm not sure," Kasia pretended to ponder, "It could be because they *are* arms manufacturers."

Aniela grimaced. "Really, Kasia, this is *not* a good day for joking."

"But I'm not joking."

Aniela stared until Kasia's innocent return gaze gave conviction to her words.

"Kasia! Tell me this isn't true. Please, Kasia, *please*."

"Didn't you know? Nela! How could you not know that?"

"I thought they sold some kind of components to the Netherlands," Aniela answered slowly, with a sensation rather like tripping in a dream—the prolonged moment of falling before startling into consciousness. Only somehow she knew she wouldn't be waking.

"Whenever I asked, the word was always just 'components'. I never thought about it much."

"They make and sell all sorts of things, to all sorts of places. Components for combines, and components for rocket-launchers, and components for bombs that go boom."

"How do you know? Did they tell you?"

"I never asked. What do I care what they do? I heard it from...men."

"How long have you known?"

"I don't know—a long time."

"I see."

Aniela sat very still and watched the certainties of her life collapse and disappear in a puff of rocket-launcher smoke.

Kasia watched her sister. "Does it bother you so much?" she asked curiously.

"Do you know the numbers of people who die every year by violence?" Aniela answered in a strangled voice. "Never mind adults; the UN says that every year more than 50,000 children die as a result of armed conflict and for every one that dies, 100 are left with permanent disabilities. I am—was—director of the ministry for disabilities, Kasia—taking advantage of the profits of my parents, who are selling the means of conflict..." She raised her hand to her forehead.

No wonder they hadn't flinched at her news about Yuri's son. What was that in the way of responsibility? Small beer indeed—piddling, picayune, nothing.

"Making weapons is shameful, immoral."

She thought of all the things she had enjoyed over the years because of her parents—education, clothes, frequent trips abroad, this house where she often spent the weekend, the dividends piling up in bank accounts, the casual confidence of never being in need, of seldom looking at a price tag, the gratification of signing over large sums to charity. "War is the mass murder that societies are indoctrinated to accept. But I reject it! I reject it! Only now—now, I find that I have been benefiting from this hideous business. Yes, it bothers me! It is unbearable."

"Oh, come on, it's not as unbearable as all that. I manage to bear it perfectly well," drawled Kasia.

Aniela hurried to a bathroom, and was sick.

CHAPTER 16

Shortly after she returned to the room, there was a sound of shuffling in the hallway and Pani Ola banged on the door. "Pani Kasia," she squalled, "dinner's waiting. Pani Iza! Dinner's ready." And her footsteps creaked heavily away again.

"Are you coming down?" asked Kasia.

Aniela rose. "No," she said, "I'm leaving." Only then, instantly, she remembered—the car was a gift from her parents. The car was paid for with the money from arms. Which dead child in which online photo had been dismembered by a device from her parents' factories? She would never drive that car again, never. She looked out the window. Evening had advanced and it was already dark. She would leave at once. She would run screaming into the night. She would walk the four miles to the highway in her kitten heels and hitchhike to Warsaw.

She looked again out the window at the utter rural blackness covering forest and wheat field. She would be reasonable and wait till morning. She had from now until morning to come to terms with everything she was losing.

She would have to face her parents some time. It might as well be tonight.

Slowly she made her way down the creaking oak stairs,

her disciplined mind attempting to force the hideous fact back into some kind of order. How had her parents come to this? How? She thought back over the years. Her parents had dropped all the manifestations of traditional life: soup and stuffed cabbage at three, crêpes and jam, compote and cheesecake; Christmas Eve with its twelve dinner dishes and straw; chalk marks from the priest on the day of the Three Magi; Easter baskets for the blessing; trips to the garden plot; the cult of graves, war-time tales and long summer vacations in the sand. They had left off going to church, left off looking over their neighbors' shoulders, and even—most un-traditional of all—left off bitterly envying other peoples' attainments. But these things had happened when she was a small child; she could not remember a time when they lived as most Poles did.

Was it that near success at scaling the steep heights into the group of the very wealthy that had changed them? In the heady early days they had first cared about appearances and then climbed so far beyond the average Pole that there was no competing. Their standard in all material goods, in so far as they had time for it, came from the international elite, not their compatriots. Was it to maintain their status with that elite that they had taken the step into arms? Or had they simply seen a business opportunity and grasped it without axiological considerations? Perhaps her mother had been blind to the ethics of what she was about, thought Aniela with depression, but her father had the background to know precisely what he was doing.

Her parents were still seated at their usual end of the plywood, but they had pushed aside various stacks of papers or moved them onto chairs, and they had dropped their electronic devices, and were waiting in attitudes of glowering expectancy. The other end of the table was set for five persons and held a variety of covered dishes. Iza had added a bottle of wine, which she was now uncorking with a smile that proved she was oblivious to the looks on her hosts' faces.

"Where's Nela?" Aniela's mother barked at her.

"She was in her room," Iza said, struggling with the wine cork, "she said she wanted to be alone, but I suppose she'll eat dinner—who wouldn't eat dinner? I brought this wine—it's a Qu-em-per, so I hope it's good. I swiped it from the caterers. Isn't it weird about Nela leaving her job—I wonder why she did that? I usually wait to get fired. I need a better corkscrew." And she left the room in the direction of the kitchen.

"She'll have some explaining to do—" Aniela's mother said to the air.

Aniela entered the room.

Aniela's father held out a tablet. "Here, read this."

Aniela took the tablet and read from a news bulletin: "Aniela Solan, director general of the ministry for disabilities, philanthropist and well-known advocate for the disabled, unexpectedly resigned yesterday from her position. No reasons have been given…"

"What's going on?" asked her father, grinding his teeth, "Why were we left to learn about this on the news? We wanted you to move on, but not like this—not like this."

"I felt I had to leave," she answered.

"What in God's name have you done?" her mother snapped.

Aniela was seriously taken aback. Clearly they had forgotten about Yuri's son and were imagining some kind of improper behavior at work, some scandal that had forced her to resign before it was discovered.

"I told you everything yesterday morning," she said as calmly as she could. "I didn't understand then why you weren't concerned. But now I understand better. You have worse on your consciences."

"What are you talking about?"

"You sell—arms components," Aniela stumbled over the words and into confrontation. "Yuri told me and Kasia confirmed it. I did not know and I am very shocked—I can't tell you how shocked I am."

Aniela's father and mother stared at her blankly.

Finally her mother repeated, "You didn't know?"

"No, I didn't."

"How could you not know? You, director general of a ministry? You sit here; you listen to us talking on the phones—"

"I never understood what you were saying. I didn't listen closely."

"You know who we meet—" said her mother.

"You've heard of Krucyk, of Malmat, of Dexidron" said her father. "You know who they are and what they do—"

Aniela raised her hands in a gesture of helplessness and ignorance.

"Does this have something to do with that Russian?" said Aniela's mother suddenly.

"No. And I don't think Russian is the right word. He's from Ukraine."

"You know," said her father, "I had my doubts about that fellow the moment I spoke to him. There's something very odd about his turning up right at this point and he's not like other Ukrainians I've met. I think…"

"That all the people in a country are alike? Yes, he's unusual. Unfortunately, we're not ordinary Poles either."

"In any case," said Aniela's mother darkly, "we'll deal with the Russian later. The question at the moment is why have you left the ministry? What is going on?"

"The question at the moment," retorted Aniela, "is why you're involved in the arms trade and when are you going to stop?"

"'Involved in the arms trade'—you make it sound like we're Boeing or Northrop Grumman," Aniela's mother brushed aside the question as if it were unworthy of her attention. "We haven't even made it very far up the country's 100 Richest list yet—though the sensors are definitely helping there. You should be glad." Aniela's mother ripped the cellophane off a box of chocolates and selected one, hovering her fingers over her prey before lifting it to her mouth and chewing slowly.

Aniela's father watched his wife and unclenched his jaw to protest nervously, "Before dinner, darling?"

"Speak to her, not to me!" Aniela's mother commanded.

"Well, Nela, you know," said Aniela's father, angry, embarrassed, and struggling, "I can hardly believe that—

you know—you weren't aware of the fact. That piece of land you inherited from your grandfather—the one we built a factory on—we spoke to you about the construction. Don't tell me you don't remember."

"That's what you built there?" Aniela gasped at this new discovery.

"You knew it was a factory."

"Yes, but—I didn't realize—I was a teenager then. You said a factory, I imagined machine parts..."

"So they are," said her mother, "Sort of. And you should be glad, because you're the chief beneficiary of all our efforts. However, *what* we sell is not the issue at the moment. The issue is what you've done."

"True," said Aniela's father, nodding to his wife, "true, Basia." He began to pace back and forth.

"We thought you'd be a help to us," Aniela's mother said, wiping her fingers with little jerks. "We're expecting you to move up, to get into politics. And now? I can't believe the way you've thrown everything away—we'll have our work cut out to overcome it. And this is a bad moment—when we're negotiating..."

"Well, never mind that now," said Aniela's father quickly.

"A scandal will be very unhelpful," said Aniela's mother forcefully, not to be suppressed. "In private, Nela, you can pretend to dislike what we do if you're such a hypocrite, but we expect your tacit support in public at least—at least that."

"My support for your business?"

"You know, I don't like your tone at all, Nela. It's hard

to believe that a daughter could be so ungrateful, so uncaring about her family's interests, as to make such a decision without a word to anyone, without considering anyone…"

"I would *never* help you in your business," said Aniela, whose tones were an unavoidable imitation of her mother's. "Your business is morally rotten."

Aniela's parents gasped.

"How dare you speak to us that way?" they rounded on her together.

She turned to her father, "How *can* you defend what you do?"

"Countries have to have militaries. There's security. There's the 'responsibility to protect'. There's 'never again.'"

"Exactly! Think about everything that a 'responsibility to protect' should mean—while military intervention has produced disaster after disaster! There are other ways to act. You know it. Individuals have a responsibility not to participate in adding to the violence. The only certain progress toward 'never again' is in the number of people who have absolutely renounced killing other people for any reason."

"No," he repeated louder, "countries have to have militaries. Someone has to supply them. There's nothing immoral about it."

"Nothing immoral about killing people?"

"We don't pull the trigger," snapped Aniela's mother, "we're not responsible for how they get used."

"If you were selling child pornography," shouted Aniela, losing her composure thoroughly for the first time in ten years, "you would end up in prison. As you are only selling the means to *kill* children, I daresay society considers you to be stellar citizens. But I won't consider you that way. Either you leave off making arms, or I cease to be your daughter."

"You're making an ultimatum to your own parents?" yelped her father, aghast. Her mother made a dry, rasping sound, like a hen trying to catch its breath.

"If the factory on my land is making any kind of arms, or parts of arms, or parts of parts of arms, I want it stopped *at once*."

"How do you imagine—" her mother began, but Iza came back into the room then and the words froze abruptly on all their lips.

It was impossible for Aniela and her parents to continue in the presence of Iza. Automatically, as if unaware of their own movements, they sat down and began to help themselves stiffly to food. Aniela hardly moved. She was torn between anger and the awareness that she had handled her parents badly, stupidly, by attacking them instead of reasoning with them. She should apologize, she thought, but couldn't do it. Here they sat—and she too—so comfortable, under the high ceiling of the room, in their expensive clothes, and their shiny shoes, with the wine glasses glinting before them, and money in their pocketbooks, and their new cars waiting outside. Here they sat with thousands of years of knowledge in their heads, all the ease of European civilization, and its suave answers. Here they sat, the real barbarians.

"Where's Yuri?" asked Iza. "Isn't he coming?"

No one answered, so Aniela roused herself. "Perhaps he ate earlier, with his son."

"I always manage to miss him," said Iza, disappointed. "Oh well, there's always tomorrow." She began to babble to the company about inconsequential matters, without noticing the monosyllabic answers. The Solans were never talkative or attentive and she was not accustomed to notice whether anyone was listening or not. Nor did she notice the decisions that were being taken as the meal progressed.

Aniela's father said to Aniela's mother, "Would you ask your daughter to pass the wine?"

"Kasia, pass the wine," said Aniela's mother.

The bottle was beside Aniela, far from Kasia.

"You mean 'Aniela'" said Kasia, catching instantly that some game was being played.

"No," said her mother, "I am asking my daughter to pass the wine. I only have *one* daughter."

Aniela rose, set the bottle of wine down in front of her father, and left the room.

Iza looked suddenly struck and Kasia, with a tight little smile, ran her eyes from face to face.

In the hallway Aniela ran into Pani Ola, standing in the door to the kitchen, listening.

"Jesus Mary, Pani Nela, you shouldn't speak to your parents that way!" she said in a scandalized tone, her unmodulated voice ringing in the confined space in spite of her efforts to whisper. "Even if they're not the best people, they're still your parents—you should have some respect.

'Honor thy father and thy mother'—that's the second commandment in the Bible after 'obey the Church' and 'pray to the Virgin Mary.' You should be ashamed. I always thought you were such a good young woman—not like your sister—but God Above, you should go to confession."

"Thank you, Pani Ola, I'll keep your words in mind," said Aniela through clenched jaws.

"And they're right about their business too. We need guns and bombs and things to protect us against Islams and Russians and those people coming from Africa, God save us."

Aniela stepped around the housekeeper and walked rapidly away.

CHAPTER 17

Aniela, rising early in the morning, slipped quietly into Iza's room. "Iza, hey Iza."

"What?" Iza moaned.

"I need you to drive me back to Warsaw," whispered Aniela.

"Now?" mumbled Iza, without moving. "Nela, darling, I'm sleeping. Wait till later."

Aniela went into her sister's room next. The room was half dark still and all she could see was a lock of blond hair, very like her own, trailing over the quilt—her sister, whose molecules of brain and body shared some close connection with her own and yet were moved by such different motives. Kasia was only a powerless bystander, not a participant in her parents' activities, Aniela reminded herself—Kasia deserved more leniency. Judge not…

"Kasia, hey Kasia," she whispered. Kasia moaned and did not open her eyes.

Aniela dropped a fold of paper onto Kasia's bedside table. "This is a few hundred zloty for Yuri—will you give it to him? It should be enough to see him through a few days. Will you do this, Kasia? And make sure he gets back to Warsaw all right. I'm going now."

"The guy can take care of himself and I think this is all

really stupid, Nela," mumbled Kasia, flouncing over in bed and going back to sleep.

Aniela left the room, picked up the small knapsack with which she always travelled, and quietly left the house. The security guards were asleep in their car, heads lolling against the side windows. She walked past unnoticed.

It was only slightly after dawn. The sun had not climbed very high yet and it was cool but going to be a beautiful clear day. The young wheat shifted gently and the eager leaves of brush and tree seemed racing to be open, to be green, to bask in the light and promise of summer. If Aniela noticed, it was only subconsciously. She trudged along the narrow road, the miles to the highway stretching ahead of her. At this hour there were no cars passing here.

When she had walked about half way she became aware that a less rural sound was joining the jubilancy of the songbirds and the crowing of a distant rooster. A few very faint bars of violin music were repeated and repeated again, as if someone was trying to remember a melody. She stopped to listen. Bach's *Jesu, Joy of My Desiring*, she thought. She searched for the source of the sound and saw a distant figure rise from the ground beneath the trees and come to stand beside the road. She walked on and soon it was clear that the figure was a man, and she knew it had to be Yuri. She had expected him to be back at the house, in bed, asleep. She stopped again and looked about. They were alone in the middle of nowhere and there wasn't really any way to avoid him—although to have left the house so early he must have wanted not to meet her again. The position was awkward. He was watching her come.

"Good morning," she said cautiously as she came even with him, keeping her eyes fixed on the dusty road at her feet.

"Good morning," he answered. "I left a note of thank you—did you find it? I did not want to wake you at such an hour to say goodbye."

She looked off into the distance, across the wheat. "I didn't know you had gone. I left some money, but you won't receive it now."

"I do not know why you should give me money."

"I feel responsible for bringing you here."

"Let us forget it all."

"Yes. I'm going to try. Goodbye." She stepped around him and continued walking.

"Madam! Wait, please!"

She turned, and he caught up with her. They stood for a few moments, he looking at her face and she looking anywhere but at him.

He had thought all night and been unable to recall a single literary precursor where the heroine offered herself as a sacrificial broodmare and was rejected. He imagined her discomfort keenly, feeling her humiliation as his own pain. "Pani Aniela…" he said gently, trying to find the right words.

"Don't," she said, "it's all right."

"No, no, I must speak. You were making me last evening such a generous offer, and I—I was rude, a lout—I was not meaning to be, but I was, and I am torturing myself about it since. I hope you will forgive me—"

"Please, let's not talk about it."

"No, I must—"

"Stop. Please."

He stopped, and they continued standing. She couldn't quite force herself again to walk away and she didn't want to hear anything he might say to her about the previous evening. Being turned down was bad enough, but what if he said he wanted to reconsider? Was the offer still on if his son hadn't suffered from her negligence? She didn't want to think about it. She said, "Where's your son?"

He gestured toward the band of trees that followed the road and her eyes followed his movement. Andrei was leaning against a tree, with his eyes closed. He was a small, still bundle wrapped up in the jacket she had bought for Yuri.

"This morning he seemed quite well," said Yuri, "so I decided to leave. But after a kilometer he grew tired of walking and couldn't stop coughing, and after another kilometer I grew tired of carrying him. So here we are, resting."

"I'm sorry. I don't know how to help you. Cabs won't come here. But the highway is only a few more kilometers. Once you get that far, you'll be able to get a ride. You'll be all right."

"And you, will you be all right?"

"What do you mean?"

"I am hearing your conversation with your sister last night. You left your door open, I think. You did not know what your parents do—about the weapons, I mean."

"No, I did not know."

"It is shocking for you."

"I don't know which is worse, the old guilt or this new one."

"But a person who causes accidental death or injury is nothing so bad as a person who supports military activity—there's deliberate intent to kill in that."

"Yes, true. I would have preferred not to be associated with either event though."

"But it is not you who are the…" he hesitated and remembered Kasia's words, "arms manufacturer."

"No, and I don't feel anything like I did then, when I thought I'd harmed your son, although I suppose I should —it's worse, as you say, and there's guilt by association. I should have realized. But what can I do now? I don't have parents anymore. I used to long for their respect and regard. Now I just despise them. And Kasia—she doesn't seem to care either—she's corrupted."

"But it is not your fault."

"No, not like the other," she agreed. She turned to leave again, but on an impulse stopped, returned two steps and held out her hands for the violin and bow. As he watched in mild surprise, she lifted the instrument to her shoulder and played with precision the rest of the phrase he had been struggling to remember.

"G, F sharp, G."

"Thank you."

She handed back the instrument. "I used to think I had to do everything perfectly. But I have learned, over and over, that I have no grounds for feeling superior."

She took a few steps away, but again turned back, as if in spite of herself. "Tell me, if your son *had* been injured—as your wife told me he was—would you still have written me that letter?"

"Absolutely. I hope—yes, I'm sure."

A pause, and then she asked, tentatively, "What is he like—your son?" Her gaze passed Yuri and rested in the distance, on Andrei, who appeared to be asleep.

Yuri nodded, understanding her interest. "He has a keen sense of humor and justice. There's something unstoppable about him. His weapon is mostly mockery and he has a sharp tongue. He will read anything, provided it has information and isn't a story. He has a great curiosity about the natural world. He likes flora and is very tender with fauna: dogs, slugs, ladybugs, anything with a soul, I guess. He's had violin lessons but prefers to listen to Russian rappers. He's bilingual and has an adult vocabulary, but—he's a child. He likes orange jelly and thinks tying shoelaces is a waste of time. He's generally polite, but sometimes he enjoys provoking his father. He's a good boy, a smart boy," he summed up, knowing he was leaving the particular charm and appeal of his son untouched.

"I'm glad," she said.

He sighed. "He misses his home."

"And now you're on the move again. I shouldn't have brought you here."

"You meant well."

Her lip twisted rather bitterly at that, but she said nothing.

"Why are you walking?" he asked suddenly, "Where is

your car?"

"I am intending to hitchhike too. The car was a gift from my parents and I am through with them."

"I see," said Yuri, looking a bit shocked. "Has this ever happened before—that you were through with them?"

"No."

"You are very catorgical."

"Categorical. You were just describing their guilt to me. And you? What would make you break off relations with your parents?" she asked in agitation. "If your father was a serial cheater with young girls? Or your mother embezzled funds from a charity? Or their business is to blow people to bits? I don't believe you'd say 'business is business' and look in the other direction. I'm sorry," she added, drawing a quick breath. "I got carried away. But you also want nothing to do with us."

"With them, yes, I do not want to be associated with them. I do not know what I would do in your case."

"Do you think I am wrong?"

"No, but where will you end? Your parents are producing the means, and many of your acquaintances— many people in the world, incredible as it seems, still believe in the idea of a military solution. Will you cut your friends too, for their beliefs?"

"I do not benefit from my acquaintances' moral choices."

"And your job at the ministry? The government is not opposed to the use of violence."

"I was a civil servant, not a member of the government."

"True, true. You are right there...But the bond between

parent and child," he looked unconsciously toward Andrei, "that is very hard to break."

"I don't think, in our case, it will be so difficult," she said in a clipped tone.

"I have caused this," he said sadly. "I seem to cross your life only to make problems for you."

"I can't believe I didn't know—I blame myself for not knowing."

"That is what *Oedipus Rex* is about: whether knowledge of unpleasant truth is better than ignorance. But sometimes the outcome is not very happy for anyone."

"Oh, happiness…" she shrugged. "Do you think that's what life is about?"

"No," he admitted and the silence lengthened between them as they contemplated the choices they had made. She was not like her parents, he thought, with a fierce kind of joy and longing—nothing like—and thus there was no reason, no reason at all, to refrain from expressing his feelings. The decision was taken in a second. He took a step nearer to her and after an intake of breath, he said quickly, passionately, "But believe me, Pani Aniela, if I could change events in my life, I would enjoyed to make your happiness my first endeavor."

She shuddered and would not look at him, not being sure what he meant but guessing he was referring to his rejection of the night before. "That's all right. Don't explain," she finished for him curtly. "Goodbye." She walked away.

Thus they missed understanding by the width of a misused verb.

I meant nothing bad, thought Yuri, why is she angry? Stop! No! Come back. Please come back.

She had walked some hundred feet, feeling his eyes on her back, when she remembered that actually there was something she could still do for Yuri and his son. She was accustomed to giving help, not asking for it, but she pulled her cell phone out of her backpack and pressed a number.

"Iza, hey,"

"Nela, what time is it?" asked Iza sleepily.

"I don't know. Early. Listen, I need a favor."

"Can't it wait till morning?" Iza asked. "Didn't you already ask me something?"

"I'm sorry to interrupt your weekend, but I'm on the road to the highway. Iza—I've never asked you for a favor before—but now I need a ride to Warsaw and so do Yuri and his son—you'll see them before you reach me."

"Yuri?" Iza's attention focused. "Oh, good, good, good. I'll be right there. Just let me put on my makeup."

Aniela walked on, and after a time, she heard the sound of a vehicle behind her. She turned and Iza drew up beside her in a small car. Its front passenger seat, shoved back against the rear bench, was much occupied by Yuri. Andrei was crowded in behind, but there was still a little empty space. Aniela, looking at the amount of road she still had to cover and peering in through the window, decided she would fit.

Iza rolled down the glass. "Nela—it's okay, I've got

them. We're a bit crowded. See you sometime—bye!" The glass rolled up and the car moved off, but not before Aniela had time to hear Yuri protesting and to see his head snap round to watch her receding in the distance.

Aniela stood in the road, dumbstruck.

"But…" said Yuri to Iza.

"Oh, it's all right, she already texted me she doesn't want to ride with us," Iza lied easily.

Yuri heard her with pain. She doesn't want to ride with me, he thought.

"I've been wanting to meet you," Iza continued, fixing her eyes on his face, "to thank you for saving me from burning up at the cocktail party last week."

"It was nothing."

"It was—it was something—look," she lifted a mass of curls and shoved it toward him, "I had to have ten centimeters cut off. What if I'd been left bald? So anything I can do to show my *deep appreciation*, you name it."

"Perhaps," said Yuri, putting a hand on the steering wheel, "watch the road now?"

"Oh, sorry," Iza turned her attention momentarily to the road and the car wobbled back on its path. "Anything else? Because, you know, I really admire a man who can act promptly in a situation. Really."

"But I think anyone there would do the same."

"But they didn't."

"Maybe they weren't looking at the moment."

"So you were looking at me? I don't mind that." She smiled at him meaningfully.

No, he thought nervously, God help us, that's not what I meant.

"Nela said you need a place to stay."

"Er…" he answered warily, keeping his eyes on the road to avoid the sight of her excessively low décolletage.

"And a job."

"A job, yes, I nude a jab. Job."

"I know lots of employers; I can help you. Why don't you come home with me: you can stay for a few days and I'll see what I can find for you. It's the least I can do."

Yuri thought of the damp shack, and Andrei, still sick, in the back seat, and of Aniela, and of Iza's probable designs and made a grasp for his dignity. "Thank you, no. I cannot do that."

Then he thought of reaching the damp shack, and of having no money, and of his already empty stomach and of how hungry he was going to be later—and Andrei too needed food. Perhaps it would not be wholly unacceptable to ask for a small loan? Just for a day or two, until he had collected some coins by busking or found another construction job. "All I would like to request, if I may be so bold," he imagined himself saying, "is a small loan of 10 zlotys."

"Well, but I'm not surprised you want to leave there," she was saying, "I mean, it's a long way out here, isn't it? And true, that's a big house, a mansion, you could say, a palace even, certainly a palace compared to anything Aniela's parents could ever have expected to live in in the old days, or my parents either, or anybody's parents, and most people can't have anything like that today either…"

Or, thought, Yuri, I could put it another way: "If you have a ten-zloty bill in your purse, Pani Iza, or a twenty, and you wouldn't miss it…"

But Iza was continuing, "It's not really a cozy house, though, is it? I mean some of that furniture is really top-notch—you wouldn't believe what they paid for it, I mean, I suppose, because actually I don't know what they paid for it, but that's what I imagine, I mean when I furnished my apartment, I spent…"

Or, I could just be blunt, mused Yuri, "Pani Iza, what I need is fifty zlotys,"—because if he was going to beg, why stop at twenty?—"to tide me over until I find a job …" But somehow he couldn't get the words out.

"But what I'm saying is, it's not really a cozy house, not really home-like, if you know what I mean? I come here often with Kasia or Aniela, but that's not because I like it there…only because I'm lonely, you know?…Lonely…"

I could hit up a lonely woman for fifty zlotys, thought Yuri, or I could just be silent. And hungry.

They were driving toward Warsaw while Iza talked and Yuri practiced self-restraint and silence; they were passing corn fields and wheat fields and farmyards as the sun rose higher in the sky and laid soft rays upon the landscape; they were driving through endless sound barriers where there was only the sun beating down on the pavement; then there were billboards, more billboards, a mad jumble of road signs and shop signs everywhere, hiding a lumber yard, a tool rental, a bathroom-fixtures warehouse, a bicycle shop; glimpses of suburban houses all in a row, and five-foot fences of chain link, of wrought iron, of plank;

smooth highway giving way to potholes and steadily in-
creasing traffic, cars dirty with exhaust and dust and yesterday's splashed mud; then blocks of apartments, grilled-
chicken stands giving way to sushi shops; city buses, tram
lines, traffic lights, new office buildings; they had arrived
in the hum and hustle of the city.

*

Some considerable time later Aniela climbed down a
weedy embankment and stood on the edge of the highway, beyond a junction. There was not much traffic even
yet, but she stopped and held out her hand at a passing
car, which screeched to a halt so abruptly—with a driver
who leaned out so lasciviously—that she hastily excused
herself and asserted that no, no, she didn't really want a
ride, it was a mistake. After this awkward interlude she
walked a ways, not daring to put out her hand again. She
only turned round at the sound of another car pulling up
right behind her. A small blue and silver police car.

This, she thought, is unfortunate.

Two young officers descended and respectfully asked
for her ID. She searched in her knapsack and handed it
over.

"You know, I suppose, madam," said one, "that it is illegal to hitchhike on the expressway."

"I have no other way to get to Warsaw."

"Unfortunately, madam, the laws are designed to
achieve the maximum safe speed for drivers, not to facili-
tate travel for all persons equally," said the policeman
civilly, "and unfortunately, I must thus fine you, hmm—

one hundred zloty: Will that be acceptable?"

She did not answer, but with an intense inner smolder at being taken to task for such a thing, such a little thing!—while her parents and their like were undisturbed! —reached in her knapsack again, produced the money, and signed the receipt.

"Aniela Solan," said the policeman, looking at her ID, "Seems like I've seen that name before."

Aniela did not help him, so he handed it back to her and turned to leave with a polite "good-day." When he reached the car he added, as an afterthought, "You'd do better hitchhiking from the other side of the underpass. You'll be able to see the drivers before they arrive." The police car departed.

By noon she had reached her apartment. In a wardrobe she found Yuri's blanket, the one he had used as a poncho, with the hole cut in the middle. It was not a beautiful object, far from it, but she brought it into her living room and sat down with it. Someday, she knew, she would pick up the pieces of her life and move on. Today she couldn't imagine it. She covered herself with the blanket and went to sleep.

CHAPTER 18

They were standing alone again in front of the lot by the lake. They had watched Iza's car turn the corner and disappear beyond the line of poplars.

"So, here we are," said Yuri unnecessarily.

"Why did we go to that place," asked Andrei, not complaining, just puzzled, "and why did we come back? I liked it there."

Yes, to sleep in a bed and eat warm food had been good.

"It's complicated," sighed Yuri.

"What, did you write another letter?" asked Andrei with a small smile.

Yuri looked at him sharply and Andrei's smile deepened.

Yuri said, "I'm glad to see you're feeling better. Look, the sun is shining. The shack will be dry again."

They climbed over the fence and wound their way through the vegetation to the shack. Yuri sensed they were not alone even before he reached the door. "Wait," he said to Andrei and looked into the interior.

An elderly man sat there, bearded and dirty, with torn sneakers. It seemed he had set a fire, as the center of the floor was blackened and there was a strong smell of smoke. He looked up at Yuri with eyes drained of intelligence, stared for a long moment, and said, in a distant voice, "Who're you?"

"Good-day," said Yuri, "Um, we live here."

"I live here. Go away."

Yuri wavered.

"Go away, before the hyenas come," said the man, and began to curse, indistinctly but obscenely.

Schizophrenia, thought Yuri, and your need is indeed greater than ours, and *damn it*, poor fellow—Why here? Why now?

He backed away and, shepherding Andrei before him, retreated through the lot to the other side of the fence. There he looked down into Andrei's pinched face.

"What now?" the boy coughed.

"Ah," said Yuri, who had no ideas, "look, it's a fine day. We don't need a shack. There are perfectly good benches in the park."

"Seems to me," said Andrei as they sat down, "like a perfectly *hard* bench."

Hours later, it was growing harder yet. Andrei dozed against Yuri's shoulder. Yuri stared at the small bundle of their belongings at his feet and tried to make plans.

Perhaps, he thought, the old man would go away after a time, but he knew he would never feel safe leaving Andrei in the shack now. Thus they must find some other form of shelter: a bridge, a railway overpass, the abandoned industrial buildings on the other side of the tracks. He roamed through them in his mind's eye: the empty window frames, broken glass, and steel girders; the scent of old rubber in the air; the scattered vodka bottles and twisted rags; the unnatural colors of the dust; the stains of rainwater and possibly urine across the floors. Outside was better: the broken pavement sprouted groundsel and stars-of-Jerusalem. To the east, toward the railway lines, there were vast stands of scrub willow, and the railway police. Where else could they go? He looked back at his temporary home with a fleeting thought for Adam after the first eviction.

But Adam at least had had Eve. And what was losing the shack compared to losing Aniela! What difference did it make where he slept when he was going to be sleeping alone and he had an empty life ahead of him in which every woman he knew—every woman he spoke to or saw or had relations with—would not be Aniela.

He closed his eyes against this thought. When he opened them after a long moment, a police car was turning the corner and proceeding along the edge of the park. Police cars passed frequently: it was nothing to cause alarm, but his muscles tensed and his eyes couldn't leave it, nevertheless.

It slowed as it reached the gate of the overgrown lot, stopped, and backed up. As Yuri watched in fright, two policemen descended, tested the gate, rattled the chain, shrugged, and climbed over. A long moment later they reappeared, herding the old man before them, alternately coaxing and commanding, and impervious to his imprecations and wild gestures. A problem arose at the gate, however. The man was unable to climb over and the policemen were unable to lift him. They were also unwilling to give up their point, which appeared to be a complaint of trespassing. Their voices came incoherently to him across the distance; other people turned to look too. A group of boys, circling the park on bicycles, wheeled like gulls and pedaled eagerly toward the commotion.

*

Aniela was woken by Kasia bursting through the door.

"There you are. Why did you leave without telling me?" Kasia's voice was aggrieved. "And Iza too. I was going to stay the weekend but I came back with Tata this afternoon since you all disappeared. And you left your car. I was going to take it, but you didn't leave the keys."

Aniela sat up and looked confusedly at Yuri's blanket, which she was clutching, and then at her familiar, neat apartment with its rows of books and elderly, polished furniture. Her eyes focused on her sister and recent events came flooding back. She would rather have stayed asleep, but she was fully awake now.

"I did try to tell you. I forgot about the keys though." Aniela frowned. It wasn't like her to forget things.

"So what's happening with you?" Kasia asked again. "That was something at dinner yesterday! And then you ran off in the night. And this morning I had so many calls asking about you I stopped answering my phone."

"You couldn't think I'd stay? And you couldn't think I'd keep the car once I knew about the business?"

"Oh well, if it was me and I was going to leave, I'd take everything I could get."

"Kasia!" Aniela felt the familiar pain of her sister's callousness. Someday Kasia would grow out of her amorality. Someday—she had to believe that.

"Well," said Kasia, not best pleased at Aniela's tone, "but this time you're wrong too, Nela. What do you expect if you talk to people like that? You act so righteous—"

"I don't—" protested Aniela, shocked to be attacked by Kasia.

"Of course they were going to be angry. You told them they should give up their livelihood. I mean, what did you expect?"

"I didn't expect any of it," Aniela tried to defend herself. "And I didn't mean they had to give up their business entirely—just anything related to weapons."

"But that's the lucrative part, you know. I wish I hadn't told you."

"Yuri told me. You only confirmed it."

Kasia didn't answer, but after a moment she said reflectively, provocatively, "I know a man who says he'll take me to a shooting range and teach me to shoot. I'm thinking of doing a piece for the blog: Girls with Guns. Ha, there are women who love that compensation stuff, so I can work it all ways!"

"Kasia!"

Kasia shrugged, "Don't Kasia-Kasia me. I don't mind the family business, you know. Because I think there are so many things wrong with the world no one can change them; smart people just accept that and try to get ahead. Like me, when I write about social things for my blog— you know what I really think?—I don't believe any of it makes a bit of difference. It just makes me look good. The world is the way it is and the way it's always going to be. Wars and weapons are part of it. Mama and Tata aren't to blame and I'm very grateful they're doing so well. I intend to take every advantage of it I can. You should get over it."

"You aren't bothered by the thought that they're part of the problem? You aren't bothered by the dead people? Maybe we don't see them because they're not in our part of the globe, but the body count exists, Kasia."

Aniela had never, she realized, had a serious conversation about anything with Kasia. Mostly any notice of Kasia's faults had been met instantly in her mind by remembrance of her own guilt. Now she looked at Kasia and tried to really see her. Kasia was posing naturally, unconsciously arranging herself in the light by the window, looking out, not answering. Aniela took in her youthful but cynical features, her cutting-edge clothing, her fingers looped with souvenir engagement rings—"so much smarter than piercings," she'd once said—her practiced performance of the in-and-out of smoking. Kasia had been to the university; she had degrees; she was indisputably clever, but Aniela doubted she thought much.

"Kasia...?"

"What about just wars?"

"There are no just wars, only losers and supposed victors, who forget their part in producing the situation and the slaughter of innocent human beings."

"How do I know they're innocent?" Kasia answered offhand.

"I don't think anyone deserves to die, for whatever reason, but one can presume innocence in the case of a child, for instance?"

"'The sins of the fathers are visited on the children'—it says that in the Bible, you know. Even I know that. How innocent can you be if you have really bad parents?"

"We have bad parents."

"No."

"Suppose we do for the sake of the argument. Do we deserve to die? Are the children on one side of a conflict more deserving of death than on the other?"

"It's pointless to talk about it. Or even think about it. You won't change the world."

"I can change my personal bit of it."

"I'd say go ahead then—have fun. But you'll take me down with you. And you won't make Mama and Tata change their minds either."

"Why, Kasia?"

"Because nobody thinks like you, Nela," Kasia's voice grated with irritation. "Don't be naïve. You're too small a minority. The only thing that changes people's ideas, our parents included, is repetition—having a whole lot of other people howling that something's okay or something's not okay. Not reason. Not arguments. Just *mass*."

"You could be a founding atom in that mass. You could help with the howling. With technology, one person has a louder loudspeaker than ever before."

"No. Leave me out of it. I give people what they want most. And it's food and clothes and feeling good about yourself because you gave something you don't need to charity. That's all." Kasia's habitual gleam of humor had disappeared. She left the window, nervously lit another cigarette from the end of the last, stubbed out the butt, and dropped the pack in her purse. She went to stand in front of a mirror and stare at herself.

"Look at me," she said grimly, exhaling smoke, "I could have been a heroine in World War II, but in today's world? There's nothing to get excited about."

"There are refugees beating at the doors of Europe—remind you of anything?"

"They aren't interesting refugees, like the Jews back then."

"Kasia—"

"No. I don't have time for any of that. In another ten years my looks will be gone. I have to make hay while the sun shines."

Aniela did not answer.

Kasia, still looking at her reflection, went on slowly, "Father asked you to come and speak to him. He's waiting in the car. I think you should go. After all, you don't have any friends except Iza, do you? And we all know what she's worth. Talk about sins of the fathers—or mothers, in her case. With no family too—you'll be all alone, Nela."

"I'll still have you, I suppose?"

"I think Mama may make me choose," she said slowly, without turning her head.

Aniela felt cold. She had her hand on the door when Kasia added, "They called somebody about that guy."

Aniela stopped. "What do you mean?"

"Tata. He called somebody he knows and asked him to find out about that guy—that Yuri. Someone in the secret services or the police from the sound of it, but I'm not sure."

Aniela walked down the hill, winding her way among the tourists, the baby carriages, and the weekend walkers, seeing and not seeing the cobblestones and the walls and the wide river, glinting blue in the sun today. Her father's Maybach was stopped along the street. It was a long vehicle, purchased from some prelate for half a million and only brought out for special occasions. Realizing she had suddenly become an event for her parents, Aniela slid into the back seat beside her father.

"Nela," he said. "Thank you for coming—darling."

Aniela considered that "darling" in silence. Did he mean it in any sense? Or was it just a habit of speech?

"Kasia said you wanted to speak to me," she said at last.

"You know, this is a regrettable business, Nela. Your mother is very upset."

"Yes, it's a regrettable business. Your business, that is."

"You know, there's no need for that—let's be reasonable, Nela."

Aniela had intended to stay calm, to be temperate and persuasive. It was harder than she'd imagined. Her father's smooth tone riled her. She was silent.

"What we want to do," her father was continuing, after a momentary pause, "is to come to some sort of agreement that will benefit all of us."

"I told you yesterday what I want," said Aniela. "I regret if I was untactful in expressing myself. I can see now that I should have approached the matter differently and

I deeply regret that I wasn't more sensitive. But the fact remains."

"The fact remains that what you ask is out of the question—out of the question. You're being ridiculous, you know. You can't think we would give up our mode of existence, give up everything we've worked for, for one of your whims."

"Mama may see it that way," said Aniela, "But *you* are capable of understanding exactly what I mean. I would have expected *you* to understand."

A telling red tinge flickered across her father's face, but he recovered. If his origins were in the urban intelligentsia, civil-minded and compassionate, and his wife's in hardened peasant stock, rising with the generations, there had been by now such a melding of the mentalities that his early life seemed far removed to him. His wife was the far stronger character and had long established her dominance over him. He could no more resist her than he could stop the Vistula from flowing.

Aniela's father was extracting papers from a briefcase, unscrewing the top of a fountain pen. "We'll have to agree to disagree then. You'll want to sign this."

"What is it?" Aniela looked suspiciously at the paper.

"Your connection with the business. You'll want to sever it, I presume." Her father's tone was dry. "Just sign."

Aniela took the paper from him and began to read. "And if I don't sign? What then? I want to close the factory."

"Then you'll be responsible for destroying the lives of all the people who work there—you'd be surprised how many work in that one factory. They won't find other jobs in these times. You wouldn't do that, I know."

"I would be sorry for them, it's true. But they shouldn't be working in such a business."

"You are hardhearted, aren't you? You always act as if you're a caring person, but in reality, it's all about what *you* want, isn't it?"

Two days ago, Aniela thought, these harsh words from her parent would have been devastating.

"I want not to be involved in producing arms."

"Regardless of who gets hurt in the process. Your mother was right—she said you're too categorical to bend. I wouldn't have thought, you know, that you'd be so selfish."

Categorical, thought Aniela, that was the word Yuri had used.

"Do you have any idea what it's like to lose your job," her father continued, "to be completely without resources? No, of course you don't. I hate to say this of my own daughter, but you're spoiled rotten, aren't you?"

"I have had many advantages, yes."

"And those advantages oblige you to take other people into account. They also oblige you, you know, I would hope, to take into account the desires of the people who gave you all those advantages. Sign this." He was holding out the pen.

"I'm sorry, but I won't. And if owning the land means I can shut down the factory, I will."

"You'll regret it, Aniela. Your mother…"

"Yes?"

"She says," he said to his daughter, not looking at her but somewhere up the street, as his hands tightened spasmodically, "that she doesn't want things to get ugly. But, you know, she's not inclined to pull her punches when she's angry."

"Get ugly," Aniela echoed, deeply shocked. "What does that mean?"

"I don't know. But I think it would be better not to find out. Think about it, Nela."

Aniela was already out of the car. For all her desire to slam the door, she closed it quietly and walked away.

She had not walked fifty strides before Pani Jadzia stepped out of a passageway. "Pani Aniela, darling," she whined in her beggar's voice, "Can you help me a little today, darling? I've got these medicines to buy and my liver is hurting me something terrible, and Lord knows I can hardly walk to the store my legs hurt so, and blessings on you, I know you're the only person I can count on in these times—"

Aniela answered rather too tartly, "Pani Jadzia, you know I arranged for you to get help with your medicines through the foundation. You don't need to beg."

"What do you know of my needs?" snapped back Pani Jadzi, abandoning the languishing tone, and Aniela, admitting to herself that Pani Jadzi's needs might be beyond her comprehension, reached for her purse and realized she'd left it at home. "I'm sorry, I don't have anything right now—"

"Of course you don't, dear," said Pani Jadzia sarcastically, turning away, "Of course you don't." She muttered over her shoulder, "I read about you in the news. Been up to no good, haven't you?"

Aniela, on returning to her apartment, found her sister still there. "I've been reading the media," Kasia said. "You should look."

It was clear to Aniela that what she would find there was not going to improve a day that was already shaping toward a memorable nadir, but she decided not to delay any longer. She looked at her phone and saw such an endless list of missed calls and messages that she turned it off and tossed it aside. She lifted the lid of her laptop: her ministry email was blocked and her private account had 137 unopened emails. She picked up the phone again and began to scroll through, looking for a message of support or friendship, but she did not find many. She returned to the emails: the first were messages about unfinished work or requests for assistance; the latter were questions from the media, mostly suggesting—what exactly? There seemed to be considerable confusion as to her reasons for leaving the ministry.

Abandoning the emails, she opened the websites of the largest national papers one after the other and found her name amid speculation her departure was related to a just-breaking Waitergate: Large numbers of officials had been covertly recorded while talking too freely in fashionable restaurants. She was not the only personage to leave her job abruptly these past hours it was noted. Undoubtedly the tapes would reveal some kind of misconduct—

"suspicious abrupt departure of director-general," said the articles. There were also hints of instability: "always a loner, always seemed a little odd" according to a former colleague who wished to remain anonymous; "a conscientious civil servant but clearly suffering from some issues —very rigid and unsociable," said another source. And to top it off, crowed a news flash, she had been found "wandering by the side of the road in the early hours of the morning and received a ticket for hitchhiking." Extraordinary behavior for a public official! Incredible bad form! Could a guilty conscience be driving Warsaw's youngest director-general to a nervous breakdown? Updates coming soon.

Underneath, in the comments section, there was a storm of invective and filth, both political—although she did not belong to any party she was ascribed to the governing one; and personal—though few or none of the commentators knew her personally. Snowballing on a sense of envy and delight at achievement brought low the mentions across the media were increasingly caustic, derisive, and hate-filled.

She closed the laptop and looked up at Kasia.

"Not too nice, is it?" said Kasia.

"I seem to have had very, very bad timing," she murmured, feeling shocked and sick all over again at this new blow. "But none of this matters now."

"Bad timing! Is that all you can say?" yelped Kasia in exasperation. "You've sunk your career and—me, my blog—"

"I just left my job, Kasia. I don't see how my problems affect you or your blog."

"They will, though. I knew this would happen—I knew it. Today there's an increase in visitors, looking for clues to a scandal, but it will fall off. Before, many people came to the blog out of curiosity—the blog of the sister of the director-general, you know, the rising star. Now it will be the blog of the sister of that politician or whoever-she-was who behaved so oddly and lost her job. No one will be interested."

"I'm sorry, Kasia, really I am."

"Not much good in that, though, is there?" Kasia was collecting her purse and heading for the door. "At least I can stop reading Bulgakov, though—that's one good thing," she added bitterly.

Before she reached the door her phone rang. She stopped and as she held the phone loosely, Aniela heard both sides of the conversation.

"This is incomprehensible," said Aniela's mother without preamble. "Who would have thought Nela could be so irrational? I always thought she was so calm."

"No," said Kasia, her eyes meeting her sister's. "Nela's not like that at all. Nela cares so much about everything that she's all emotion, a boiling kettle of emotion."

"Nonsense," retorted their mother.

"I, on the other hand," continued Kasia, "don't really feel anything about anything."

"What?"

"Come to think of it—since we're all telling each other the truth these days—I haven't since you broke up my relationship with Artur."

"Who?"

"Artur. You know which Artur."

"What are you talking about? Why are you bringing that up now? I have more important things to think about," snapped her mother. "Don't be absurd. You, at least, know there are more important things than—than—"

"Yes, yes. Altruism is for show; self-seeking is for real. *I* know it, but Nela doesn't."

"I'm glad one of my daughters has her head screwed on properly."

The apartment door closed on the conversation.

I was wrong, thought Aniela, Kasia does think—she's just come to sad, rearguard conclusions.

*

The standoff between the two policemen and the elderly trespasser on Yuri's lot had continued so long that even the small boys had tired of the dispute and departed. Yuri inwardly, fervently, thanked the providence that had prevented them from still dwelling in the shack.

"Man is fond of counting his troubles; he does not count his joys"—the line from Dostoyevsky floated through Yuri's mind as Andrei woke from a long nap, lifted his head off his father's shoulder, smiled, stretched, and looked about with the renewed vigor of a plant after rain. Yuri, finally able to move, rose and stretched too.

"Why did we come back here?" asked Andrei, who was tenacious of a subject, "I liked it there at that house. I liked that lady."

"I liked Pani Aniela too."

"No, I mean that old lady—Pani Ola, the cook."

"Oh."

"Just joking."

Andrei twinkled at the look on his father's face and added, watching his father curiously, "Pani Aniela was nice too."

But his father wasn't listening. Yuri's eyes had fastened on the driver of a car that was proceeding slowly along the street. The car stopped and a woman descended. Even at this distance, he knew it was Aniela.

"Speak of the devil," he murmured, his heart beginning to pound. She must be looking for them. He couldn't shout, or wave, as he didn't want to attract the attention of the policemen. She was standing uncertainly by the car, looking toward the police vehicle, when a second police van came briskly around the corner and halted by the gate of the lot. Yuri looked about nervously. This was too many policemen all together. Where could they go to hide? The park was open and while they were beyond a hedge and at a considerable distance, they must be clearly visible as two figures, sitting or walking, even if their identities were not obvious.

"Shouldn't we get out of here?" asked Andrei, his eyes also fixed on the van.

"Yes, yes, we should," said Yuri. "But wait a moment— if we move at once, we're more likely to attract attention than if we sit here quietly."

"Okay," said Andrei, in a small voice. "That's Pani Aniela."

"Yes."

"Do you think she called the police?"

The idea had flitted across Yuri's mind and been rejected. "No. Why would you think that?"

"They never came before we met her and now they're here together."

"That's called the *post hoc* fallacy in logic," said Yuri quietly, "and while this may not seem like the time for rigorous standards, it is in precisely such moments that we should keep our wits about us." He paused, as he was curiously out of breath. "On the other hand, if our *intuition* tells us she's not trustworthy, we had better attend to the impulse."

"You mean run?"

"Yes."

"Is that why you're shaking?"

"I'm not."

"Do you think she told them about us?"

"No."

Andrei touched his father's trembling hand with the tip of a finger and frowned. "Do you think they're going to catch us?"

"I think they're here because of the old man, not us. But listen, sonny, I want you to get up and walk casually across the park. Go hide among the trees between the portable toilets and the library. We'll meet there later, okay? It may be a while."

Andrei nodded and Yuri said, "Go, then."

He watched his son glide casually away—his son, who in a few short months had hardened so strikingly into street life that his father's odd commandments raised no puzzlement in his eyes. Yuri watched him for a hundred feet and then was distracted by a renewed commotion at the lot. When he glanced back to check Andrei's progress, the boy had disappeared. Startled, Yuri looked all about, but the child was nowhere to be seen.

He rose and took a step or two forward. From here, his view of the property with the shack was clear. Beyond the backs of the uniforms clustered round the old man, he saw Andrei appear at the top of a neighboring fence and drop into the lot. What on earth was he doing? "No!" Yuri wanted to shout, "Get out of there!" But he could only watch as his son, with an eye on the policemen, began to search for something in the grass.

As Yuri stared, Aniela appeared through the gap in the hedge and began to walk toward him. His attention then was shattered. *She* was walking toward him. His son was there. Andrei appeared to find what he was looking for— he straightened abruptly from the grass, whisked over the fence like a squirrel and was gone again. The policemen gave no sign of having noticed his presence.

Aniela was approaching.

"Why are you here?" she said rapidly, without even a greeting, "You need to get away from this place. Walk to the other side of the park—I'll get my car and meet you there."

He nodded and she left. A few minutes later, he slid into the car beside her.

"New car," he said.

"A rental," she murmured, accelerating.

They drove around the lake, past the rushes and the

fishermen and the dog walkers, until they came to a small intersection. Yuri jumped out and ran through the park gates to collect Andrei from among the chestnut trees. He found him clutching a familiar-looking plastic tub.

"What have you got there?" he asked, as he hurried the boy to Aniela's car.

"Oleg. My snail. I went back for him. I want to keep him."

"I doubt if we can afford to feed him. Get in," he shooed Andrei into the car and barely had time to pull his own foot through the door before Aniela had the car in motion again.

No one spoke until they were several streets away and it was clear no police vehicles were following them.

"So you didn't call them?" he asked.

"No, of course not. But my parents might have," she answered. Then, on second thought, she shook her head, "No, that's not right. They wouldn't have known where to look for you…Unless they learned the address from Iza—and I doubt that. Nevertheless, I had to come to warn you…I'm sorry, it's my fault." She told him what Kasia had said.

There was a long pause.

"Err…" said Yuri.

"Thanks to me, you are no longer safe here—or anywhere in Warsaw, perhaps. It is unfortunate."

"Yes."

This was where Aniela would normally have taken charge, with ideas and practical steps for Yuri to follow. Yuri, however, had not only mortifyingly refused her help the previous evening he had also made it plain in the morning that their paths would have to diverge. She wasn't going to put herself forward again or even say "Where shall I take you?" He could get out here.

"Oh madam," thought Yuri, "if only we could sweep aside the anfractuosities of fate so I could accept with alacrity and infinite gratefulness the offer you made me yesterday and have the opportunity to exert myself in making the experience one of..."

"Err," he said.

"So," she said,

• "I've done what I came to do.

• You're warned.

• Do you want to get out here?

• Or shall I take you someplace else?"

"No, no, thank you," he said, his heart breaking, "we'll get out here."

"There's *nothing* here," said Andrei in alarm, as Aniela slowed, searching for a place to stop.

"I can take you someplace else—it's no problem," conceded Aniela, not looking at Yuri.

"Vinni Pukh Street," said Andrei, taking the lead with a chuckle. He knew nothing of the street, but had heard his father mention it.

"Kubuś Puchatka?"

"If you would be so kind. Thank you," said Yuri, submitting to fate.

CHAPTER 19

Winnie the Pooh Street was a cul-de-sac. Ten paces off the bustling prosperity of Nowy Świat one stepped into clean worlds like this of apartments, government institutes, and lawyers' offices, or, as chance would have it, into smaller courtyards, where men with broken noses held pit bulls as they sat on dirty steps, below graffiti. Andrei looked around with interest as they crossed one of these, but Yuri led him onward.

They walked downhill toward the river, through a small park occupied by modernist sculpture and an occasional reader, past the music school. Someone's scales crossed with someone's *Hungarian Dance.* A bench gave forth a few canned bars of Chopin for a couple of tiny Asians. Yuri would have liked to sit, listen to the cacophony, and feel surrounded by the striving, however mutilated, for higher culture. But they did not linger. Following the edge of the escarpment downwards they came across the shanty of a homeless man, hidden between branches and a brick wall blackened by fires. Lower yet they found themselves staring up at a buttress with a plaque: "*Here at the foot of the Kazanowskis' castle, Zagłoba fought with monkeys.*"

"An episode," said Yuri in response to Andrei's question, "from Sienkiewicz's novel of the Second Northern War. The monkeys had escaped from a zoo, if I remember correctly."

"Chimpanzees or macaques?"

"I don't know."

"Why fight with monkeys?" said Andrei. "That's cruel."

"And with people it's okay? Zagłoba fought with everybody," said Yuri. "He's the grotesque, swashbuckling hero of the Polish national imagination. Sienkiewicz won the Nobel prize."

"Is that good?"

"Of course not—all these stories where the hero is the best basher prop up an outworn morality and impede progress toward a greater kindness." But he was talking for his own pleasure; Andrei was interested in monkeys not literature. So they continued walking until they came to the unused entrance of a large monastery, whose doors and tympanum were set about with weeds and pigeons and the carved words, *Salus Nostra in Manus Maria.*

Salus nostra in manus Aniela, salus nostra..., he thought, but he didn't know where their salvation lay really. "We've taken the wrong path for the crossing, I think," he managed finally.

"Maybe this way," said Andrei, taking charge again between bouts of coughing.

The river was close. A period of walking and they crossed the boulevard through an underpass and came out onto a square scattered with broken glass, empty bottles, and plastic cups rolling in the breeze.

"Wait," said Yuri, and in spite of his blistered feet and riven heart, he picked up three Lech bottles from the wall and deposited them in a garbage can. With his foot he caught a piece of paper beginning to tumble in the wind and put that in too. Andrei came wordlessly to help him and before long the square was mostly clean. Then they followed the bank back to a sluice and a line of small houseboats and came to a poplar five feet across. There they stopped—not because it was a good place to camp, but only because they felt they could walk no further, and the time had come to sit, and stare at the water, and wait for time to pass.

But this is unacceptable, thought Yuri with a sense of fright, half an hour later: could a homeless life really reduce them to a desire to vegetate? He began to sketch out for Andrei in the sand the tributaries of the river before them, the Little White Vistula and Little Black Vistula—

"Does it flood often?" asked Andrei, surveying the gradations in the banks.

"What? I don't know," said Yuri, distracted from the mental composition of a lecture involving a detour eastwards up the Narew to the Bug River and its significance as a dividing line between Catholicism and Orthodoxy, German and Soviet armies in the Second World War—

"What fish live in it?"

"I don't know."

"Do you think fish that live in north-flowing rivers are different from ones that swim south?

"I never thought about it," said Yuri, feeling useless.

"How am I going to be a scientist if I don't go to school?"

"I don't know," said Yuri, feeling worse than useless.

In the morning, Yuri and Andrei sat in the sand still, their backs against a tree trunk, and stared out at the deep blue of the Vistula. Above them, branches swayed in the breeze. Yuri, musing dismally on the variability of weather in this part of the world, shivered and looked down at Andrei. "Are you cold?"

"I'm okay," Andrei lied for his father.

Yuri rubbed his arms and yawned. The night had been much disturbed by sand fleas and traffic noise, and morning brought no breakfast. Somehow their gazes shifted to Andrei's pet.

"I read that French people eat snails," said Andrei.

"Yes," said Yuri, hoping his son was not considering this perfidious expedient, although his own hunger pangs were making the thought less unappealing than usual. He waved his arms about his head. A cloud of midges had found the shelter of their tree and descended around their heads in an irritating mist.

"They boil them. I wouldn't do that to Oleg no matter how hungry I was," said Andrei, flapping his hand to shoo the insects from his snail.

"No," said Yuri. "It's hard to be hungry, though, isn't it?"

"It's okay," shrugged Andrei.

"Come," said Yuri, and rose abruptly. He couldn't let his son down. Twenty minutes later, he handed Andrei a napkin enfolding five thick french fries—the leftovers of a skinny biker's meal, acquired from a riverside café at the price of some contemptuous looks.

Humiliation, he thought, was a recurrent theme in Russian culture, but not one he'd ever cared to dwell on, nor did he agree with that morbid English poet—Donne was it?—who called it the first step to sanctification. No, it only gave him a new sympathy for the rapacity of gutter rats and the stoniness of cloakroom cleaners.

*

Yuri wasn't playing his violin when Aniela saw him next, on her way to the bakery. First a group of gadabouts hid him from sight, then there he was beside his usual step and she knew instantly that a reckless subconscious will had guided her and she could have, should have, taken the other street. Now there was no alternative but to stop and speak. In spite of the people about, only a few coins lay in his violin case.

He was still wearing the clothes she had bought him, but they had already acquired a patina of grime and the dubious creases of nights in hard places. He was turned away and did not notice her arrival.

"Hello. How are you?" she said.

He jumped, startled, and turned to her. The pleasure on his face was so vivid she couldn't help but see it. Possibly he was a good actor, she thought.

"Ah, it is you. I am fine, fine, thank you," he said.

She couldn't think what else to say. He was standing, looking down at her, bow and violin dangling in his hands. Nearly every possible question or statement seemed impertinent.

"Where is your son?"

"I have sent him to look in garbage barrels."

"To find something to eat?" she asked, shocked at the idea.

"No, to sell the cans for scrip."

She didn't bother to correct him. "Where are you staying?"

"By the river, in the woods," he shrugged.

"I'm sorry to hear it."

She waited to hear him say it was okay, but he didn't.

"You didn't leave. You aren't worried about the police here?"

"I admit it is making me very nerves to be so close to such representatives of the laws. Particularly now. But in the Old Town they are mostly municipal guards and those are not bothering immigrantic buskers. And I must make money."

She heard herself saying, "I wanted to ask your advice. Although I realize…You're busy."

"No, I am at liberty to listen to you…please," he gestured invitingly. He had collected his violin case as he spoke, and now she found herself following him a few steps into an alley, where they were out of the path of passersby.

She thought:

•He's sleeping rough, with a child.

•I keep throwing myself at him.

"Please," said Yuri invitingly.

"I'm sorry. You have other things on your mind. Forget it."

"You make me happy. Please."

"It's partly a philosophical and partly a practical matter."

"Madam, I am at your service, but I doubt...my advice is not perhaps worth much, you know. I am not such a proctical person."

"Praaactical."

"Praaactical, thank you."

Aniela, thrown off stride by Yuri's linguistic failings, hobbled through her tale of factory ownership and threats.

"So I was wondering," she concluded carefully, "what you would do in my situation? You're the only person I know who might understand how I feel."

"Madam," said Yuri, "I am so flattered."

There was a pause while he thought.

"You must close the factory if you can. That is clear."

"Yes, but the people who will lose their jobs—do I owe them anything?"

"They made their choices. They could have taken other jobs, in other industries. You are not responsible."

"The factory is outside of Warsaw, in the countryside. I doubt there are many other jobs available. If people are very hard up, they can't be blamed for taking any kind of work."

Yuri pondered again.

"You have been benefiting from this industry, yes? You have thus some sums of money from it. Or not?"

"Yes, a considerable amount."

"You wish to keep it, of course." She would not like his suggestion, he knew, with a semi-conscious awareness of the expensive drape of her skirt, the texture of her sweater.

"No."

"If you divided it among the workers as severing pay —would it come to any significant amount for them?"

Aniela did some quick sums in her head. "It would not be as good as a job, but it would be something. Yes, I could do that," she said, giving a decisive *coup de grâce* to what was left of Yuri's emotional life. She smiled at him then, a real smile, and they stood smiling at one another, not knowing why—as their two situations were not very positive-looking—they were suddenly so brimmingly happy.

Andrei appeared. He was holding the snail tub and a plastic bag with a number of sticky-looking cans. His clothes were even dirtier than his father's, but, glad to see his father smiling, he gave Aniela an appealing grin.

"How is cat?" he asked, after the greetings were over.

"I'm sorry? I don't understand?"

"Homeless cat. Cat without name. Little, beautiful, gray cat. Your father feeds him."

Aniela did not know her father fed a cat. It seemed out of character to her, and she did not know what to say. She stared at Andrei—this boy she had worried about so much and who was quite clearly just as he should be. She remembered the sharp chin, the peaked hair, the mischievous sparkle.

Suddenly she found herself speaking too rapidly, unaccustomedly nervous. "You must be hungry too. Will you come home and have lunch with me? I mean, if you want to—although doubtless you have other things to do, other places to eat..."

"Yes, I like." Andrei jumped at the opportunity as his father hung back.

She had been taught her way around a kitchen by her grandmother—an author and professor *habilitus* who had insisted that cooking was a more certain means of giving pleasure than any other activity. Still, Aniela felt unexpectedly anxious at making a meal for such important visitors. It was a relief thus to watch her guests demolish dish after dish and to be assured by Yuri that she was the cordon bleu of impromptu lunch-makers. Then she could take part in a lively tricorn conversation of broken phrases and repeated words, and even, often, find herself on the verge of laughter.

In the midst of it, Iza called. "Nela," she said without preamble, "I went looking for Yuri, there where I dropped him off, and I can't find him anywhere. What should I do?"

"He's here," Aniela said reluctantly, but Iza wasn't listening.

"Where do you think he's gone? Isn't it odd the way he just disappeared? I wanted to invite him to stay with me again. I mean, he turned me down before but maybe he'll reconsider? Because where he lived didn't look so good to me, you know? And I have a washing machine, at least. I bet there's no washing machine there. What do you think? Only I can't find him, so what does it matter? Unless you know where he is?"

Aniela couldn't lie. "He's here, Iza."

"She says she has a washing machine," she said to

Yuri, as she put the phone in his hand. "She wants you to stay with her—I can't invite you to stay because of my parents." She could not mention now that for the past hour she had been revolving again the idea of renting an apartment for Yuri and Andrei. It would be like competing with her friend.

Hesitating, Yuri's eyes fell on Andrei's neck, thin and insect-bitten, and he gave in.

Iza, when they had descended from Aniela's car before a Powiśle apartment building and taken a small elevator up four flights, was as ebullient as Yuri expected. Her apartment was also very much as he had imagined it. It was new and tidy and filled too full. She appeared to have been tempted by every bin in an Ikea store: a quantity of candles, baskets, boxes, photo frames, ceramics, and crystal doodads littered the shiny surfaces. There was a white rug on the floor and an overstuffed sofa and a pashmina throw. "Don't touch anything," Yuri whispered to Andrei.

There were two bedrooms, said Iza. She would make one up for him, she said, speaking to Yuri, and did he prefer pink sheets with a lavender comforter or lavender sheets with a fuchsia comforter? The kid could sleep on the sofa. Sit down there, she said—sit, sit, sit—and disappeared. Andrei and Yuri crossed the white carpet carefully and sat down gingerly on the sofa, knees together and elbows tucked in close to their sides. Andrei clutched his plastic tub and snail protectively—Iza had already recoiled in disgust and he didn't trust her. Yuri held the violin in his arms and almost regretted the hard stone surfaces and pigeon dirt of the Warsaw street.

*

Andrei's thin limbs had arranged themselves crookedly on a chair facing a table where an unfamiliar helping of muesli was growing soggy in a bowl of yogurt. Yuri was cramped into the seat across from him. Iza had disappeared into her bedroom to prepare for work.

"I want to go back to the shack," said Andrei in a strident undertone as soon as they were alone.

"We can't go back. How could we live there, with the police about and that old man?"

"I don't like it here."

"Shh. Keep your voice down. She might understand. Our present situation does not fill me with satisfaction either, but we have to be grateful. It's very kind of Pani Iza to take us in."

"She doesn't do it for kindness."

Yuri opened his mouth and shut it again, rather astonished at his son's perception. The boy must surely have been asleep when Iza, in a short tee, had come to stand in the shadowed doorway of his bedroom that night. Yuri had feigned a furious, snoring sleep and the seconds had ticked by while his face burned in the dark and still she stood. He had kept his eyes closed and thought of Aniela and eventually, when he opened them again, he was alone.

His eyes met his son's and read a judgment there. He jerked his gaze away, embarrassed. Was he taking advantage of Iza by staying? Was it a kind of prostitution, even if nothing happened, if he knew her motivations? A series of possible other habitats flashed through his mind—the riverbank, under a bridge—and were compared to a bed with a down comforter, a shower with hot water, a stove with a flame, and he knew, uncomfortably, that he wasn't intending to leave their present refuge until forced.

"I don't know what you mean," he said sternly to Andrei, and watched self-doubt flicker in his son's eyes. He had never lied to Andrei before and the boy believed him implicitly.

"Or, yes, actually, I do. You're right," he amended hastily, ashamed of himself. "But it means we have to be particularly sympathetic and forbearing ourselves, so no one gets hurt."

"She doesn't like me," Andrei went on. "She looks at me the same way she looks at my snail."

"Well…We'll move as soon as possible. Now eat your whatever-that-is before it gets any worse."

"I hate maesli. And Oleg doesn't like it here either. He's becoming less mobile. Maybe he's pining for his home."

"Did you give him enough food and water?"

"I took the leaves off that plant there," Andrei gestured toward one of Iza's houseplants, now somewhat denuded. "But he won't eat it. Maybe snails don't like apartments. Look, I think he's getting sick here. We should take him back to his home."

Yuri bent over the snail, whose health had sadly acquired the projections of his son's anxieties. "He looks all right to me."

Iza emerged from the bedroom in a cloud of perfume and departed for work, with a wave, a toss of curls, and a reminder that Natalya, the cleaning woman, would be coming shortly.

After Iza's departure the minutes crawled, their seconds marked by the tick of a loud electric clock but unreal-seeming in that encapsulated space with no vistas. Outside, beyond lace curtains, they could see only walls of windows and, looking down, a small courtyard with tiny squares of grass and a shed for garbage containers. The noise of the city and the building's other inhabitants was muted.

The sound of the doorbell made them both jump but was a welcome relief. Yuri leapt up and opened the door to a grim middle-aged woman whose greeting and clothes marked her at once as a compatriot.

"Good-day, good-day," Yuri and Andrei chorused in eager Ukrainian and received a smile of joy in return and then, as Natalya set to mopping and dusting dirt-free surfaces, a flood of words—about Natalya's home town, and her husband, who had a job in a Russian oil field, and her son, who was out of work, and how she was terribly afraid he was going to be drafted—all men from twenty-four to sixty they were saying!—here she gave Yuri a stricken look and then changed the subject—and how she should be home helping her daughter-in-law with her grandchild, but one had to live, one had to go where there was work, and if families were torn apart, well, what was one to do? Though it was hard to make enough here even to send home, the cost of living was so high. She was only working thirty hours a week and she wanted to work more, but just that morning she'd had to turn down a job—right close, too—because it was at the same time as this one. That was just the way of it: some people had no luck in life and others had too much, but if only the war didn't spread and they didn't take her son she'd give thanks to God—a quick touch to her crucifix and a self-conscious glance here at Yuri; perhaps he was a non-believer, perhaps he was a patriot—and now, she'd better get back to work, or Pani Iza would come home and be angry with her.

"I'm looking for a job, too," said Yuri, "Maybe I could do the one you turned down."

This brought Natalya up short. "You! Do housecleaning?" she laughed.

"Why not? It's a job—I need a job."

"It's not men's work," Natalya said uneasily, but when Yuri pleaded, she agreed to make the arrangements.

"I don't think," said Natalya, after ending her phone conversation, "she understood you're a man."

"She will get the idea when she sees me," shrugged Yuri.

He pressed a doorbell and the door opened at once.

"Good-day, madam," he said, "Pani Natalya sent me."

His prospective employer stared at him blankly and then appeared to come to herself. "To work?" she repeated tentatively.

"Yes," said Yuri definitely, "if you please, madam. I very much want to purify. It is my dream to be a purifier."

Pani Marta was sophisticated. If he had said he was a transvestite she would have accepted the fact with only a blink or two. As it was she raised her eyebrows and appeared to hesitate before stepping back to let him enter, "Okay, it's unusual, but whatever suits you," she said.

Yuri knew she was a journalist—a person who might once by age and education have belonged to his own social circle. She was now, by possessions and nationality, a being of a different, higher sphere. Her tone to him was not uncivil, just matter-of-fact, with none of the interest it would have held if she had considered him a possible equal. He made a quick mental adjustment to his non-personhood and looked around at the apartment.

Pani Marta and her husband travelled—they had objects from Africa, Thailand, and Venice. They were sporting—their bicycles and tennis rackets cluttered the entry. They smoked, and every flat surface held an ashtray. Their closets were insufficient, and parts of their wardrobes were scattered over chairs, sofas, and the floor.

"It's a bit of a mess," said Pani Marta, "Our last Ukrainian's visa ran out two weeks ago and we haven't been able to find a replacement." She walked through the apartment, opening doors.

"This is the bathroom." Yuri got a glimpse of damp towels and tubes enough for a chemical factory.

"The kitchen. The dishwasher's broken." The counters were heaped with dishes and the remains of a week's food preparation.

"Right. So, you'll find the cleaning things under the

sink or in the cupboard there. I'm going out, and I'll leave you to it," said Pani Marta, and was gone.

It was not that he had never cleaned a home before. He had fairly regularly used the broom, and he had been known to run the vacuum and even to wipe off the kitchen counters. But it was only a sort of surface cleaning. There had been a neighbor woman who came in daily to do the in-depth housekeeping and also the cooking. He had never actually tackled a dirty dwelling and turned it out from top to bottom. He picked up a cleaning cloth and hesitated, his mind veering from the present to Aniela, to Ukraine, to the draft and the fighting, to Aniela, to Spencer's theory of the state as the product of war, where—he dabbed at a cluttered table—"the aggressiveness of a ruling power inside a state increases with its aggressiveness outside of the society…"

There was a bookshelf with a fair number of books. He found himself in front of it, head tilted, dust rag dangling. No Korolenko, no Sholokov, no Astafyev. Political scandal, alpine adventures, a translated American thriller or two, nothing much to his taste. It was very odd not to be reading. He was hungry for books: he yearned for an enormous helping of story, served with great dollops of neatly said thing—or so he phrased it to himself—a narrative that would inspire or at least distract him.

Come, he said to himself, you must stop thinking. You have a task—you must do it well, beyond all expectations. This apartment has to be the cleanest it's ever been when Pani Marta comes back.

He did the dishes and scrubbed the counters and sink.

It took him too long. He rushed about emptying ash trays. He tossed all the clothes in a heap on the bed, until it occurred to him that he should hang them in the closet. His fingers hesitated over the too intimate task of handling a stranger's clothes—a dirty tee-shirt, a bra—it was worse than doing their dishes. The bathroom next. The bathtub was stained with orange rings. He began to scrub—no, he mustn't think of sitting at his university desk, writing, preparing lecture notes, correcting his students' work; or of his colleagues—Ala bringing him tea, setting it among the books; Grigori passing, saluting him with a cigarette—"off to pound knowledge into my captives," feet ringing in the space between the marble floor and the high ceiling—Grigori his friend who had stood with the others when he was turned out. He mustn't think at all about his previous life, his usual occupation of a morning—he must just scrub. The rings didn't seem to be yielding to pressure. He mustn't think about the contrast between his present occupation and what he had thought to be his main task in life: to pass on to students the beauty and power of words. No—never mind. They also serve who only bend and scrub. Perhaps this period of adversity would have its uses. He realized, for instance, that he had never adequately appreciated the Cinderella story.

He stopped for a moment and stared at his ineffective efforts on the tub. It was really not as white-white as it might-might be. Not white, for instance, like the sleeve of Aniela's blouse. But he would probably never see her again, so what was the point of thinking of her—it just made him ache. He got some bleach and splashed it about, then recoiled as the rising vapors grabbed him by the throat. He gasped for breath, opened the window, and leaned out over a four-story abyss to drink the oxygen and give way, for a moment, to his sadness.

A meter below him, a turtle dove clung to a crevice in the cement and cooing, called its mate to it. Far below in the courtyard two small children pedaled tiny bicycles in circles. He closed the window gently and went back to work.

The hours passed as he rubbed, scrubbed, vacuumed, and mopped. He cleaned the bathroom and closed the window. When he heard Pani Marta's key in the lock, he was putting away the cleaning materials.

"Madam," he said, gesturing about with pride. "Your apartment."

Pani Marta swept her eyes casually over his work, pointed out the dust he'd overlooked on a shelf, and said, "Okay, well then, can you come twice a week?" She handed him two twenty-zloty bills.

Outside the apartment, in the ugly concrete hallway, Yuri looked at the money with elation. More money than he'd had in months. It gave him a joy far greater than his first university paycheck.

Clutching the two bills, he set out toward Iza's apartment, but after a short distance, on an impulse, he turned around and hurried in the direction of the Old Town. A determined, long-strided walk and he was soon pushing the intercom button of Aniela's apartment building.

"Aniela, darling," he wanted to say, "I made forty zlo-ty!" A ridiculously small sum and there was no reason at all why she should be interested, but he badly needed to share his emotion. The words were already tumbling in his mind. He would tell her over the intercom and walk on—she would be pleased for him.

"Aniela, darling"—only he wouldn't say "darling" out loud, only think it—"I've made forty zlotys! Forty zlotys in three hours, can you believe it? Cleaning! Forty zlotys, Aniela, I'm rich!"

"Hello?" Aniela's cautious, low voice cut across his thoughts, halting them like a splash of cold water.

"Hello."

"Yes, hello?"

"Er…" How ridiculous. What was exciting when an intellectual became a menial—or a man became a maid? She was a beautiful, busy woman who had her own problems of a higher order. She didn't want to hear about his forty zlotys. "Hello."

"Yes, we've established that. Who is this? Yuri?"

"Yes…I…How are you?"

"I'm okay. And you?"

"Good, I'm good."

"So…good then…"

"Yes…"

"I don't usually have conversations over the inter-com...Do you want to come up?"

"No…no."

"Do you…need something?"

"No."

The silence stretched, filled with a bookshelf's worth of unsaid words.

He had to say something, Yuri thought in panic, and grabbing his courage, babbled out an invitation "to walk, or have tea, or coffee, or kimchee or whatever you like. Please."

There was a long pause and then, in quite a different tone of voice, she agreed to meet him.

It would be a short walk, they said to each other shyly, and promptly forgot their resolution. The time lengthened as they strolled along the Vistula, heads bent in conversation. They lingered over flutes of raspberry beer in a waterfront café and hardly noticed as the evening filled the paths with bicyclists and picnickers. They took a ferry to the other side of the river and walked down a plank onto a sandy beach.

The warm weather had sifted people out of their high rises onto the riverbank, where, as if hankering for a darker age, they delighted in building bonfires. Yuri and Aniela trod gingerly past sprawling sunbathers and wet dogs, breathing in the scent of smoke and sausages, of water caught in pools and mussels in silt. They sat on a driftwood log, talking unabatedly while the colors retreated from the walls and spires of the old town and the skyscrapers beyond.

Aniela spoke of her city, which was trundling toward the future with buildings, roads, and even trees appearing and disappearing as if on a fast-forward film, and Yuri spoke nostalgically of his own home, a somnolent city of

roses that had awaited the moment to wake and be re-
furbished, only to be blasted apart instead. He began to
wonder aloud about his friends and neighbors but stopped
abruptly. Instead, they talked of her visit the next day to
her parents' factory and her ensuing poverty.

"You will not be able to dress like this anymore," said
Yuri, touching the sleeve of her blouse. "It is very beautiful cloth. I am imagining it has a fancy name like gossa-
mer, or mousseline, or baize."

"Baize—no." She didn't laugh at him. "I think that's
for pool tables."

She looked down at his fingers on her forearm, and he
withdrew them, embarrassed. She regretted it.

"My ancestors survived the Holodomor," he said, re-
verting rapidly to their previous subject, "the purges, the
Second World War, the forced migrations. Most of my
family was spared. We lived on that street, in that house,
and as the world changed, we continued to drink tea from
the same samovar, walk under the same lime trees, sit by
the same city fountain, attend concerts in the same philharmonic hall. Now…It must be very different already."
He let the words trail off and shrugged. "I am whole; I
have my child—I am nothing of a victim compared with
some."

"You will return someday," she said.

"Perhaps. I cannot see the future. And now, everything has changed," he said, meaning he had met her. He
was bursting to say more, but all their cross-purposes and
misunderstandings, his position and hers, inhibited him.
A silence fell.

He thought: her hair at the temples looks endearingly soft. The tint of her skin, the glide of her walk, the brave tilt of her head—all captivating. His fingertips retained the sensation of her sleeve and entreated for another touch. Did he dare? He didn't. If only she would turn to him! He could live a week on any contact, however slight. He fantasized momentarily that she reached for his hand, let her knee touch his own. Idiocies, he knew. Anyway, he acknowledged, as he willed himself to stare at the water and not at her fingers clasping her knees, her long limbs above the sand, it wasn't really—really—these that moved him, but how little they mattered in comparison with her mind. Here at last was a rational, trustworthy woman, a deeply caring woman with an unshakeable core. One could grow old with someone like that, and not grow bored. One could accept a lesser job, adapt to a foreign city, find compensation for all losses with a person like that. He imagined a household where generosity of spirit and not pettiness was the norm. No playing games, no shallow squabbles, no foul-mouthed rants over nothing, just certainty and pleasure in each other's company. All she felt for him was compassion, though. There was a Dostoyevsky poem about a pomegranate heart. Perhaps Aniela had given him one bit of her pomegranate heart, but she had pity and a small piece for everyone. That was all it was. He was here and she was there, beside him but a kilometer distant, and he had nothing to expect.

She sat beside him yearning, willing him to make a gesture toward her and not daring to speak herself. She fixed her eyes on the river before them, where the sundown turned it to pink and silver and dove gray, and the water swayed lap-lap, lap-lap against the side of a wooden rowboat.

He sensed her withdrawal—doubtless because he had touched her, he imagined. Moving away from her on the log, he searched for whatever small rock was within reach. He had an urge to hurl it at the water, an age-old gesture of frustration, but she turned her head to look at him and he froze then.

"We should go back," she said.

CHAPTER 20

They had parted with no word of meeting again. Two days later, he was her first thought on waking: Yuri—with an ache of pain. The succeeding thoughts were jumbled images from her visit to her parents' factory.

She had taken the expressway to the outskirts of a rural community and driven down a lane of houses arranged evenly in the ugly Mazovian style. There were peonies pushing through fences and neighbors chatting on the sidewalk, and no hint of anything sinister in the neighborhood.

Where the houses ended the road passed on through fields. She followed it to a wide gravel parking lot and looked about at what was left of her grandparents' property. Ahead was a chain-link fence with a security booth, a barrier, and a row of retractable spikes. Beyond were two aluminum-sided warehouses or factory buildings. She asked for the manager and said she wanted to speak to all the workers about a bonus. The manager was puzzled but eager to please—Aniela Solan, daughter of the owners—he was not suspicious.

The employees that streamed out of the building and came to stand ten feet from her were mostly men. They regarded her unsmiling face with growing distrust as she waited and their numbers increased.

Then she told them, over their murmurings of surprise and dismay, that she intended to close the factory and while she imagined her parents—their employers—would find another facility, she hoped it would not be soon. "I realize this may cause hardship and therefore in order to ameliorate—"

"What? What? What?"

"...your injury from this situation, I intend to offer payment—"

Suddenly there was complete silence.

"I am prepared to sign bills of exchange for any of you who will leave the business and promise not to seek reemployment in the arms industry...It will not be a huge amount, but it should help anyone willing to look for other work."

When she finished there had been a momentary lull and then a cannonade of angry comments and questions. "She's crazy," someone said, spitting, "I heard it in the news. Don't believe her." A few of the workers had not taken the bills, but when she drove away, an hour later, she had been very, very much poorer.

How many would keep their promises, she wondered again as she rose. Not most. She had suggested they pool their resources to buy machine stock for a different kind of production; she had offered the premises, but no one had been interested. She had done what she could.

She drank her morning coffee, ate her morning slice of bread, and contemplated, with sympathy for the factory workers and a deep sense of disjunction, a day without work. The mundane task of seeking a new job would not suffice to distract her. She would have all day to ponder an existence that had come to pieces as emphatically as— but no, she was sitting in the comfort of her apartment and had no right to conjure images of wreckage.

The morning news was before her. The victims of a plane crash were portrayed in detail while the overnight casualties of bombing in Ukraine and Syria and Libya were only vague numbers.

"I know nothing," Yuri had said, "of my friends and neighbors. The street beside my son's school has been destroyed."

"There is a historian," he added, "who says war is the result of miscalculations. I am less indulgent. I think wars are prosecuted for the benefit of very small groups of people—the benighted masses go along with it."

She was right; she wasn't behaving hysterically. It was while she was reassuring herself that her phone rang. It was her parents, asking her to meet them at a restaurant that evening to talk.

*

The restaurant was one she never frequented; one where, she knew by reputation, the cost of a meal could run to a month's average salary, a place where ministers dined on baby octopus, and business and politics sleeked each other's wheels with champagne and lobster bisque. As she followed the red carpet, her eyes adjusted to the lights of the chandeliers, the glint of cutlery and glasses, the whiteness of the napery, the well-fed look of power and the murmur of low voices. There were her parents, at the far end of the room. Her mother saw her first, and then her father's head snapped round and they watched her follow a subtly fawning maitre d' to their table and hand her over to an openly obsequious waiter. Other people had noticed her too and the murmurs turned to whispers as she passed through the room. Heads swiveled forthrightly or with attempts at discretion until she slid into the chair the waiter was holding.

"Thank you," she said grimly, as she was handed a menu.

Looking up she caught the eye of an acquaintance across the room. She nodded. His return nod was a facial contraction that fell just short of a cut, after which he concentrated on his meal.

But I've done nothing—nothing *now!*—except resign my position abruptly, she protested inwardly. Never mind, she told herself, her feelings were not the point at the moment. The point was what was she doing here? Did her parents really know so little about her—have so little clue about her motives—as to think she would be swayed by a display of wealth and gastronomic extravagance? And yet she had accepted the invitation without hesitating. She had not said, "No, not in the Emerald Club, I won't go there"; she had automatically agreed and put on a suitable dress and walked out the door. Maybe she didn't know herself to what degree she had been molded by her surroundings.

To her parents, as she pretended to study the menu and

the waiter stepped back, she said, "Why here? We could have met anywhere. In the park, for instance."

"Aniela, darling," objected her father.

"Do you think we're lowlifes," her mother's tone was crisp, "to skulk around in parks?" Below a thick gold and amber necklace, hills of green silk filled the space between the chair back and the table.

"We are civilized people," continued her father smoothly, "and it is normal that we should avail ourselves of the achievements of our society's material culture."

"At a thousand the bottle?" Aniela read from the menu.

"We've worked hard and been successful. There is no disgrace in our enjoyment of the position we have earned." Aniela's father's cheek twitched rapidly, but he had obviously determined to maintain his suavity.

"But my question is, whether your business really entitles you to the claim of 'civilized' and whether you have in fact earned your entitlements—your meal that you are going to pay mountains for, and so on and so on—and whether in fact your manner of making a living doesn't make you a great deal worse than any…say, 'lowlife' in the park." She stopped abruptly. This was not how she had intended to talk with her parents.

Her father was looking around nervously. "Keep your voice down!" People were beginning to cast curious glances at their table.

"I'm sorry," she said, but couldn't stop. "It seems to me that the material accoutrements of civilization should not lend stature where civilization's essence, its concern for each human life, is absent."

Here the waiter glided forward.

"Let's order," said Aniela's father with an effort at restraint, and when the waiter departed with their order, he added slowly, "I thought this was about our business, but I see I was mistaken. I see it's about your general attitude to wealth. This is a new departure for you. You never minded your advantages in the past."

"It's a sort of delayed adolescent rebellion," snorted Aniela's mother. "It's absurd. This whole situation is absurd."

Aniela ignored her mother and answered her father, trying to speak as carefully as he had. "It's not about wealth. It's about your business. Only I always imagined—now I see wrongly—that your business was a legitimate one—that you hadn't hurt anyone, but only provided some service or good—and that made having more than other people all right somehow. But your business isn't legitimate and as I look back at my own naivety I wonder how much else I overlooked."

"Keep your voice down. Our business is perfectly legitimate."

"It's legal, you mean. You're legitimate operators in the arms trade. It's also highly immoral."

"I don't have to listen to this," said Aniela's mother to her father, who patted his wife's hand placatingly and said, between gritted teeth, that they should eat.

They ate in silence for a while. The salsify and the truffles followed the raspberry tomato consommé. The Grand Cru succeeded Le Paradou Rose. Aniela's mother ate with vigor, stabbing with slightly more force than was necessary. Aniela picked at her food.

"When did you begin this business?"

"Twelve-thirteen years ago, when world affairs took such a dangerous turn," said her father.

"Propaganda."

"It's easy to be wise in hindsight. Maybe you saw matters clearly but you certainly didn't express your views to your parents."

No, that was true; they had never discussed world affairs. She had never raised any international issue with her parents nor they with her. Talk, when there had been any, had glanced on personalities in domestic politics.

"But then it became clear, in any case, that if the danger was not quite the one imagined in Washington, there was more than enough to worry about from our near, dear neighbors here. The Georgian war? That shook things up all right."

"We're ensuring that Poland can defend itself," put in Aniela's mother. "And its neighbors can defend themselves."

"You sell to Ukraine—and the government?"

"Some…we're working on it," said Aniela's father. "Your recent behavior has been very unhelpful in that regard. Very."

Aniela addressed herself to her father, "You've studied history. You know that no one is defended, no one is made *safer* by military action—that that idea is just part of the myth-making of war culture. The numbers of the dead, before and after, speak for themselves."

"And the Second World War? What about that?"

Aniela's mother jumped in as if the sole mention of that war trumped all arguments, "What about the Second World War?"

"What about it? 27 million Soviet citizens died and Russia brags of its 'triumph.' 60 to 80 million dead around the world—"

"Maybe more would have died if they hadn't fought."

"All those millions for a 'maybe'! That pseudo ethic of sacrificing some to save others is used to cover every crime by every regime."

"Freedom is worth fighting for—"

"The dead aren't free; those who mourn them aren't free; more countries weren't freer at the end than before. Enough with romanticizing the Second World War. The powers on both sides were fighting for empire."

"And the Jews? What would have happened to them? Your father's own mother's father, you remember…"

"Shhh, shhh…" Said Aniela's father sharply, nervously.

Aniela continued in a fierce whisper.

"It's the war that made the Holocaust possible. That the Allies were fighting to save the Jews is one of those false tropes imposed on the past—"

Their voices rose. Heads turned, some in curiosity and some in irritation.

"Why," said Aniela, "do you speak as if the only means of resisting an evil is violence? How—"

"They—the Nazis, the Soviets—"

"It's easy to speak of a 'they,' but if the Second World War teaches anything it is that in the right circumstances we are almost all capable of inhumanity, of *bestiality* even, and indifference. The persistence of militaries trains us from birth to accept killing. That has to change. We all have a responsibility to protect others by rejecting military culture."

Aniela's mother broke in, "You always think you know best, but no one who matters agrees with you. Your proofs and your prescriptions mean nothing because all the *important* people, all over the world, disagree with you. But you were always so stubborn, so arrogant in your beliefs."

The enmity in her mother's voice, palpable as her presence, startled Aniela into silence. She said nothing more but stared hard at the tablecloth, summoning up from the past her relations with her mother, this stranger who suddenly seemed capable of anything. Her mind reeled back quickly through ten years of barren conversations, back through high school to her mother's hovering presence at the time of her school leaving exams, back to a childhood illness and her mother's brief hand on her feverish forehead. She had been taken by her mother on shopping trips, on vacations to resorts and foreign cities, to tutors, to the dentist...her mother had been the giver of gifts, and also the person she must always strive to please by being successful, by being exact, by not bothering her when she was preoccupied, by not insisting on a response to her needs when it was clear none would be forthcoming.

The decision was confirmed during the dessert course. There would be repercussions and revenge, because her parents' self-respect required vigorous defense from the truth.

"We want the apartment back," said Aniela's mother, "in exchange for the work you've interrupted at the factory. Not that it will begin to make up for our losses, but maybe it would be good for you to know what it's like to lose something you care about."

"Which apartment?"

"The one your grandparents left you."

"It's mine."

"Yes, but we think you should sign it over to us. Either that, or we might let the authorities know about your friend."

"Which friend?"

"The one who's probably a Russian spy."

Aniela choked on a bite of marinated rhubarb.

"Have some of the Moscato," said her father, gesturing to the bottle. "And maybe we can think of a way to resolve all this. You know. Darling."

"Maybe not," said Aniela, and rose.

Aniela's father exchanged glances with her mother.

"Sit down. We have another suggestion to make—it's about the boy."

Aniela hesitated, and sat down again, on the edge of the seat.

"What boy?"

"'Which apartment? What boy?'" Aniela's mother mocked, "Don't play stupid, daughter."

"The one you nearly drowned," inserted Aniela's father coolly, "the one you're so concerned about. He's with Iza at the moment in her apartment. Your friend is in the Old

Town, playing his violin. He hasn't made much this evening—around seven zloty as of an hour ago—but never mind that. It might be because of the rain, and not because he's just a really poor musician."

Aniela stared.

"Over there, at that table" her father gestured slightly with his chin, "is our notary. He has the papers drawn up and is waiting for our signal. You'll sign them and we'll be done with one another."

The man he indicated was a small bald man in a suit and tie, dining alone. He looked up then, startled to be caught in mid-bite, but asking with his eyes if he were needed yet. Aniela and her father looked away.

"I give you the apartment and you don't turn Yuri in?"

"Actually, we were going to call and have them pick up his son. Mr.—Romen, is it?—can come second."

"I see."

"And given your recalcitrance," added Aniela's mother, "it's not just the apartment, but also the land where the factory stands."

"Both?"

"Yes, so that next time you remember not to make life difficult for us."

Aniela continued to stare at her mother, who said these words with deep hostility and resentment but no special excitement, as if such modes of pressure were standard fare for her. She looked at her father, who looked away, with only a muscle jumping in his cheek. He too, was accustomed, she realized.

"Your choice, darling," he prompted, "the boy goes to

the detention center or your signature goes on the paper—what's it going to be?"

Aniela, in her professional career, had dealt often with unpleasant situations, with colleagues or counterparts whose intentions were opposed to her own. She had kept her detachment. Now she struggled for the appearance if not the reality of that objectivity. She took a slow sip of wine and ran rapidly through her alternatives.

She had thought she was indifferent to her surroundings, but the thought of losing the apartment was surprisingly painful—the view, her memories of her grandparents, the last piece of continuity and stability in her life. It was her retreat, her *home*. For the first time she was about to lose materially, and badly.

And the arms manufacturing—she wouldn't be able to stop that. They would go on pumping out parts from their factory. She would be tied to their name and their malign activities forever.

She felt for the edge of the table to steady herself, but it slipped under the linen and offered no support.

She put these thoughts aside in the matter of seconds to concentrate on saving Yuri and Andrei. Perhaps if she went to the lavatory and called Iza from there, she could warn them to flee? She turned her head, searching.

"Don't think of rising from your seat until you've signed," murmured her mother.

If she left now, would she be able to get to Iza's apartment before her parents could mobilize the authorities? Would there be a chance, if the police were slow in responding, that she could get Yuri and his son away? If her father knew the contents of Yuri's violin case, he had someone watching. She hated the idea that Yuri was being spied on unawares, hated—almost—her parents.

Her mother sat brooding, placid but fanged, a spider prepared to defend its web. Her mother's hand lay on the tablecloth: chubby, diamond-studded, and with just enough likeness to her own slimmer version to make her avert her gaze. Who were these people, after all? How could she have been their daughter all these years and known them so little that she never understood their utter selfishness.

"I never realized what sort of person you are," she said to her mother.

"We feel exactly the same," responded her mother.

To sign or not to sign? But even if she signed away her apartment and the factory land, Yuri and Andrei might be picked up anyway. The lawyer had said they wouldn't last long. She thought of the two of them in her apartment three days before: of Andrei trying to tell her, in his broken Polish, about the habits of gastropods; of Yuri talking with animation of the Vaplite movement and smiling at her as he took down another book from the shelf.

Andrei would end in an orphanage, he had said. But their fate was already sealed; there was nothing she could do for them.

Yuri had applauded her closure of the factory. "You have the opportunity to do something rare. To take a conscious decision that will cost you a great deal but will add to the total of human dignity," he had said.

If she signed she would be giving in to blackmail; she would lose her apartment; and she would have done nothing to stop her parents from manufacturing arms.

"We're waiting," said her father impatiently, taking out his cell phone.

"Maybe you should make that call," said Aniela's mother to him.

In Aniela's imagination Yuri was being thrust into a cell, the metal door was slamming shut with a clang.

"I'll sign."

The waiter, summoned, swept their dishes from the table. The notary glided over apologetically and, fumbling, laid out sheets of paper. Someone produced a pen. Aniela ran her eyes over the names, numbers, and addresses typed out in full. Some of the information was generally written wrong in such documents; usually no one noticed until later. She'd never heard that it affected the legality of the document though. All that mattered was the signature. She signed with a ministerial flourish of spikes, twice, handed over the papers, and rose.

"We're done then. And you'll leave Yuri alone."

"I will. Darling. But, you know, the police—once a crime has been reported, they have to investigate it. *Ex officio*, you know."

"You reported them already? I signed for nothing then." It was a horrified statement, not a question.

Aniela's father looked off in the distance and did not answer.

"I will never forget it."

"That's the idea, darling," Aniela's father smiled without mirth.

CHAPTER 21

Aniela walked out of the restaurant into a night of strolling pedestrians, perfume, streetlight, car hoods, and concrete littered with acacia flowers—all of which she perceived only through a fragmented glaze. Mama! Tata!—an inner voice wailed. If this was how they behaved when crossed by their daughter, how did they comport themselves with strangers, she wondered, images of perverse darkness flashing across her mind. But why was she surprised? If one was in the arms business, one had already decided for force over justice; one already saw the world through one's own sick lens of threat and retribution. And she had loved her parents! With an effort she swallowed her nausea. These thoughts would have to wait for later. She couldn't stand on the sidewalk with her knees knocking. She had to focus.

First, she had to get Andrei away from Iza's apartment and then warn Yuri. Next, she had to get back to her own apartment before her parents sent someone to change the locks and she lost everything inside. She knew she had only the smallest window of time.

She called for a taxi and soon one was pulling up. "Hurry," she said, and gave Iza's address. As the taxi veered into traffic, she tried Iza's number again and again—please answer, she thought—but Iza didn't answer either

her cell phone or her home phone.

The ride took mere minutes. "Wait for me," she said to the taxi driver, and ran to the building. Her father had said that Andrei was in the apartment, and while she supposed it might be untrue, she had to make sure. No one answered the intercom, but she knew the code and let herself in. As she simmered with haste, the elevator carried her slowly, impassibly upwards.

Iza flung the door open at her knock, a furious look on her face. "I'm going to—Oh, it's you, Nela." She grabbed her friend's arm and pulled her into the apartment, jabbering loudly, "Do you know what that, that, that—"

"What happened? Where's Andrei?"

"What happened? A massacre! I'm going to murder that little brat when I see him! Murder him! Look what he's done—look! Can you believe it? I give him a place to stay, I feed him, I'm nice to his father, and that's the thanks I get—I mean, I've seen some ungrateful people before, but this takes the cake, I mean—never, ever, whatever, I'm going to kill him! With my bare hands!"

"Iza—"

"I thought it was that brat ringing the doorbell. But I'm not going to let him in!"

"Iza—"

"He can stay out all night for all I care. He's an animal —he shouldn't be living in a house. Look!" Iza grabbed Aniela's sleeve and pulled her toward an open window. He threw everything out! Can you believe it? Look, look, look!" She bent out the open window. Aniela followed her pointing finger down four floors. In the pale light of a street lamp, the courtyard appeared to be littered with a strange half-circle of debris, as if someone had dumped a garbage pail out the window.

"Everything—he threw everything out—candles, pots, vases, cushions, everything!"

"Who—?"

"That kid—that devil."

"But why—?"

"And my phone—I can't find my phone—oh!" Iza's voice rose to a shriek, "Maybe he threw that out too. I have to go look." She whirled away from the window.

"Wait, Iza!" Aniela caught her friend by the arm and was dragged half across the room by the impetus. "Where is he now? I have to find him."

"I want to find him too, and when I do…" Iza flounced across the hall and into the elevator.

There was no point in waiting to get sense from Iza, Aniela realized. It was clear some dramatic upset had occurred—the point now was to find the boy and deal with the damage. Rather than wait for the elevator she rushed down the stairs, three at a time, high heels striking loudly.

At the bottom she was brought up short. Andrei was squeezed into a dark corner, almost out of sight behind the elevator shaft. Iza was nowhere in sight.

"Andrei?" she said. "What happened?"

The boy didn't answer, and as she came closer she saw with distress that his face was damp and his eyes swollen.

"What happened?" she asked again gently.

He gulped. "She threw Oleg out the window. My snail."

Aniela stood mute, forgetting for a moment all the rest of the problem before such petty cruelty.

"That's...Why did she do that?" she stuttered.

"He crawled on her table and leaved sleme, and she tell me"—Andrei sniffed and Aniela leaned closer, concentrating to understand him, "not to be darty fireigner, and get rid of him, or she do it, and I say she stupid and I no want to live with her and I no want her to be with father," he gulped. "But that not Oleg's fault." His lips trembled as he tried to hold back the tears. "And then she grab him and throw him out."

Aniela's own eyes began to fill in response to the child's emotion.

"I'm so sorry. I'm really sorry. I never would have thought she'd do something like that...Maybe it survived the fall?"

"No. He smashed, sure. I want bury, but no find because dark."

"I'm sorry."

"He was my friend."

"I'm sorry."

"I hate Iza."

"That's why you threw her things out the window."

"I want go to Ukraine. I hate this stupid place."

But right now it wouldn't be so good for you, thought Aniela. Time was passing.

"Look, I'm really, really sorry, but right now I have to find your father. Will you come with me to look for him? I have a taxi waiting."

Andrei scrubbed his eyes with a sleeve and shook his

head. "I wait for father," he muttered.

"Listen," said Aniela, "I don't think you're safe here. I think some police may come for you—and then for your father. I don't know if I can help you. But I think I'm your best bet at the moment." She tried to speak simply, but she didn't know how much he understood.

"You take me to father?"

"I'll try to."

Andrei rubbed his face again, nodded, and made an effort to pull himself together.

They pushed through the apartment doors together and found themselves facing a policeman, who was standing by the intercom.

"Excuse me, madam," he said, "I'm looking for..." His eyes dropped to a clipboard. "A Ukrainian family. Romen —father and son. Do you know which apartment that is?"

"Number 45," said Aniela. "But I think they've left."

Andrei was sidling away but the courtyard was surrounded by the apartment complex; there was nowhere to run. The policeman's eyes fastened on him.

"Your son?" he asked Aniela. "He doesn't look very happy."

"Yes," said Aniela, putting her arm around the boy and pulling him close, even though he stiffened, even though she was unused to such familiarity. "He's just lost his pet."

"Ah," said the policeman, losing interest and turning back to the intercom. "That's all."

Aniela and Andrei walked to the waiting taxi and got

in as a tear slid down Andrei's cheek again. The taxi driver turned and looked them over but said nothing except "Where to?"

"Wait," said Aniela, struck by a thought. Iza wouldn't have picked up a snail, even to discard it. "Andrei, did Iza throw the container out too?"

"No. She go like that—" he choked on the words as he imitated the motion of someone tossing something underhand.

"Wait here a moment, will you? You won't move? I have to check something."

Andrei nodded, and Aniela hurried back to the building. She passed the policeman, who was still waiting for someone to answer the intercom at the nonexistent apartment 45, pushed through the door, jabbed the elevator buttons, and waited impatiently as the lift hummed her up four floors. In Iza's apartment she swept her eyes around the denuded interior but found no plastic container. She crossed rapidly to the kitchen, jerked open the cupboard hiding the garbage bin, and lifted out the tub. There was no snail inside, but another look in the garbage and her heart gave a funny hop. The snail was perched on a mound of cucumber peelings, whole and undamaged, waving its eyestalks. Carefully, she unstuck it from its moorings, plopped it in the container, and rushed back to the elevator.

"Here," she said, handing the tub and snail to Andrei, who gasped and then smiled through his tears, a large smile.

"Oh, thank you, madam, thank you."

"I think he stuck to the container. You owe Iza an apology."

Andrei shook his head. "No! She meaning to do it. Oleg save himself."

"Well, he's a smart snail. Now let's go find your father. The faster the better."

As the taxi pulled into traffic, Aniela leaned back and reflected that it had been easier to stay calm in the days when nothing mattered in the present, only the past.

*

Aniela's father and mother came out of the restaurant and breathed the damp night air as they waited for their taxi. "Well," said Aniela's mother, "that was very satisfactory. I think we showed her."

"Very satisfactory," echoed her husband.

"We're minus a daughter," said Aniela's mother briskly, "but perhaps she would have been no use anyway." A pause, and then, "We'll want to get that apartment cleared out and on the market right away. I wonder what it'll bring?"

"Not more than a million, I suppose. Small change, but I'll contact the agents tomorrow."

The taxi arrived and took them to their Warsaw apartment building. They rode the elevator to the top floor in silence, opened the door to their home, and paused briefly in the entry to take satisfaction in the modern luxury space with its shades of gray and bling.

"Kasia's not in. She's never in. It's dark in here, isn't it?" muttered Aniela's mother, pressing buttons to turn on more floodlights. When that was done, she took off her gold and amber necklace and stood sifting it through her fingers.

"I'll call her to see what she's doing," said Aniela's father. "Maybe she'll come with us to the country tomorrow."

"In the morning we have meetings at the office," Aniela's mother reminded him.

"Yes," said Aniela's father musingly. "Though I suddenly feel so tired—so tired somehow. I'd like a rest. To tell the truth, what with this Nela business, I feel a bit sick of it all at the moment. Not because she's right, of course —not that—but I simply can't get over her ingratitude for all our hard work."

"Yes. All these years to get where we are…I don't know how she thinks she can dictate to us."

"She's being completely unreasonable. We were right to take steps. It was just."

"Of course it was."

"So tomorrow—we'll set things right at the factory and carry on. We'll get over this. We don't need Nela— too bad for her but it was her choice."

"Nela will come round," said Aniela's mother. "She's lost her head at present, but it'll be a passing thing. Maybe there was some difficulty at work that we don't know about; maybe she has some hormonal problem; maybe she's been working too hard or maybe she's been spending too much time with those basket cases of hers. I should have got her out of that ministry sooner—that's the problem. She's always been tractable. She just needs to be steered in the right direction, shown what's right—even if we have to twist her arm to make her see it."

"You think she'll change her mind about it all?" asked her husband, startled. "Because I thought she seemed very determined, very angry. I was surprised she signed, to tell the truth."

"She'll get over it. It might take a bit longer now, is all," added Aniela's mother thoughtfully.

"Do you think we shouldn't have made her sign things over to us after all?"

"No, no, of course not. She had to be brought to reason. We can't let anyone get away with that sort of opposition—not even—or particularly not—a family member."

"No, of course not. You're right, darling."

"You agreed to it, you know."

"Yes, although it was your idea."

"That's very convenient for you."

"But since we're in agreement, darling…"

"We better be."

Aniela's father headed for his bottle of vodka and poured himself a generous nightcap.

Aniela's mother put the deeds down on a table and flipped idly through them. Suddenly her gaze sharpened and she gave a squawk.

"Marek! Look at this!" She waved one set of papers at him furiously then dropped it to flip rapidly through to the end of the other.

"*Myszka Miki?*" Aniela had signed, with a great many spikes and strike-throughs, "Mickey Mouse."

"That—!" shouted Aniela's mother.

"*Really*, darling," protested Aniela's father.

*

"Come," Aniela said to Andrei, and "hurry," as the taxi set them down and they were left alone on the edge of the Old Town. Andrei followed her, puzzled, as she made her way through an unexpectedly dense crowd in the Barbakan gate, hurrying as fast as her heels and the other pedestrians would allow.

"Why is hurry?" he asked. "What is happen?"

"It's complicated," she replied over her shoulder. In his sharp eyes she read his wariness and his effort to understand the strangeness of his new world, but she couldn't stop to reassure him.

In the distance they could see Yuri's usual place across from the church, but it had been taken by a man with a display of toys on strings.

"Listen," said Andrei. "Maybe is."

Aniela listened hard and could hear the strains of a violin, faint between the walls and the echo of evening pedestrian traffic. She couldn't make out the tune, though it seemed to come from the next street over. As they hurried toward it, Aniela tried not to let her hopes rise: probably it wasn't Yuri, probably they would turn the corner and see a quite different busker—a young woman in jeans or an old man on a campstool, not Yuri at all. She achingly wanted him to be there.

He was. They rushed towards him and then almost simultaneously slowed and held back—Andrei, no doubt, out of dignity and possibly the memory of what he had done to Iza's apartment, and Aniela because, after all, the feeling of alleviation at the sight of him and the wild up-surge of some fluttering, struggling emotion that might be happiness was probably aberrant.

He stopped playing and looked at them in surprise, his eyes fastening on Andrei's blotchy face.

"Come with me, please," said Aniela, coming up to him, "There's no time for explanations—just come quickly."

He put up his violin and was following her almost at once. As they scurried toward the Barbakan she looked about but couldn't spot any obvious surveillant. It was as they were squashing themselves into the back of the wait-ing taxi that a car pulled up behind. A man stepped out of the crowd and got in—a man whose ox-eyed visage sug-gested his employment by the uniformed services.

"Are we being followed?" Aniela asked the taxi driver when they had driven a short ways.

"There's a BMW that's turned twice with us."

"Can you lose it?"

The taxi driver pulled to the curb with an abruptness that had them grabbing the front seat for support.

"What are you doing?"

"Madam, I'm not interested in getting involved in any-thing. You can all get out here, please. No need to pay me—just get out."

Aniela jumped from the car. Several cars behind, the BMW sat in traffic.

"This way," said Aniela, and led the way, heels click-clicking, through an open gate between buildings. As they crossed the courtyard, she looked back and saw they were being trailed again, this time on foot.

"This way," she repeated, stifling a leaping impulse of fear and wonder at being pursued. Fortunately, she knew the area. She rushed Yuri and Andrei into a restaurant, past the garden tables in the back. Where? Why? a wide-eyed Yuri tried to ask, but followed her trustingly, tremblingly up an alley to a department store, up the stairs and down an escalator, dodging the other customers, and out again into the street. They turned a corner and, panting, ducked a little too rapidly into a café, causing the staff and customers to look up in surprise. But no one followed them in. They were safe for the moment.

Aniela pulled herself together, strolled with grace to a table, and sat down.

Yuri, after sending Andrei to the lavatory to wash his face, sat beside her.

Aniela put her hands on the table and clasped them together. Yuri clasped his hands together in the same manner and set them down very deliberately a centimeter from her own. For long moments neither spoke but only took deep breaths.

She felt dizzy, unable to keep breathing. Nonsense, she told herself valiantly, it was just their escape. And now she was succumbing to the coffeehouse air, so dark, so cocoa, so suffocating, nothing more. But it wasn't true. He was too close, dwarfing his chair, crammed between the tables. She was aware of his hands, his knee, the stubble on his jaw, his unbearable silent attention crushing her. She pulled her hands back; he stared at the top of the table, while she felt herself blushing. So this was how it was, she thought with a kind of hopeless anger. She was relentlessly drawn to this man, maybe even in love with him, maybe even badly so, but she would tell him her news and he would leave the country. There was no future for her feelings.

"I must explain…" she said.

"No," he said, "Wait." He was leaning toward her, speaking rapidly, in an undertone. "I see that something has happened and we are in trouble, but I must take this chance to tell you that I am so very, very glad to see you again. My heart is…"

"No, no, forget that now," she interrupted him.

"But I…"

"Don't say anything—please. I have to tell you, first, that you are being followed. You're in danger and I strongly advise you to leave the country. Go to Germany. Or France. Somewhere where no one will be interested in you. Anywhere but here."

"Who is following us?" asked Yuri, after a moment of keen disappointment at having his declaration chopped short. He leaned back in his chair. Would they never get it right? Would their messages always just slide past each other, two seconds too late or two words wrong? Would he never be free to get on with matters of vital importance to him?

"I don't know." Aniela was still out of breath. "It might be someone sent by my parents, or it might be an undercover policeman—also sent by my parents, maybe someone from the Border Patrol.

"They're after me?"

"Yes. To get at me. It's complicated."

"Yes, but…You could tell me? Please."

But Andrei was rejoining them already. He and Yuri had a rapid exchange in Russian about Iza and the snail. Andrei looked ready to cry again.

"I would not have expected this of Pani Iza," said Yuri soberly. It was not exactly Turgenev's tale of the lady ordering the dispatch of Mumu the dog, but still. Protectiveness for his son surged, along with anger at all cruelty.

"I'm sorry," said Aniela in a rush, "You'll have to forgive Iza. I think she may be slightly affected by some fetal alcohol disorder. Her mother drank. It may be why her life is one error of judgment after another. It's not really her fault."

"Ah," said Yuri, "that is sad too."

"Yes," said Aniela, "But right now, there are other things to think about. I'm going to leave you here, because I have to get back to my apartment before they change the locks. I'll come back, if you can wait...Order something, and I'll pay when I return." Just please wait, she thought, please, but she had no way of knowing whether Yuri would or not, and no right to ask it.

She left the café, rang for another taxi, and stopped on the corner to wait for it. Yuri caught up with her there.

"Change the locks? What does it mean? Please tell me."

She said hurriedly. "My parents told me that I must sign over my apartment and the factory or they would call their contacts in the police or Frontex or I don't know whom and have you picked up. I signed over the apartment but not the factory. Only they haven't realized that yet. And afterwards, they told me that you would be pursued anyway—*ex officio*."

"You gave up your apartment for us? Why? Why did you do that?"

"Because…" she said, gazing unseeing into the distance and shrugging as she turned away. The answer was so obvious.

He followed her. He was too close. He stopped her with the lightest of touches to her bare arm and the longing of that minute contact jolted her whole being, fracturing her previously iron poise.

Here was where she should move away, say goodbye with dignity, put a foot, a yard between her evening dress and his rough jacket. She didn't move. She looked up at him, into his serious, sensitive eyes that mirrored her own shaken state.

"Be-because," she said again.

"Don't go," he said.

There was no longer any distance between them; she was imprisoned and clinging, an element becoming a compound, a matter of syncope and darkness, probably, definitely, fainting.

A taxi had stopped beside them and was idling impatiently.

"Wait for me, please," she gasped, and pulling away from him gently, got in the taxi.

CHAPTER 22

Yuri, half thrilled, half terrified, returned to the restaurant and found Andrei standing at a window, looking out.

"Why were you kissing Pani Aniela?" he asked.

"Er…"

"I ordered some pie," said Andrei, skipping to the important subject without waiting for an answer. Relieved, Yuri followed Andrei back to the table, where they were served large slabs of apple charlotte. Yuri was too excited to eat, but Andrei dug into his dessert. After several bites he stopped though and asked again, "Why were you kissing Pani Aniela?"

This time, Yuri was ready. "Because I love her." He watched his son digest this news along with several more bites of pie. It didn't seem to upset him unduly.

"Does she love you?"

"I don't know. I'm not sure—that's what's killing me. Frankly, I don't know why she would."

Yuri watched his son attempt to imagine an adult relationship. "Mmm…No. But maybe you'll get lucky?"

"Thank you," returned Yuri drily. "I'll have to wait and see."

"She kissed you—that's probably a good sign, isn't it?"

"I don't know, I don't know—maybe it was just, er, the pressure of the moment."

"Will she come back to Ukraine with us?"

So here they were again. "We can't go back to Ukraine."

"I'm not going back to Pani Iza's! I'm *not!*" The tears welled again.

"No."

"Where then?"

"I don't know. We have to wait for Pani Aniela to come back."

*

Aniela, with Yuri's embrace the towering main mast of her thoughts, let herself into her apartment with the knowledge that she should be terribly sad and upset about losing everything, and yet totally unable to stop grinning.

She had to call the movers, and she had to put things in suitcases, and instead she leaned against the wall and giggled—a strange, unaccustomed sound.

After a moment, her habitual efficiency asserted itself. She called a moving company, promised a bonus for after-hours work and expedition, kicked off her heels in order to work faster, and hurriedly began to place valuables in what boxes and suitcases she had available. The movers arrived and began to cart off items. Burly young men and wiry-muscled older ones maneuvered out the door with wobbling loads. Unexpected quantities of dust and strange bits of debris trailed across the floor. At any other time, the sight of her home being stripped bare, hole after hole appearing where familiar objects had once stood, would have filled her with a kind of despair. Today she only thought of Yuri, of a possible new turn to life, and of working faster, because packing, even when items are thrown into containers, is time consuming. She glanced at her clock and decided to call the café where she'd left Yuri. Stepping out of the way of men with boxes, of men moving a table, she rang the number.

"The large man, at the corner table, with a young boy," she said. Could she speak to him? The waiter, hands busy, phone squeezed between his shoulder and his ear, looked over at Yuri, ran his eyes over his foreignness, surmised his poverty, resented his manliness, recoiled mentally, and with the odd atavistic aggression of the herd member against the outcast answered, "They've left."

"Left?"

"That's right, madam, left."

"Did he leave a message?"

"Nope."

Aniela put down her phone. He hadn't waited. She looked around then at her emptying dwelling and began to shake.

*

In the café an hour passed, then two; the waiters began to hover and look disapproving. Yuri glanced in the menu, shuddered, and realized he couldn't pay for their orders. The minutes ticked past and Andrei grew bored and squirmed in his seat. Customers came and went, but Aniela didn't return.

The streets were emptying; the café was closing. Yuri, having humbly received a number of insults from the manager and having left the violin in pawn for the unpaid bill, stood on the sidewalk with Andrei.

"She's not coming."

"No."

"Where will we go?"

"To the riverbank again. Tomorrow…I don't know." He felt like lead. She must have changed her mind. Go to Germany or France? Walk or hitchhike? What difference did it make?

"We don't even have our blanket any more. And with no violin you can't make any money. Except that cleaning job, but that's not for several days."

"That's right. Tomorrow we'll head west."

Andrei, startled by the heaviness of his father's voice, looked up at him and wanted to cheer him. "Now things are getting interesting?"

Yuri tried to smile.

*

Aniela's phone rang. It was Kasia, impatient and more than slightly hostile. She'd just talked to their parents, she said. They'd reminded her she didn't have a sister and invited her to accompany them to the country.

"I think they're going to want me to take on all their plans for you."

"Well, I never agreed to those plans, so that aspect of it doesn't bother me. I hope you'll think about what you're doing. Listen, I've got to pack, so I can't talk now."

"Are you all right, Nela? Because this isn't like you. You know, what you're doing isn't rational at all. You have no place to live, no way of buying another apartment. I'm not even sure you can rent when you don't have a job. I'm sure you're broke because you always give your money away and now you've given what was left to some workers—who were doing something you think is wrong? All this doesn't make sense, Aniela."

"I'll have to get another job."

"Yes, but what will you do? I don't know if you've been looking at the media, but—what I showed you the other day?—it hasn't got any better during the week, it's just beginning to die off a little in volume. I don't know who'd hire you when there are all these rumors about you. And to do what? If you can't be a director, what can you do? No one can live on the salary of a social aid worker or administrative help."

"I'll manage."

"Live in a tiny apartment in the suburbs? Go to work on the bus? You'll be just like a common person…like, like—anybody."

"You know what's common, Kasia? It's people who accept the status quo. It's being part of the gray mass that says, whatever happens to someone else, it's not worth making a fuss over or taking a stand about. Don't be like that, Kasia."

Kasia cut Aniela off briskly, as if to prevent herself from hearing more. "Mama and Tata offered me your apartment. You don't mind, do you? Since you've given it up."

There was a long, long pause, then Aniela said, "If I'd known that, I could have left Grandma and Grandpa's furniture for you."

"No, that's okay. I don't want that old stuff. Mama and Tata said I could redecorate. I can make something of it for my blog."

"Kasia?"

"What?"

"What they're doing is wrong. Don't be part of it. Think about it. Please. Arms manufacturers do not provide heroic soldiers with the means of protecting people. All those high-sounding phrases are just propaganda. Arms manufacturers provide the means of death—"

"Nela, stop it!" Kasia tried to interrupt.

"They provide benefit to no one except themselves. The cost to ordinary people is suffering beyond your imagining. You can't want to be that kind of person."

"Leave me alone, Nela."

"Kasia?" but Kasia had hung up.

A man was standing by the open door, knocking on the frame. "Hello? I've come to change the locks."

Aniela looked around her home. There was next to nothing left. "Okay, that's okay. I'm just leaving."

"I was told there might be someone here, but I was to carry on anyway. I'm sorry, but those were my instructions." The man was attempting to look neutral but was embarrassed enough to find it hard to meet her eyes—such a pretty lady, so proper-looking and soft-spoken. "They paid me a lot to come at this hour," he added, as if to exonerate himself.

"I'm not the owner any more. You can carry on."

The man began to attack the lock with a screwdriver.

"I was told to ask you to leave before I put on the new one," he said to the door.

"I'm going."

Aniela looked about for her shoes and purse and the knapsack she had set aside. The room was quite empty—all the rooms were empty. She thought back—she had put down her purse on the table, and later taken off her shoes and placed them on top of a box. All must have been carried off by the moving men.

This, thought Aniela, is unfortunate.

Hesitatingly, she stepped out onto the landing in her bare feet. But there she was caught between the wall and the locksmith, hunched around the door, so she went tentatively down the steps to the next landing. The surface was strange to the soles of her feet, which had never travelled these stairs nude. She held down the light switch to see her watch and found it was almost one o'clock. She would have to call Kasia and ask her to come to the rescue with a pair of shoes. Then she remembered she couldn't call because her phone was in her purse, and her money and credit cards too. She tried to think whose doorbell she could ring at that hour of the night, but as she pondered a mental list of faces and doors, she knew her neighbors were all too elderly to be disturbed or too new and unfamiliar to her.

She also knew that the last thing she wanted was to have to hold herself together while she explained her situation to any one on whose door she might conceivably knock. She sat down on the cold marble of the staircase and leaned against the balusters. Yuri, she thought, Yuri, where are you?

She should be worrying about her own situation, but he was all she could think about. Had he left because he didn't want to wait, or had he been forced to flee or been picked up by the police?

She shivered. She could sit here until morning, she supposed, or go out into the night air and shiver there. Iza's apartment was within walking distance. She would have liked to avoid seeing Iza again, but her options were limited.

Despite the hour, there were quite a lot of people about in the street and the lamps lit the sidewalks with an almost noontime brightness. She would have preferred a more discreet illumination. The cobbles and pavement bruised her feet, but she tried to walk without concession to grit and barbs. She marched past elderly American tourists, still out with their canes, past groups of thirtyish Britons, weaving and loud, past trios or quartets of local youngsters, still seeking some mild adventure at midnight. Most passed her without noticing her unshod state; others fixed their eyes on her feet as she approached; one man took a photo with his phone. At that she plunged off the pedestrian thoroughfare of Krakowskie Przedmieście and strode between the buildings, alone and in the dark, past empty-eyed windows and boxes of red geraniums, over bits of broken glass noticed just too late, down a series of brick staircases to Dynasy Street, the sad corruption of a prince de Nassau's former domain. There, beneath the engulfing branches of the escarpment's brief wilderness, she stopped suddenly in the obscurity, prey to such a sense of loss that she sat down on a damp wall, regardless of the damage to her dress, and felt powerless to move on—or move at all. She could only shiver. Perhaps she would never see Yuri again. He would leave the country, go to France or Germany or somewhere else in the wide world, and she would never find him. Perhaps he did not want to be found. Perhaps the kiss she had understood as a commencement he had meant as a farewell.

After a while, she rose and walked on, with feet that were first sore and then bleeding, until she came to Iza's apartment. She let herself in, rode the elevator up, and pressed the doorbell. Nothing happened, so she held her finger to the bell and listened to it ring futilely inside the apartment for long minutes. Eventually there was a cursing, shuffling sound and Iza's voice behind the door asked angrily and suspiciously, "Who's there?"

"Iza, it's me, Nela."

The door was yanked wide and Iza stood foursquare in front of her in a rumpled robe and hair over her eyes. "At this hour, Nela? What do you want? Some friend you are." Iza jerked her head. "Come inside, the neighbors'll hear." Aniela stepped inside and Iza continued, "You've got some nerve getting me out of bed like this—and you've got some nerve foisting your refugees on me."

It was not the first time Iza had leveled accusations at her, but such sentiments always took Aniela by surprise. She began to defend herself, "But you wanted them to come—" and then stopped abruptly.

"But you didn't tell me not to, did you? I always relied on you, Nela, and you let me down. My home is ruined. *Ruined.* That kid was a maniac. And Yuri—I thought there'd be some use of him, but *nothing*, not a thing. He just used me."

"*Used* you?"

"He just wanted a place to sleep, that's *all*, nothing more. And you didn't warn me, or anything—." Iza broke off suddenly. "Why are you here now, in the middle of the night? And where are your shoes?" snorted Iza, "And what did you do to your dress? Were you sitting in a mud puddle or something?"

"No, it's—I need your help."

Iza laughed sarcastically. "No way, darling. I'm still mad at you."

Iza, Aniela reminded herself, wasn't entirely responsible for herself. She took a deep breath and tried again. "Okay. I understand you're angry. Could I call Kasia from your phone? Just that?"

Kasia was scarcely more supportive. "I thought you were eager to experience living without your family. Anyway, I'm not supposed to be associating with you. Mama and Tata's orders," she said coolly. "Get Iza to help you."

"She won't."

"'She can't help being the way she is. We have to be forgiving'," Kasia quoted mockingly. "Do you still think that?"

"Yes."

"You're unbelievable, but I have better things to do

than listen to goody-goody speeches."

"Just bring me the shoes and I won't say anything but 'thank you'," said Aniela.

"Hmm," said Kasia, and after a long and wounding silence, agreed to come to Aniela's rescue.

Aniela prepared to wait, standing wearily in the entryway of Iza's apartment.

"I'm going back to bed," said Iza in irritation.

"There's something I want to tell you first," said Aniela.

"What?"

"I'm in love with Yuri," said Aniela.

"*What?*"

"I think he's probably left Warsaw, and I'll probably never see him again, but all the same, I wanted you to know."

"I always thought you were my friend," said Iza with a look of consternation and disgust. "And you cut me out like that?"

"No, Iza, he wasn't your boyfriend. He's not mine either. I'm just in love."

"Well, you can have him. The jerk. And his kid. Especially his kid. Not only is that boy a devil but did you know he has nightmares or something and wakes up every night shouting? I didn't get a wink of sleep. But I think you behaved really badly to me." She stomped out of the room.

Kasia arrived in Aniela's car, and in near total silence, handed her sister a pair of shoes and a change of clothes.

She drove her to a bargain hotel, paid for a room while Aniela waited in the vehicle, and then came back with the key. She held it out.

"Thank you," said Aniela.

"Since you're here, I'd like you to sign the car over to me, if you don't mind. Mama and Tata agree. You won't be using it," said Kasia harshly, "I brought the paper."

Aniela signed. "I love you too," she said.

It was the first time she remembered saying those words to Kasia. The first time in ten years that she had said them to anyone.

"I'm the one who sacrificed for the family," said Kasia defensively, "I deserve what I can get."

"Kasia," said Aniela, struck by a thought, "Do you mean you sacrificed your boyfriend—the one you've been mentioning recently? Do you wish you hadn't? Because you could have refused Mama's dictates, couldn't you? You were of age."

"No, he gave *me* up, remember. But it was just as well. What, give up all this money, this lifestyle, for love? Of course not. I'm not stupid. Money and power are the only tangible, worthwhile things in the world. You know that."

"I can't believe you think that."

Kasia wouldn't look at her sister, but fixed her gaze somewhere up the dark street. "Anyway…he got married last week."

"I'm sorry, Kasia. I'm really, really, sorry I wasn't available when you needed me."

"You were only going to say 'thank you.' Get out."

"Thank you. Goodbye."

Aniela passed the night in a room the size of a chicken cage, in a high-rise building stuffed with such coops. In the morning she collected her belongings from the movers.

Then she began to search for Yuri. She returned to the café where she had left him and Andrei the night before, on the chance he might have left word for her with a different waiter than the one she'd reached on the phone. He had left no message, she was told, only his violin in surety for the price of pie, and—the manager was happy to say—he had not been back. It was early yet. She paid the bill, collected the violin, and left a message for Yuri should he return, though she doubted it would be passed on. If he wanted to reach her he wouldn't find her at home, the email address he'd used once was her work one, and he didn't know her phone number—but he could ask Iza. Hopefully, he would call. She was disappointed her phone showed no missed calls, but she invented myriad explanations: he had no money; he hadn't wanted to call during the night; he was waiting for Iza to cool off after the contretemps with Andrei. She could expect to hear from him during the day, she assured herself. But as the hours passed, this hope diminished. Perhaps he had been picked up by the Border Patrol—but in that case, surely he would have tried to contact her, as his last, only, recourse, she reasoned.

In the afternoon she set out to search, quartering the Old Town before walking several miles of the Vistula banks on either side, along the walkways and into the woods. She encountered walkers, bikers, beaver dams, the flattened grass of picnickers, evidence of drunken parties, some fishermen, random nature lovers, cranes, ducks, gulls, and dogs, but no Yuri. She pushed through willow thickets and stepped in ant hills. Thinking it more circumspect than bellowing his name in bovine fashion, she periodically took out the violin and played the first bars of Pachelbel's *Canon*, but no one came crashing through the bushes in answer. Very tired and discouraged, she finally had to accept that if he wanted to get in touch with her, he would.

*

It was as she was heading wearily into the underpass of the boulevard that her phone rang. She snatched for it with such haste that it jumped from her hand like a minnow and she managed to drop it, a kind of clumsiness that almost never afflicted her. She picked it up and, calming herself, raised it in measured fashion to her ear.

"Hello?"

"Nela, you have to help me!" came Iza's chirping voice. "I decided to leave my job today, and you have to help me find a new one."

"Iza," said Aniela struggling with disappointment. She looked up to find herself facing the bristling concrete guns and soldiers of a large bas-relief on the underpass wall. She stared down the barrels as she answered, "I thought you were angry with me."

"I was, but never mind that—now I need your help, darling, so listen—I need a new job. What do you think?

Do you have any ideas? Because I don't like my boss and I think he was really unreasonable to be so upset about one *small* mistake…"

Aniela didn't bother to ask what small mistake. Quite possibly it wasn't so small. Sometimes Iza kept a job for a year, maybe two, sometimes only for a couple of months or less. Sooner or later, in spite of having considerable abilities, she became too much of a burden on the workplace and was let go. For years, Aniela had used her contacts, sought the aid of her parents, made telephone calls on Iza's behalf, written her CVs, helped her find another position and supported her once she was hired.

"I'd help you if I could, but you know, I'm out of work myself."

"What—you mean you're g-going to be all offended and not help me? Really? You're not a very g-g-good friend." Iza began to cry.

"I only mean I'm not in a position to help you the way I used to," said Aniela wearily, feeling a slight jolt at this first evidence of the forfeits involved in her loss of status.

"Well, whose fault is that?" said Iza with a return of anger, "Why should I have to suffer? I think you're being selfish."

"Iza, I'll do what I can. Tonight there's a wedding I have to attend…"

She had mentioned it to Yuri as they sat together on the riverbank, pointing out to him the distant contours of the building where the reception would be held. It had been an offhand comment, but perhaps, just perhaps, he might remember?

"You don't like weddings. I bet you hardly know the couple. Skip it and come to me."

"I don't like weddings. But when I say I'll be somewhere, I try to be there. I'll call tomorrow and we'll think of a plan of action."

*

A line of cars with thick, shiny lacquer—Mercedes, BMWs, a Bentley—drew up in turn before the lighted canopy of a palace hotel. Passenger doors opened. Heavy older men in dark suits hauled themselves upright. Women —it was always a high-heeled leg that appeared first and hung in mid-air before being followed by a round or svelte body and a head of dyed hair. The women hurried inside, out of the wind, while the men came together with a certain strut, like pigeons before a feeding. The younger, fitter members, alert for some crumb of opportunity, hung about the portico.

Aniela descended from a taxi and slipped in quietly, past the swagged tulle and the massed white roses and the men who meant nothing to her.

When Yuri arrived the guests had already been swallowed by the red-carpeted entrance. He waited in front of the palace, to the side, until it became clear he was drawing the attention of the doormen and moved further away, to sit on the concrete base of a wrought-iron fence.

Inside they were eating, he knew, and tried not to let his imagination dwell on rows of plates blockaded with silver and crystal, on decorative starters, on steaming main dishes brought round in repetition. He hadn't eaten in twenty-four hours. From inside came the sound of music—danceable, decades-old tunes meant to stir and cheer the listener. His mind was empty of everything but food and Aniela and not even the music could distract him.

After a time he was joined on the sidewalk by an older man in a dirty apron.

"Let me guess. You're here for the wedding," the man joked as he took in Yuri's squatting perch and unfed gaze. He added, as if to assert that his status, however lowly, was higher than Yuri's, "Me too—I work in the kitchen."

"You are fortunate," said Yuri.

The man took out a cigarette. "I'd move on, if I were you," he continued, half officious, half good-natured, "if security sees you, they can be unpleasant. They've been chasing photographers away."

"I want to talk to someone inside."

"Who's that then?"

"Pani Aniela Solan."

Curiosity and uncertainty flickered in the man's eyes; he shrugged to indicate he didn't know any Pani Aniela. "I doubt they'll let you in. Why don't you call her?"

"No telephone."

The man held out his own and Yuri, not wanting to admit he didn't know the number, pressed buttons at random.

"No one answers. With such loud music maybe she can't hear. Or maybe she's turned it off."

"Or maybe she doesn't want to answer," said the man.

"That is also possible."

"Come around to the back," said the man, with a look

of compassion at Yuri's sadness. "Maybe I can find some-one to take a message for you. Here," he gestured toward the front of the hotel, "no one will help you."

Inside, dinner was over. There had been toasts and ten courses of food and the price of the proceedings had been discussed with disapproval and envy. The drinking and dancing had become steady. The music drowned all conversation. Aniela had spent the meal being profoundly grateful that her parents were seated at a different table, and had had the opportunity to count—with chagrin but no surprise by now—the number of her acquaintances who had decided to navigate between not quite noticing her and openly snubbing her. As the evening progressed, however, she began to be importuned with invitations to dance by men who had drunk enough to forget that she was a repressively chilly woman with an aura of scandal about her.

Champagne glass in hand, she was edging round a pillar to avoid another such encounter when she found herself face to face with her mother. She started, her drink splashed down her fingers, and she saw her mother's eyes narrow. Her mother leaned toward her and Aniela saw her lips moving but she couldn't hear over the pounding of the music. She bent nearer.

Her mother yelled in her ear, "I didn't think you'd have the nerve to show yourself in a public place."

Aniela yelled back, "Why not? I haven't done anything wrong." As she said the words, she realized, with a lift of her sad heart, that it was a beautiful thing to have a clean conscience.

Her mother shouted, certain that no one three feet away could hear them, "What about tricking your parents? That signature was *base*. And what about disrespecting your parents?"

When Aniela looked unrepentant, she continued, "And you know something else? Your *Professor* Yuri Romen—he doesn't exist."

"What do you mean?" thought Aniela, startled, but she retained the presence of mind to be silent.

"No one can find a trace of him anywhere. There is not, nor was, any such professor at any Ukrainian university. Everything he told you is *lies*. Lies, lies, lies. What a dupe you are."

Aniela didn't answer, and her mother, seeing that her words had hit their mark, turned and walked away.

Of course, thought Aniela, Yuri would be using an alias—that made sense. On the other hand, it was unsettling to realize that she had been prepared to give herself entirely—bodily—to a man whose name she didn't even know. She put a hand on the pillar for balance as she felt the ground slip a little between her feet. But no, at once memories of Yuri came crowding—his words, and more, his actions. She believed in him.

As soon as she could she made her way to the entrance of the palace for a breath of air and to search for Yuri in the street. When she had made this trip three times, she knew she was deluding herself—he had not remembered or he did not want to come—but still she did it. She had another half hour to endure, she thought, before she could decently slip away.

A man detached himself from the building opposite and hurried across to her. A long-haired youngish man in tight black pants, carrying a camera and a notepad—a journalist, he said. He had thought she might be here—he was pleased with himself for being right—he was stepping in front of her, eager to know the truth of the rumors about her. She said she didn't know of any rumors. Surely she'd read the speculation as to why she'd left her position so abruptly? Was it because she was one of the persons recorded in the Taping Affair? No, she said to the journalist, she hadn't been taped—that is, she didn't know if she had been or not, but she hadn't been informed of such an occurrence. She deplored the invasion of privacy but felt certain she hadn't said anything that couldn't be heard by everyone.

"So your problems have nothing to do with being taped?"

"I don't have any problems."

"Really?"

"No."

"Oh, so you left the ministry on a whim?"

She had known well that those in the public eye walk a tightrope with the media; she had known that a single slip could send a person tumbling to social death. If the relative scale of transgressions seemed unjust to her, she held no grudge against the journalists. She paused and said calmly, "No, it was a considered decision for personal reasons. Excuse me." She tried to pass on, but the journalist stepped in front of her again.

"The personal reasons aren't problems? Because I read you were upset about your parents' business."

"Really? Where did you read that?"

"Twitter."

"I don't have a Twitter account."

"Well, not yours. Somebody else's."

Iza probably, thought Aniela, wretched Iza.

"So it isn't true?"

"I was very sorry to learn that my parents are engaged in the arms trade, yes," she said reluctantly.

"Why? What's wrong with that?"

"No comment. Excuse me, please," she tried to leave.

"No comment—that means they're doing something illegal?"

"No. Immoral," said Aniela, pushed to the wall, "We disagree on a point of ethics."

"Your parents are immoral? You're saying that? Can I quote you?"

"No, leave my parents out of it, please! You can quote this: I say manufacturing arms is the cause of more suffering and is more unethical than drug dealing, human trafficking, or producing child pornography. Everyone can see the evil in those and lets the other pass, but it's the difference between abetting abuse and abetting murder."

"Do your parents deal in child pornography?"

"Of course not! Listen to what I'm saying!"

"So I'll say that you see a link between your parents' business activities and sexual misconduct and have left your position as a result." He was backing away.

"I never said anything of the kind! I was trying to make a point about the industry," cried Aniela in alarm, but he was already retreating through the crowd. "Wait!" But he wouldn't.

Aniela raised her hand to her forehead. A taxi was approaching; the driver was looking her over. She gestured and he pulled to the curb.

Behind the palace, Yuri was waiting under the baleful eye of a distant guard, planted with arms akimbo at the service door. Eventually the man in the apron came out and waved to him. Yuri bounded up in hope, but no, the man was sorry, the servers had looked for the lady but she seemed to have disappeared. The place with her name card remained empty. Yuri started to leave, but his eye was caught by the contents of an open dumpster. He reached in and extracted a carrot—"Hey! Leave that there!" shouted the guard—but Yuri brushed off the dirt and walked away munching it, to the diminishing and derisively cheerful tune of *La Bamba*.

*

Aniela sat on the bed in her bargain hotel room, trying to block out its frightening beige sterility as she made phone calls. No, it wasn't possible to discover the name of a young academic on a fellowship in Cambridge ten years ago. Or the true name of a literature professor no longer employed by one of the now-closed universities in the eastern provinces of Ukraine.

As she was searching for some clue to Yuri's identity,

her phone rang. It was Iza.

"What are you doing, Nela? Are you looking for jobs for me?"

"No, I'm looking for Yuri."

"Kasia says your parents say he's not who he pretends to be because there's no trace of him and no one even knows what his name is."

"His identity is more than his vitae and I don't need his name to know who he is—I already know that. I just want to find him. You're sure you haven't heard from him?"

"No," lied Iza.

"Iza, are you *sure*? Please, Iza. It matters so much to me."

"No. And anyway, why should you get him if I can't have him?"

"Iza, I want to make sure he's all right. I want to know if I can help him. I want…"

"I'm not stupid, Nela. I know what you want."

"I really, really, want to find him, Iza. So if you've heard anything of him—please."

"Let him go back where he came from. I mean, he's just a foreigner, Nela."

Aniela put down the phone and tried not to give in to uncontrollable shaking, to the ache of every muscle from the idea that it was increasingly likely she would never see Yuri again and never know if everything that might have been—shared joys, sorrows, conversations, kisses, touches, union, minor pleasures, household routines, major events, ideas, differences, everything day in, day out, down half a century of life ahead of her—would not happen because

he had not wanted it to or because they could not find
each other.

CHAPTER 23

Yuri and Andrei sat in the sand, watching the embers of their fire send an occasional tipsy spark into the darkness. It was late and the last of the beachgoers had departed.

"We should get some sleep," said Yuri, "Tomorrow we'll leave Warsaw."

"You say that every day," said Andrei. "You've been saying it for days."

"This time I mean it," said Yuri, his eyes avoiding those of his son, and travelling into the distance, to the river, to the far bank, to the city where Aniela was hidden somewhere, to the nearest bridge, where the pedestrians had been reduced by the lateness of the hour to a sole figure standing in the middle of the span. Yuri's gaze travelled on, over shafts of light in the water and barely bobbing boats, and back again, to the figure on the bridge. His imagination toyed with the idea that it might be Aniela and his rational mind rejected the notion. It was hard to tell because of the distance, but he thought the figure was a man.

"It seems so random."

"What's random?"

The word took him back in memory to his afternoon with Aniela on this same beach.

"My mother thinks you're a Russian agent," she said,

"because the fall of the angel was too much of a coincidence. I think she's wrong, but it seems there should be some significance in our meeting that way—only I don't know if it's suggestive of something good or something bad."

"Ah, yes. You mean it should symbolize our imperfect natures or the imperative to help each other against the defec—"

"Defective."

"—defective structures we erect—something like that. But no," he replied, smiling at her, "I think it suggests randomness, nothing more." Her eyes had met his and what he had seen there hinted at some more intimate, more passionately felt message. Then she had turned her face away and he had felt abandoned, in a sudden cold breeze.

Now, to Andrei, he asked again, "What's random?"

"Everything that's happened to us—the people burning our house, and our coming here, and you meeting Pani Aniela, and now we're just leaving. It doesn't make sense. We're like a branch in the river—we just get carried along downstream or washed up on a sandbar but we don't have any say in the matter."

Even if one's thoughts were wrapped python-like round a certain woman, serious questions raised by a young son had to receive their due or they might never be asked again.

"No," said Yuri, making an effort, "I'd say we're not like that branch, because we're animate; we have minds. Maybe there are forces that carry us along and maybe they seem overwhelming, but we can react. We can make choices. We can try to be our best selves no matter what happens."

"I don't feel like I'm myself at all. I'm somebody different than I used to be back home."

"You've grown—and that's good," said Yuri, wondering what scars his son carried. "Listen," he said seriously, "some events are accidents and some are consequences, but our task is to face each difficult occurrence as if it were an opportunity to prove our worth by being brave or honest or compassionate or thinking or whatever. If anything happens to me, I hope you'll remember that."

"Why? What's going to happen to you?"

"Nothing, undoubtedly nothing. I'm the first immortal man. My point is we have to try to be honorable. How would it be if we never had to make an effort?"

Andrei shrugged. "Better."

"Don't shrug. Really? What do you think?—When I learned that Aniela's parents were arms manufacturers should I have pretended it didn't matter? They have influence. We might have got asylum. You'd go to school. All our problems might have been over—no more being hungry, no more sleeping in the cold…"

To himself he added, "no more worries of ending up in jail or dead, of you going to an orphanage, of you being abused, of growing up ignorant and warped. All I had to do was look in the other direction. Was that really so hard? Just not to notice?"

Out loud, he said, "We'd live in comfort, happily ever after…what do you think?"

"Do you regret it?" asked Andrei, uncertainly.

"No."

"But Pani Aniela isn't like her parents, is she?" said Andrei. "Why didn't she come back that night?"

"I don't know. Perhaps she couldn't, or perhaps she doesn't want to. Her situation is difficult, I suppose." He grasped a handful of sand and felt it trickle from his fist, like all the hopes he couldn't hold.

"Why don't you call her?"

"I don't know her number."

"Why don't you go to her apartment?"

Yuri shook his head, not bothering to explain. "If the border guard is looking for us, we can't stay."

"I thought you were in love with her."

"I'll learn to live without her," said Yuri.

"But," said Andrei, "it's not really fair, is it?"

"What's not fair?"

"You lose everything. And other people," he waved toward the bridge with its diminishing stream of cars and bicyclists, toward the illuminated city sprawled on the other bank, "have everything."

"No," said Yuri, leaning back on his elbows, and closing his eyes, "most don't have everything. Not everyone is healthy; not everyone is happy. Not everyone has a great son like I do."

Andrei declined to notice this unusual bit of sentiment, "But what are you going to do?"

"What can I do? I'll just have to concentrate on being a good person."

"I bet you wish you were with Pani Aniela instead."

"Well…"

Andrei glanced at his father and sat up straighter. "Are you all right?"

Yuri made a giant effort for his son and answered in a level voice, "I'm all right."

Yuri pulled apart the last burning branches of their fire, and with his cracked shoes, pushed sand over the remaining embers until he was quite sure the fire was extinguished. When he was done, his gaze traveled again to the bridge. To his surprise, the figure was still there, still in the middle of the span, bending now over the railing a little, head and shoulders hunched toward the water.

Of course, thought Yuri, it was absurd suddenly to start imagining that the man—he was certain the figure was a man—was intending to jump from the bridge. He mustn't start envisioning dangers where there were none. On the other hand, he had sat opposite the church and seen the crumbling cornice, and although he had felt obliged to point it out to the authorities, he hadn't really, truly, expected anything to happen. And then the angel had come smashing down and almost killed the woman he loved. He rose, undecided.

"Andrei," he said, but Andrei had fallen asleep in the sand. He shook him slightly, "Andrei, I'll be right back— I'm going to talk to a man on the bridge."

Andrei nodded without opening his eyes and Yuri set off for the bridge, walking only slightly more rapidly than normal and feeling certain he was being ridiculous, that the man would simply be enjoying the sight of the river, or be immersed in thought, or composing a poem, or drunk, but not suicidal. Nevertheless, after a moment he broke into a jog. Ahead of him, on the bridge, the man put a foot on the railings and raised himself a foot or two. Yuri began to run pell-mell. A couple of bicyclists pedaled onto the bridge and sped rapidly, bent over their handle-bars, toward the figure in the center of the bridge. The man stepped down again and waited as the cyclists raced past and onwards.

Yuri bolted onto the bridge as the cyclists whizzed by. Yelling "Hey! Hey!" he pounded toward the middle of the span and as he drew nearer he realized that the man, who was once again putting his foot on the railing, was Aniela's father. The idea that this was an arms manufac-turer, a man willing to harm his own daughter, a man who'd informed on him out of spite, flashed through his mind but didn't stick.

"Wait!" he called as he ran and the words came out breathless and quavering with the thuds of his feet.

The man hoisted himself a little higher.

"Wait!" Yuri shouted across the distance, "Mr. Solan! Mr. Solan!"

On hearing his name, the man looked round startled. He stepped down and waited until Yuri was near enough to recognize.

"You! Here!" he said in a strangled voice. "Don't come any closer."

Yuri stopped, some thirty feet away.

"What are you doing, Panie Marku?" he panted. "I saw you from the beach—"

"I am, as you have properly surmised," said Aniela's father testily, "about to jump." His eyes glittered. "Very appropriate you should be here to watch. If I thought you had a conscience it would be satisfying, but I know you don't.—Don't come any closer!"

"But sir—"

"It was you who told Nela to close the factory, wasn't it? And the media—that was your idea too?"

"Your daughter," said Yuri, in a voice that trembled, "will be very graved—."

"Gri*e*ved," corrected Aniela's father automatically, angrily. "It doesn't seem to *grieve* her that we're going to lose everything—everything we've worked for all these years. It doesn't *grieve* her that she's made me into a pariah."

Yuri reached his hand pleadingly toward the other man, "Don't do something you'll regret."

Aniela's father snorted. "I can't regret anything when I'm dead, you fool. Don't come closer." He lifted himself onto the edge of the railing, swung his legs over, and teetered on the outside of the railing, hanging on still, but looking down. "I mean it! Don't come any closer! Let me have some p-p-peace in my last moments, for G-God's sake."

Yuri froze. He was too far away—if Aniela's father let go of the railing, he would never reach him before he fell.

"But that's what I'm trying to tell you—" Yuri's heart skipped beats as he thought fast and his mind dredged up something Aniela had told him—"you can't kill yourself here. The water isn't deep enough."

"*What?*"

"Global warming. Or maybe just cyclical droot. I don't know. But the river is very low now. I assure you—the fishermen walk across the river in their high boots. You can't drown yourself. You probably just break your legs. Or your back. Then maybe you drown, but it won't be the swift death in the strong undertow like you imagine. You have to rethank this."

Aniela's father peered at the black water for a moment and then gave a cracked laugh. "I don't even know if you're telling me the truth."

Yuri nodded vigorously and lied through his teeth. "True, true, true."

Slowly, Aniela's father climbed back over the railing and leaned against it, turned away from the river, looking up at the sky. Eventually he sought relief in a quiet string of obscenities, which he enunciated without any particular vigor or emphasis, as if they were the only words surfacing from his subconscious in this extremity. Soon he came to the end of all he knew, and only occasionally tossed out a new one, as it occurred to him, like a car coughing as it runs out of fuel.

"What has perspiritated this?" asked Yuri, coming to stand beside him.

"Precirp—oh, forget it," said Aniela's father irritably, folding his arms across his stomach as if in pain. "You ask that? You? When you started it all? We didn't have these problems with Nela before you came along—"

"*Post hoc ergo...*" Yuri tried to defend himself, but he was again interrupted.

"Don't tell me you haven't seen the news this week?"

"I am living on a damp sandbank. I don't read the news."

"We're ruined—"

"Ah. Good. How so?"

Aniela's father gave Yuri a long unreadable look. "Our name is mud. What was being said about Nela is nothing in comparison—the Vistula doesn't hold that much mud. Twenty-five years of building up our business, our name, our position—twenty-five years. Our daughter gives an interview to a reporter and in five minutes, maybe ten, it's all over." His voice faltered. "Ten minutes to ruin a reputation it took twenty-five years to build. I don't know what she said—something brainless about the arms trade being as bad as selling child pornography or something crazy like that—she said that to us once before. Now we're supposed to be sex offenders or something. I am, at least—my wife gets less of it. There's so much talk in the media the prosecutor is making inquiries. It doesn't matter that they won't find anything because we're branded forever. It's so ironic—our only fault is having a disloyal daughter and caring about the security of our country."

"Yes, it's ironic to be ruined for an offense you did not commit, when you were actually doing something much worse."

"It is *not* worse."

"Killing children is not worse than abusing them?"

"*Protection.* We were providing the means of *protection.*"

"Where's that then—all these protected people? Because when the two sides got their guns in my part of the world, protected is not what we felt."

"No one can help the collateral damage."

"Yes, they can. They can not start shooting."

Aniela's father turned his head slowly and gave Yuri a long stare. "Some rescuer you are."

"You don't believe it yourself. I see that—You don't believe your own slogans even."

"I knew you were behind all this. You brainwashed our daughter. I hope you're happy." Aniela's father tipped his head back again, but closed his eyes, and began to repeat the string of obscenities, slowly, savoring each.

Yuri wasn't sure what Aniela's father was talking about. He said cautiously, "I have not washbrained your daughter. I have not known her enough to wash her brain. She has her own ideas. But I can not believe she wanted this with the media. It seems not like her. She wanted only to stop your war business, I think."

Without opening his eyes or moving his head, Aniela's father answered, "I don't know. I hardly know her, I realize, but I always thought she felt some affection for us. I was wrong, obviously…Oh, what difference does any of it make now? You know what's the worst of it? You're right—deep down I feel I deserve it, and what Nela thinks is true. But my wife will never understand that. And this will follow me now for the rest of my life. Which I hope will be short."

"I did not know you are a curward."

"What?"

"Croward?"

"I'm baring my soul to you, as the last person ever, and you speak to me that way?" Aniela's father managed a brief surge of anger.

"Looks like it to me. At least *you* have a roof over your head. Two of them. Roofs, that is."

"I'm an outcast. Even my daughter has turned against me. And my wife—my wife doesn't understand. What can I do? What am I going to do?"

"Well, not kill yourself….Man needs a little adversity in his life. It's good to do new things."

"What do you know of it?"

"Something. A little something by now."

Aniela's father made a small sound that might have been either admission or rejection of Yuri's viewpoint. "What are you doing here?" he asked suddenly. "How did you turn up here?"

"I live here," said Yuri, gesturing toward the riverbank. He would be gone tomorrow.

Aniela's father peered at the dark band of trees and brush along the water's edge. "You have no home and no name. I wish I could escape that way."

No you don't, thought Yuri. Out loud he said gently, "Come. I've left my son sleeping down there. It makes me nerves to leave him for so long. Come with me to collect him, and then we will go to your home."

"Ah, the boy who likes cats. He's a good boy."

"Yes, although you are trying to get him deported, and me, back to where someone could drop a bomb on him. One of yours, perhaps."

"Well, nothing personal, you know." Aniela's father struck the iron barrier with his palm, lightly, and pushed away from it. "You go to him—I'll say goodbye to you here. I've taken up enough of your time. Good evening," He bowed slightly, and turned away.

"Wait!" said Yuri, uncertain what to do and imagining Aniela's father climbing to the top of the nearest high rise or hanging himself with his belt. "I do not want to leave you alone. Please come with me."

Aniela's father looked all about, vaguely, as if seeking other ideas, and then with a hopeless gesture of his hands, he shook his head, and moving a bit like a sleepwalker, began to walk away.

"No," he said in a polite tone, "You can go to hell."

Yuri watched him retreat, torn between his son below, alone, on the dark and deserted beach, and this self-pitying and suicidal idiot, who also happened to be Aniela's father and was, in any case, a human being in need. He calculated the time it would take for the man to cross the bridge at this slow pace. If he ran, perhaps he would have time to collect Andrei and then return and catch up with him.

He was starting to turn when out of the corner of his eye he saw a bus loom onto the far end of the bridge, and at the same time Aniela's father headed across the street toward it. Yuri ran and caught up with him, putting a hand on his arm. Aniela's father shook him off.

"Leave me alone, I said."

"Please," said Yuri, "please come with me. I cannot leave you—"

"How touching."

"Sir, I cannot tell what facts are weighting your mind, but I am sure it is never too late to be a better person, and someday you will be glad that I do not let you kill yourself, and besides, under a bus, it is very massy and not nice for the driver."

"What?"

"Never mind. Don't do it. Please, come with me." Yuri tried to pull him along. Aniela's father resisted, attempting to shake him off, but Yuri was much larger and heavier.

"You're really very irritating, you know. This is ridiculous. Let go of me!"

"Yes, but come."

"If I come with you to your son, you'll leave me in peace?"

"Yes. Maybe."

Aniela's father allowed himself to be shepherded to the end of the bridge and through the woods. After a time they were trudging in the heavy sand of the beach, Yuri some meters ahead, trying to hurry his companion.

Here were the stands of swamp grass and willow that hid the camp site. He stepped into the clearing. It was empty. In the dim light he could make out the darker spot of their fire on the sand and the impression where Andrei had lain.

"Andrei!" he called softly, but there was no answer.

Yuri looked all around. Surely this was the place. "Andrei?" he called louder and waited, but the only the sounds were the usual ones of traffic, and distant music, and small rustlings of leaves.

"Andrei!" he shouted, really bellowing now and beginning to be frightened.

Still there was no answer.

He listened but again all he heard was the sudden rasping of his own breath and the nighttime noise of the city.

"Andrei!"

"Maybe you've got the wrong place?" said Aniela's father.

"No." Forgetting his companion entirely, Yuri began to search, quartering back and forth through the reeds and brush, falling into holes and stumbling over buried branches and concrete blocks, but finding no one. When he had run all the way back and forth again to the bridge, he returned to Aniela's father.

"Where could he have gone?" said Aniela's father, in the confused tone of someone emerging from a coma to find his help is urgently needed.

"I don't know," panted Yuri, "I don't think he'd leave —unless he came to find me. Where would he go? What has happen to him? I am afraid—there are sometimes strange people around here."

"Be calm," said Aniela's father, his voice shaking slightly. "Let's be calm and think. Maybe he fell in the water."

"No. He is eleven and not stupid. In water he will not fall. I am afraid he is kidnapped."

"No. No. This does not happen much in Poland," said Aniela's father, his national pride piqued and pleased to one-up Yuri. "Maybe in Ukraine, but we don't do that here. Poland is a very safe place. Maybe he went to look for you on the other bridge." He waved toward it.

They hurried toward it, searching and calling.

At the bridge, Yuri turned in every direction. What to

do now? What on earth to do now? Above them, a dark cage of steel girders rose out of the deeper shadows of the embankment. Beyond, the bulk of the national stadium hovered, lit, like an enormous tartar tent with lances.

"If I call the police, maybe they will help me find him, but then they will arrest us—"

"Great," muttered Aniela's father, "now I'm going to be involved in a disappearance."

"You were going to kill yourself, anyway."

"It's looking more attractive every moment."

"You *egotist!*—Will you stop thinking of yourself for one damn second and try to help me?" shouted Yuri. "Anyway, if you kill yourself after being in spot where a child has disappearated the two events will be forever joined in everyone's mind."

"You have a point," said Aniela's father, quivering a little.

"So it is in your interest to help me! And also you owe me, because I save you from a terrible death! So now you must stop a taxi and drive about the streets here, looking—he can't have gone far in this time. I must stay here, in case he comes back to find me. Will you do this? And after that, I promise, you can jump off any bridge you like."

"I can't stop a taxi. I left my wallet at home."

"Walk then. Go look now, go!"

Aniela's father hesitated and then nodded his head.

"If he comes back here, I will light a fire. You can see it from far."

Yuri turned away, but he was called back by Aniela's

father. "Did your son give you any idea where he might go? Was he talking about doing something or going somewhere?"

"He talks always about going back to Ukraine. But I am one hundred percent sure he will not go without me."

"Someplace else then. Maybe if you think back, there's a clue somewhere—what were you talking about this evening?"

"Only about your daughter," said Yuri with an impatient wave. He watched for a moment as Aniela's father retreated with uncertain step and then ran to catch up with him. "Please," he said, "Please tell me the phone number of Aniela."

Aniela's father eyed him obstinately and then shook his head brusquely—"That, no!"—and walked away.

Yuri ran in the other direction and then back toward the street and the bike paths, to find a bicyclist. The first three to pass refused to stop; the fourth agreed reluctantly to let Yuri use his phone. Yuri called Iza, and after he insisted, time and again, that it could be a matter of life and death, she gave him the number of Aniela's mother. Yuri counted the rings as the bicyclist stood by, foot on the pedal, wary and impatient, ready to take off again. At last Aniela's mother picked up.

"Hello? Who's calling at this hour?" the voice was sharp and suspicious.

"It is I, the Ukrainian—"

"What do you want?"

"It's about your husband," Yuri spoke fast, afraid she would hang up on him. There was no time to wrap it up nicely. "He tried to jump off a bridge half hour ago—"

"What?"

"Yes, I think you should know—I am afraid he is maybe still—"

"What nonsense. How could he *try* to jump off a bridge? Either he jumped or he didn't. Even Marek could manage that. I don't believe a word of it. What kind of sick plot is this? Why are you calling me?"

"Because I am very worried about him—"

"You have some nerve. After everything you've done to ruin us."

"No. It wasn't me—it was not much me, I mean. But that is not the point now—the point is that I think the mental status of your husband leaves much to be wished and you should speak to him—"

"Go to *hell*." And the phone went dead.

The bicyclist had his hand out for the phone. Yuri backed away with a placating gesture and tried Aniela's mother again. He listened to it ring and ring, then sent a text message—"This is not a joke. Look for your husband"—and handed back the phone. The bicyclist pocketed it and was gone in a second.

Well, he had tried. He didn't know if Aniela's father was even now looking for a tree branch from which to suspend himself, or if he was in fact looking for Andrei.

And worst of all, he didn't know where Andrei was. He made his way back to the campsite and sat down on the message his son had carefully scratched in the sand. Staring across at the far bank, he prepared to wait, with the stymied adrenalin creeping like knives along his arms and a dread awareness of his son's fragility when set against the wide, uncaring universe.

*

Some time previously, Andrei had woken to find himself alone. Having sat up and surveyed the southern bridge, he found it empty of pedestrians. On the other bank, the lights of two floating restaurants bobbed in the water and the science museum looked like a giant twist of rusty metal. But those westward features were a world away from his sandy sleeping place. He had as much connection with the city as the ducks sleeping along the shoreline—he hoped they were asleep there, anyway. He imagined the snuffling jaws of the giant catfish patrolling the waters and wrapped his arms around his legs.

He did not much care to sit on his own, in the dark, waiting. He smoothed the unseen sand, wishing his father would return. They should be sleeping because tomorrow they were going to get up early and hitchhike out of the country, so his father said. He didn't understand why they had to go. He was sure his father didn't want to leave and he didn't either. Warsaw wasn't his place yet, but he was growing used to its geography and customs. The subtle differences between its concrete and buses and clothing and those of his home town had ceased to seem glaring to him. He could speak Polish, sort of. He didn't think he wanted to go to Germany, which he associated, by a kind of genetic frisson, with coldness and cruelty. He didn't think he wanted to have "*Achtung! Achtung!*" shouted at him. He didn't think he wanted to learn German at all. But what could he do about it? He wasn't even a branch in the river; he was just a tiny little twig being swept along.

Or was he?

On an impulse, he scratched a message in the sand, jumped up, and set off at a run.

He bounded up and down the sandbanks, pushing his way rapidly through the tall grass and brush and hugging the shoreline until he came to the upstream bridge, the railway one. It was forbidden to pedestrians—cars and people used the next bridge over, but that was half a kilometer on and well lit. He and his father avoided crossing bridges at night because police cars passed often and where could they run? On the railway bridge, no one would see him now.

The tracks were protected by a fence of metal stakes, but he knew it was overgrown with vines at the embankment. He crossed the street, swarmed up the bank, climbed the creepers with only an unpleasant moment or two when they started to rip loose, and was soon on the bridge, brushing off his clothing and wincing at his scratches. There was not much room to walk—narrow grills had been set on either side of the tracks for use in emergencies or by the railway personnel perhaps. Viewed up close, they seemed much less inviting than from below and not very solid underfoot. They clanked and the dark gaps between the girders went down, far down, to the river below. He jerked his gaze away. The empty tracks stretching into the distance ahead of him were eerie and powerfully repellent. His good idea suddenly seemed much less appealing.

He paused to imbibe half a minute of nighttime loneliness then shrugged. He'd faced worse things. He set off
across the bridge, determinedly not looking down too
often but only ahead, his worn-out shoes shuffling along
the grills. The first train came past on the other side, going in the opposite direction, and though the noise was
considerable and the shaking of the bridge unpleasant, it
rather amused him to see a startled face or two snap round
in a carriage window at the sight of him.

It was the train that passed close, on his side of the
bridge, that unnerved him. A *pendolino*, one of the fast
ones. He pressed himself to the edge of the walkway, as
far from it as he could, but it came closer and closer at
dizzying speed. For a split second he saw the face of the
engineer, mouth open, before the train passed in a blur of
green and white—close, close, so near that seemingly
every moment it was about to tear him from the walkway
and drag him under. He put his hands over his ears and
closed his eyes, his whole body shaken by the rhythmic
whoosh and whang of the train. Then it was past and he
stood still for a moment, his legs weak enough that he
thought he might fall. If he lost his footing he would drop
between the walkway and the tracks, strike on the girders,
and end in the river below. He felt an unaccustomed
prick of pity for his father. "*March forward—that's my testa-
ment*"—his father had made him learn those lines. He
fixed his eyes on the end of the tracks and kept walking,
faster and faster, as the strength came back to him. It
occurred to him that the train employees might alert the

authorities to his presence there.

He had crossed the river, to his relief, but the bridge continued for some ways on its high embankment before coming to a station. He was on solid earth, jogging awkwardly over large gravel and pine girders and breathing the scent of tar and petroleum. Somewhere he needed to get off the tracks and over the fence. He could see ahead that the viaduct passed over a street, and he hoped to find a way down there. The shaking of the ground gave him warning. A train was emerging from the tunnel ahead. He froze. Its hypnotic light was approaching at a speed it was impossible to gage. Tearing his eyes from it, he moved to the right and was jolted by the sight of two men in uniform approaching along the track.

Without a second's hesitation he turned and ran in front of the train. As he sprang across the rails he felt himself caught full in its lights. He realized he'd misjudged its distance and felt his torn shoe catch on a crosstie. He was stumbling. He would get run over—in terror he jumped and rolled, jerking his foot out of his shoe as his knee struck the iron rail. Then he was tumbling on gravel, clawing and sliding. Above him, the train was a loud, continuous flash of colors. He scrabbled along the embankment to the bridge, his heart pounding so that he was hardly conscious of his own movements. Here, where the street met the buttress, the fence ended. He dropped from the embankment onto the pavement and ran. The pain in his knee stabbed with every step but he paid no attention. He scurried around buildings, turning into alleys and passing through courtyards, until he felt certain that he was far, and the policemen weren't following him, and he could stop and gasp and gasp. And eventually, when he was able to breathe again and his heart had climbed down from his throat, he set out to walk, or rather limp, the rest of the way to the Old Town.

CHAPTER 24

He knew the Old Town fairly well and thought he would recognize Aniela's building again from having been there for lunch. This, he felt sure, was the right door. Unfortunately, it was locked now and he didn't know which button of the intercom to press. He estimated the probable apartment number from the quantity of stairs he remembered and pushed a button.

"Pani Aniela?" he asked when he heard a faint hello.

"No," said an elderly voice, slow as his snail. "Pani Aniela lives at number 8."

Andrei pressed the 8, but the bell just rang and rang. What now? he wondered in despair. After all he'd been through he didn't want to walk all the way back to the river and his father—who was going to be annoyed, no doubt about it—with nothing to show for his expedition. He left his thumb on the bell—maybe Pani Aniela was wearing headphones.

"Hey, what're you doing, kid?" said a voice. "You're going to break that thing."

He looked up and saw a woman who looked like Pani Aniela but was younger, and also, somehow, different. The woman was regarding him from under a cocked eyebrow, over a cloud of cigarette smoke. A movie-star sort of young woman. Also not a person to mess with, Andrei sensed, taking his finger off the button and backing up a few feet.

"I'm looking for Pani Aniela," he said in a shaky voice.

"She doesn't live here anymore," said Kasia. "Beat it, kid."

She tapped out the code and let herself into the building. The door closed behind her. Andrei waited a few moments to give her time to disappear, then, hoping he'd seen correctly, pressed in the same numbers. The buzzer rang and he slipped inside and up the stairs, two at a time. Number 8. He knocked on the door, praying for Pani Aniela to open it.

Instead it was opened by the same blond young woman. "How'd you get in? Never mind. Go let yourself out again. I told you my sister doesn't live here. Look," she stepped back a little so he could see the empty interior, "See? There's nothing here—no one here."

"You're here."

"I just came to take measurements. But who are you anyway? I don't have to explain myself to you. Go away."

"Please. Where I find her?"

"What do you want with her?" Kasia stared at the boy for a minute, enlightenment striking. "Ah, I know. You're that Ukrainian's kid, aren't you?"

Andrei nodded. Kasia's eyes measured him from head to foot.

"Aren't you a bit young to be out on your own at this time of night? Where are your shoes? Or do you always run around like that?"

"I lose one, so I throw other."

"You and Aniela both barefoot. Hmm. I could make it into a fad on my blog," the corner of Kasia's mouth had an ironical quirk.

"Where Aniela?"

"Do I look like an information booth? If my sister didn't tell you where she lives, I'm not going to either. Off with you. Bye." Kasia started to close the door.

Andrei didn't move and Kasia hesitated, subject to an unusual feeling of doubt or contrition.

"Where's your father? Is he out there busking? You go to him now. Go on."

"I not know where father. I want Pani Aniela."

"That's all I need," Kasia muttered to herself, "an orphan. Mother of God. *Out*!" She spoke almost gently—for her—as if moved to pity in spite of herself, but she shut the door on him and listened as his feet went down the stairs.

Then her phone rang.

"Kasia!" said her mother without preamble, stammering slightly, "This can't be true, but that man, that Ukrainian or Russian or whatever, that Yuri, called and said your father tried to jump off a bridge this evening. And I don't believe a word—I still don't—but I tried to call your father and his phone rang in the bedroom—he's left his phone and his wallet too. And that's just incredible. Have you heard from him? Although how could you hear from him?"

"No," said Kasia, deeply startled, "Tata wouldn't? Surely? Mama? And how would the Ukrainian know?

This is odd—his son was just here. Tata wouldn't? I know things are really bad with the media and all that, but…"

"Bad? Bad? Did you see that article in *The Gazette* or the one in the *Republic*? They don't say a word we can sue them for and they make us out to be monsters. But still—it's absurd. Of course it's absurd. Your father wouldn't do that to me. I don't believe it."

"Where could he be?"

"I don't know. I have no idea."

"Could he have gone to a friend?"

"What friend? You know he doesn't have that kind of friends. And I tried to call the Ukrainian back but I got some stranger—he made the call from someone else's phone, somewhere by the Świętokrzyskie Bridge."

"By the bridge?"

"Yes."

"Maybe we should call Nela and ask if she's heard from him?" asked Kasia, beginning to panic. "From Yuri, I mean?"

"No. Nela? Definitely not. Nela who?"

"Yes…but…"

"We agreed we were never speaking to her again. Your father agreed too."

"Yes, but—"

"Out of the question. I'm not calling her." A long pause, and then: "You call her. Oh God, oh God, maybe it's true! I'm getting a very bad feeling. Kasia, you might be left with only a mother."

"God, no!" said Kasia. And if her reaction was only

partly concern for her father, it was genuine. "Have you looked for a note? Wouldn't he leave a note?"

As Kasia was listening to her mother, there was a tiny knock on the door. A tiny knock that continued and continued. In exasperation, Kasia jerked open the door. Andrei stood there again.

"Where Pani Aniela?"

"Look, kid," Kasia snarled, "I have my own problems. I don't have time for you. Beat it!" She slammed the door and turned her attention back to her cell phone.

Knock, knock, knock.

She opened the door again and was about to shout "*Go away!*" but Andrei got his word in first. "I no have time for you either. Where Pani Aniela?"

His bare foot was over the sill but she didn't bother to slam the door on it. She was brushing past him and hurrying down the stairs, phone still to her ear. He heard her say, "I'm coming to you..." and then she was gone.

Andrei felt himself growing terribly weary as he grappled with acute disappointment. Uncertain what his next step should be, he crept down the stairs and out of the building. What could he do but return in defeat to his father? It had all been for nothing, his trip. They would go to Germany and his father would never smile again— he imagined his father hunched over a beer mug, sighing *ach, ach*. The picture seemed to him so miserably sad that he wanted to cry too. He realized for the first time how much he cared about his father's happiness. But he was bone tired, hungry, and his knee hurt. His feet hurt too. It was going to be a long, long walk back over the bridge.

The street still held a fair number of people. Ahead of him, he saw the old woman he thought of as the Green-Sweater Grandma. His father gave her money, but he, Andrei, didn't have any. She hailed him as he came past. "Where's your daddy, child?"

He didn't feel like talking over the lump in his throat so he just raised his hands in a gesture of ignorance.

But Pani Jadzia wasn't put off that easily. "Come, child, what're you doing running around at midnight? Because I'm surprised your father allows that—such a good man."

"I don't know."

"What are you doing here alone?"

"I want find Pani Aniela—that blond lady—but she not here."

"No. She moved. Why don't you call her?"

"How?"

Pani Jadzia shook her head at his ignorance, looked all about to make sure no one was watching, then carefully slid a new smartphone from her purse and pressed a number. "Here," she said, and handed it over.

"Hello?" said Aniela.

"I very glad talk to you."

"Andrei?" gasped Aniela.

"I try find you—"

"Andrei?" repeated Aniela.

"Yes, is me," said Andrei, and continued rapidly. "Listen. Look. I try find you because father very sad and I no want to go Germany and father is love you and so I want know you love him and if yes why you no help us? You hear me?"

"Is he there? Could I talk to him?" asked Aniela eagerly.

"No, he not here," said Andrei, somewhat worried by not getting an answer to his question. "You love or you no love?"

"Where are you? Are you alone?"

"Alone, yes. I am in Old Town. Close where you live."

"Will you stay there till I come? I'm on my way and I'll be with you as fast as I can."

Aniela's phone rang again as soon as she'd turned it off. She raised the phone to her ear as the doors to the hotel elevator closed and she began the descent.

"Mama?"

There was a pause, then her mother's voice, a little defiant but with a tremor in it, stating that she was only calling because it was an emergency.

"What emergency?" asked Aniela in alarm.

"That Ukrainian called—"

"Yuri! What happened?"

"I don't know. Listen—the point is—the point is—he says your father tried to kill himself. I can't believe it's true, but—"

Aniela was speechless with shock for a moment.

•This is unfortunate.

•I'll feel guilty forever.

•Tata!

"If Yuri said it, then it's true," she said at last. "Where is Tata now? You say 'tried'—is he all right? Is he in a hospital?"

"I don't know—I don't know anything. He left this evening saying he was going out for some air and then I got the call from the Ukrainian. Your father left his phone here, Nela—he never leaves his phone—he takes it to bed and to the bathroom with him. I'm at my wit's end now. Will you help us look for him? Maybe he's still there, by the bridge? But I don't think so, because the Ukrainian said I should look for him—"

"Which bridge?"

"The Świętokrzyskie. The Ukrainian used someone's phone near there."

There was a pause while Aniela wrestled with fear and various darker emotions.

"You'll help us, won't you?"

"Yes. Though I doubt I'm the person Tata wants to see at the moment."

"But *you're* responsible, you know!" shouted her mother. "You drove him to this."

"No! I never told him to sell arms. I never told him to do anything so vile."

"Oh, for God's sake, you're still harping on it—at this time!"

"You're right.—Did Tata leave a note? Or any hint where he might have gone?"

"No, nothing. Wait a moment. I'm leaving the apartment. I can't talk where people might hear."

The phone went dead, and rang again, almost immediately. This time it was Kasia, repeating their mother's message. "Do you think it's true?" she asked, hoping for reassurance. "You're going to help us, aren't you? Or do you still want nothing to do with us?"

"Selling arms is evil. But strictly speaking, *I'm* the one who was disinherited!"

"So you won't help us?"

"It's a life—I have to."

"A '*life*'—Nela, it's our father."

"Yes," said Aniela grimly. "We need to talk to Yuri and find out if he knows where Tata might be now."

"But we don't know where Yuri is either—"

"Andrei must know. I'm meeting him in front of my apartment—your apartment, I mean—let's all meet there as soon as we can."

Kasia made a strangled sound. "Aniela, I'm sorry. You can have your apartment as far as I'm concerned. This has gotten way out of hand. I just want it all to stop. I want to go back to being your sister. I want us to go back to being a family. I never thought I cared about Tata much but now—I really hope nothing has happened to him."

"I hope not too—and I never stopped thinking of you as my sister, Kasia."

"And Tata? Will you forgive him? Because when we find him—if he's feeling suicidal—I don't think stressing his business is going to be helpful."

A number of thoughts passed rapidly through Aniela's mind, including seething resentment and distaste, but she made an effort to be compassionate. "I won't mention it today, you can be certain."

*

"This way," said Andrei and led the three women into

the woods by the Świętokrzyskie bridge. Aniela's mother lagged behind, hindered by weight and the wrong shoes, but Aniela and Kasia were in close pursuit as Andrei, with the exuberance of a puppy walking its people, half-bounded, half limped along the path to the beach, finding his way in the dark with no problem.

"Andrei!" Yuri was already standing when his son burst grinning into the clearing. Aniela followed the boy, stopping uncertainly some distance from Yuri.

"Aniela!" Yuri's immense relief at the return of his son was followed by an upswing of pure joy. This was succeeded by an equally rapid downswing in mood on the dampening conclusion that she had come for her father, not for him. Kasia pushed past her sister and began questioning him; he tried to focus on her and explain what he knew of her father. Aniela's mother had just arrived when Aniela's phone beeped.

"It's Tata," she said, "a text message." The tiny words glowed in the dark—banal letters of immense importance.

"I'm typing this on the phone of a passerby so don't try to answer. Two messages. First: Mr. Romen's son has disappeared. I've searched for him in the Praga area with no luck. Nothing more I can do. Hope he's okay. Second: You were right about the business. I know you think the worst of me now, but at least you'll know I had the honesty to admit it. I hope you remember I always admired and cared for you, in my way. Perhaps we'll meet in some afterlife and I can explain myself. Give my love to your mother and sister. Goodbye."

Her gooseflesh rising at the valedictory words, Aniela instantly called the number.

"Hello?" said an unknown voice.

"The man who just used your phone—is he still there?"

"It's usual to say 'good evening,' you know."

"Good evening. That man?"

"Um, no, he's crossing the street."

"Please—it's of the utmost importance. Please go after him and tell him—"

"Are you serious? You're joking, right?"

"Please, he may be suicidal—"

"What? Say that again?"

"He may be suicidal, please go after him—"

"No, if it's something like that, I don't want to get involved."

"Please—it could be a matter of life and death—"

"Is he dangerous?"

"No, no. Please, tell him—"

"No, I don't know…"

"Tell him I won't judge. Tell him I forgive him," Aniela lied fervently. "Tell him to call me. Tell him we are all waiting for him with Yuri. *Tell him* or I'll have you prosecuted for failure to assist in a life-threatening emergency."

"What? What did you say? My phone's running out of battery—"

And then there was silence.

There was nothing to do but wait. Yuri did not speak. He was aware that the three women were thinking continuously of the absent man, wondering if he were even now, this moment, taking last looks, last breaths, passing that inconceivable barrier between the living and the irretrievably gone. It was not a time for talking.

Andrei dozed, his head resting on a piece of driftwood. Aniela and Kasia sat beside him. Their mother stood first on one foot then the other to pour the sand out of her shoes, and then she just stood, phone in hand, waiting. Only once did she address Yuri, as he walked back and forth thoughtfully on the edge of the beach. She gestured toward Andrei's sleeping form. "Don't you even have a blanket for him?"

"No."

She shook her head at that, because she was not a woman devoid of all feeling, only one whose empathy was hampered by her usual sphere and habits. This evening the rough shaking of her world and the possibility of personal loss allowed a momentary, unaccustomed, softness to appear.

"Thank you—for stopping my husband on the bridge. I hope it wasn't for nothing—"

"I hope for the best."

"Perhaps we shouldn't have squealed on you."

"I do not understand."

"Perhaps we were wrong to tell the authorities about you."

"Yes."

"Never mind."

Yuri did not reply but his eyes fell on Aniela, who was listening, and who looked away then.

An hour later there was another text message. This time it was on Aniela's mother's phone. "It's Marek!" she shrieked.

"I'm calling from the neighbor's. You have the key. I'm locked out," she read aloud. "Thank God!" she exclaimed, "thank God," and without another word stampeded through the sand and nettles into the woods, closely pursued by Kasia.

Aniela rose from the piece of driftwood on which she had been sitting but did not follow them. Her own phone beeped. "Got your message. Thank you," her father had texted. The words swam before her eyes.

Yuri was watching her. She read the message to him.

"It is a great relief," he said.

"Yes."

"I thought—if he did not do it at once, he will not do it. But I have been wrong about many things. I am glad he is home."

"Now I will have to have some kind of relationship with him. Not close, I hope."

"You will find it in your heart—a way. I am for for-giveness, as a negotiating point, at least."

"We are linked forever. I cannot escape them—or their reputation."

"Your father feels very bad."

"For the wrong reasons probably. I can't believe he's had a change of mind. I'm sure my mother hasn't."

"No. But perhaps it is a departure place for new think-ing."

"Yes. Maybe there's a slight hope of a new start."

She fell silent, having no desire to talk about her parents. What did they matter to her at this point, when she was about to learn she had nothing to look forward to from now to eternity? She swallowed and tried to concentrate on breathing evenly, in and out, in and out. Since Yuri had been able to contact her for the sake of her father, it must mean that he hadn't wanted to earlier, for her sake.

He did not speak. He was standing six feet away, and though his features were somewhat obscured by the night, she was intensely aware of his gaze on her. Round about there was only darkness and the quiet flowing of the water. He was going to say goodbye and was thinking how to do it nicely. Here was where she had to do it first, with dignity, but the words wouldn't form. Breathe in, breathe out, was all she could think.

"I also want a new start," said Yuri passionately, suddenly, making her jump.

"Yes, Andrei told me you are going to Germany. You are right to leave." If her eyes filled, it was too dark for him to see.

He was moving toward her, but he stopped at that. "You want me to leave?"

"No, but—"

"So why—why are you telling me such a revulting idea?"

"I want what's best for you—that's all."

She thought—in as much as she could think when he was standing so close, so very close—that she hardly knew him, he hardly knew her, their attraction was no excuse for disrupting his plans, there was not much she could do for him, and any future they shared was bound to be difficult and possibly dangerous.

He thought that perhaps in a better world he could have told her his only concerns were for her, that he had no ambition but her happiness, no will to step further from her side than was demanded by daily living, and no desire to imagine a future she did not share. Caught, though, by a surging emotion too rich for language, his elegant words took leave of him. He could not have strung together a long sentence to save his life.

"So come," he said, "here!"

Andrei opened his eyes briefly, saw two figures embracing on the riverbank, smiled but was too tired to lift his head, and was just falling back to sleep when a noise startled him awake.

Kasia came crashing out of the bushes and said breathlessly to Yuri, "Mama sent me back. She says to invite you to the apartment to spend the night or at least make sure you have somewhere to go. She says it's the least we can do."

"I'll take care of them," said Aniela.

CHAPTER 25

Breakfast in the Solan apartment the next morning was a tense affair, not early, and attended only by the three women, plus Andrei's snail, in a large, clean jar.

"Nonsense," said Aniela's mother. "Nonsense, nonsense, nonsense. I won't listen to this."

"But," said Aniela, "we really hope you will consider what we are saying. We really think you will have to. We are determined—Kasia and I—that there will have to be changes in the family."

"We were doing fine before you fouled things up."

"We are going to live better—"

"Better? You call this better? Have you been reading the news? Do you know what's happened to our business? We're going to be *poor*. Poor! Poor! How will that be better?"

"Better for the world—and for our consciences."

"Gaagh!"

"You're not going to have any connection with the arms business; Tata needs a long vacation; I'm not going into politics—"

"You couldn't anyway now. Your reputation is shot, just like ours."

"Kasia is going to be guided by her own judgment instead of your aspirations—"

Kasia nodded, a little uncertainly, and Aniela's mother waved a hand in disparagement. "What do you know about anything?"

"You will be far from penniless, I think," said Aniela, slowly, "and I'm sure you'll be able to build up the other branches of your business—"

"Nothing is as profitable."

But then, to the amazement of her daughters, a tear slid down her cheek, and in a moment she was openly weeping. "I thought—I really thought—that all our efforts were for you two. I always wanted the best for you."

Aniela was aware that her mother's tears, if expressing genuine grief, were calculated, but over the croissants and coffee her loyalty and compassion quietly won the day over her still simmering outrage. She could make believe her parents had been blind, not evil. Some kind of relationship would still be possible.

"You don't need to worry about me," she said. "My future is with Yuri—at least, I think that's his name."

*

Aniela's mother came out onto the terrace of the house in the country, a can of cat food in her hand. She sat down on the fallen pediment, a sad, hunched, brooding figure—plotting. This couldn't be the end. At last she roused herself.

"Cat, cat!" she called. "Come here, cat." A gray shadow flitted through the stone balustrade and skittered toward her.

"Look," she muttered, "this is what my life has come

down to. Feeding a cat. I used to be one of Poland's top businesswomen."

A thin shadow fell across the terrace stones.

Andrei knelt by the cat. "Feeding good cat is better than doing bad business."

"Don't be impertinent."

"What is 'impertinent'?"

"You are. You're a very impertinent boy. I don't know how your father stands you."

"Ah. 'Impertinent' is to say true things that big people don't like, yes?"

"You know nothing about it, brat. My life is a shambles. No one listens to me—not my husband, not my daughters, not anyone. I've lost a heap of money. What on earth am I doing here with you?"

Andrei shrugged, unconcerned. "Cat needs a name."

A sigh. "Go ahead then. Name it."

"Yevgeniy."

"Why Yevgeniy?"

"Is father's real name." Andrei's smile deepened as his companion shot him a glance. "Or not."

"Hmpf."

"What I call you?"

"Whatever you like—just not Grandma."

"But you will be like grandma for me, no? Because father and Aniela—"

"Well. Well. We'll see about that."

EPILOGUE

Republic of Poland
Civil Records Office in Warsaw
Abridged Excerpt of Birth Certificate

Surname: Solan
First name (names): Julianna
Date of birth: 14th day of April, two thousand and fifteen (14-4-2015)
Place of birth: Warsaw, Poland
Name and surname (father): Pending
Name and maiden name (mother): Aniela Solan

THE END